THE NATION THIEF

THE
NATION
THIEF
ROBERT
HOUSTON

PANTHEON BOOKS, NEW YORK

Library of Congress Cataloging in Publication Data

Houston, Robert
The nation thief.

1. Walker, William, 1824–1860—Fiction.
2. Nicaragua—History—Filibuster War,
1855–1860—Fiction.
I. Title.
PS3558.O873N3   1984   813′.54   83–42820
ISBN 0–394–50992–7

Manufactured in the United States of America

First Edition

BOOK DESIGN BY GINA DAVIS

Art on the title page shows General Walker reviewing
troops on the Grand Plaza, Granada, Nicaragua, 1850.
From a print in the New York Public Library.

Once more with feeling,
for Pat

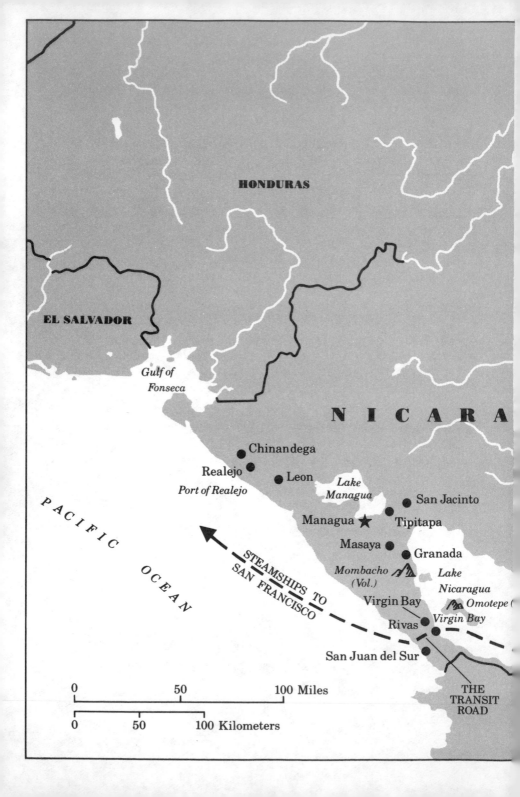

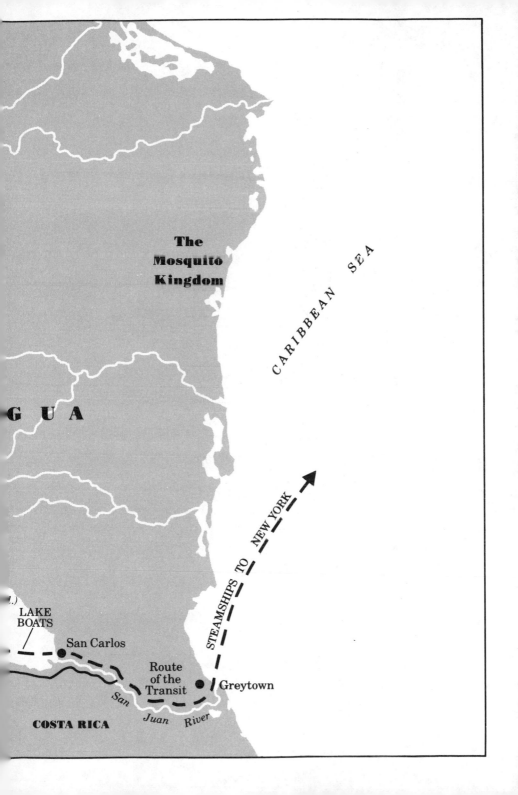

PROLOGUE

WILLIAM WALKER

THEY HAVE SAID that twelve thousand people are dead because William Walker came to Central America. I do not know of what consequence those numbers are; numbers can no longer concern me. What is of true consequence is the fact that I have done something few other men have been given to do: I created myself. I am William Walker. I created William Walker in Central America, and it is that single, overwhelming event which must concern me. That alone, not mere numbers.

Outside my window, I hear the sound of the Honduran sergeant calling cadence, and the barefoot soldiers' sloppy shuffle on the paving stones of this fort's parade ground. In the distance, I can hear the waves of the Caribbean and now and again the cry of a woman selling *tamarindo* juice at the gates of the fort, or the bark of a dog in the wind from the sea. This is a lonely place, like St. Helena must have been. I would be pleased to have a copy of Bonaparte's memoirs with me while I endure this, but there are no books in this town except for those in a few private homes. I would have changed that. William Walker would have changed that.

These facts are true about William Walker. He is five feet, two inches tall. He is president of the Republic of Nicaragua and general-in-chief of its armies. He weighed at one time one hundred and twenty-five pounds. He now weighs no more than one hundred fifteen pounds at the most; he will take no food save bread from these people. He is as of last May thirty-six years old, the age at which Lord Byron died. He has never been married. His father is a banker in Nashville, in the state of Tennessee. He has not heard from his father nor written to him in several years. Since his mother died, there has been little between them. He is aware that he ought to be bothered by that.

I know this also to be true about William Walker: he has come not to fear death because he knows that if his political life is truly over, it is right that he dies—just as he has always known that unless he embraced death, he would have no political life. So now he is listening while there is still a little time to understand what he has done and what he means and whether he is a hero or, God have mercy on him, a monster.

PART ONE

TALMEDGE WARNER

THE MOST I knowed was that I was cold, and that the man said that before we was through we would control the trade of the whole world. I come out there to California to find the gold, but the gold was all gone. I'd never set eyes on Colonel Walker till I got on the ship, which was a leaky old brig that had more sheriff's impounds on it than a politician has lies. In May of 1855, that was. None of us ever truly expected we would get out of San Francisco Bay without the sheriff jailing us all. There wasn't even money for stevedores, so we spent most of the night sneaking our supplies outen the warehouse by torchlight—powder and guns mainly, Sharps rifles, and one old three-pounder cannon. There was rings around the torches in the fog, I remember, and people was speechifying on hogsheads about us being immortals and changing history and such, but I was more worried that we wasn't loading much to eat but some bully beef and ship's biscuit, which wouldn't carry us near all the way to Nicaragua. We was going to get right hungry, I thought, but Colonel Walker's officers kept a-telling us that we would pick up what we needed by some raids along the coast of Mexico on the way down, and nobody else seemed fixing to argue, so I let it go.

There must of been a hundred ships anchored in the harbor, most abandoned by their crews who had took off for the goldfields or that was short a cargo. When there wasn't

3

no fog, you could see their masts a-sticking up like weeds with spiderwebs all over them. I wasn't sure right where Nicaragua was, but they'd promised me two hundred and fifty acres of good land there and a salary, and all I had to do was kill a few greasers to get it. Fruit just fell off the trees in your hands down there, and there was seven women to ever man because they had been a-killing off one another in this civil war for near on thirty years. Well, I wasn't but twenty-five or so, and nobody in particular, and times was hard for a poor man, so it sounded good to me. There wasn't hardly none of us over thirty. We wasn't but babies, but we was a mean enough bunch to handle most greasers, I reckoned. I'd been told how in the war with Mexico they had to tie them to trees to get them to stand and fight sometimes, because they was conscripts and didn't want no part of it. I didn't mind that.

They stowed us down in the hold with the cargo, but none of us stayed. The wind was colder'n a nun's cunt, but we all wanted to be on deck to see Colonel Walker when he come on board. If he did. The crowd on the dock spit and chewed and taken bets that he wouldn't show, and argued what we'd find when we got down there where we was shipping for.

What we'd been told we would find is this: them that recruited us said that Colonel Walker had signed a contract. There was these two bunches, the Conservatives and the Democrats, that was at one another. They had two presidents and all, each one claiming he was the real one, but the Conservative bunch had the capital city, which was called Granada, and they were more or less the official ones. Well, there was this man named Byron Cole, he had went down to Nicaragua and got a contract for Colonel Walker to bring in three hundred fighting men for the other side, the Democrats, who had set up their own president in this other town called León. They had all heard of Colonel Walker because he had taken some boys and took over Lower California for a while the year before—and him not but twenty-nine then and only a colonel because he called himself that.

Well, Colonel Walker didn't have money but to round up fifty-seven or -eight of us but that didn't seem to faze him none. He put it out that he was going to be after a deal more than a little land. It was like this, the recruiters said, and they talked right good: as everybody in California knowed, old Commodore Vanderbilt run the fastest ships there was between New York and San Francisco through Nicaragua— up the river and across the lake and then by wagon a few miles till you got to the Pacific side and then onto another ship for San Francisco. In a little while, they was going to put a canal through there. And when they did, ever ship in the world would have to pass through it. *That* was why we wanted to get set up in Nicaragua, they told us. Hell, wouldn't take much and we'd be set up for good, I figured.

Great God A'mighty, I wish I'd known some things then!

Anyway, I was shivering like Franklin's bald mule even though it was May, and it was about coming up dawn and I figured that if I stood at that deck railing much longer I was going to turn flat to a icicle. He ain't coming, I decided, and picked up my bedroll and started toward the gangplank when this snare drum commenced and some feller tooted on a flute and there he was. William Walker himself! Famousest man I had ever seen.

But was I set back! The man wasn't but a twelve-year-old undertaker! No bigger'n a minute, and dressed in a old black suit you wouldn't want to put on a corpse in a Mexican funeral. Well now, I'm surely leaving, I thought, until he passed a little closer on his way to the captain's cabin. And then he laid them great staring gray eyes on me and I thought, no, that ain't no man you want to mess with. They was the flattest and coldest things I had ever seen in my life. And then when he climbed up on this hatch and commenced to speak, I heard that thin Tennessee voice that was even colder than them eyes and I settled down some. I had knowed some mean hardshell preachers in my life, and this man there could have run with the meanest of them. I don't recollect well what he talked about—destiny and progress and democracy and such that sounded right fine, though. But when he stepped down offen that hatch, I mean to tell you he had us ever one. We was whooping and clapping like we had just heard the best tent-meeting preacher in California. He had ever one of us convinced we wasn't going off to some place like Nicaragua, wherever that was, but that we was a-going straight to the Garden of Eden with him.

And when we slipped out the bay yonder past the Heads, and I heard the steam tug casting off and knowed we was really on the ocean where the sheriff couldn't get to us, I didn't go down below where it smelled like old varnish and whale oil and farts. No sir. I went below all right. But I wasn't smelling nothing but native women and oranges and bananas and pure glory. Hallelujah!

GUY SARTAIN

THEY HAVE ASKED me, sir, why a Negro would want to go down there with William Walker. Well, first he wasn't then what he was later. He was an abolitionist and I would even say a radical in those days. He wore an old Kossuth hat, in honor of the revolution in Europe, he would tell you, and they even jailed him for writing articles in his newspaper about the corruption of San Francisco's judges. He spoke out about the rights of women and art and even a little for socialism. And where else would I go? I was a surgeon. He was a surgeon. He knew I was having a hard time in San Francisco —I was a very good surgeon, sir, but most there wouldn't let me work on them, especially the women. It doesn't matter, Colonel Walker said to me. Some in my expedition won't let you work on them either. But they are trash, and when the blood starts to flow, they'll change quickly enough. And besides, the native troops I intend to have will surely be grateful for you. I would be proud to have you, Dr. Sartain, he said, and so I went.

We were five weeks at sea. I kept to myself for the most part, except for dinner with Colonel Walker now and then. He was the quietest man I had ever known; he could sit for an hour and listen to a conversation and be so silent you almost forgot he was there. But sometimes when we ate alone, he would talk as if he were starving for talk. He knew I had studied in Europe, too, and he would ask me if I remembered such and such a place in Heidelberg or Paris or Edinburgh, or if such and such a professor had been there in my time (he was just thirty, I think, and I was a few years older). And then he would seem to check himself and those great eyes of his would go flat and he would say something like, "I hated European medicine because it was only used to cure the excesses of the rich," and we would pass the rest of the meal talking about politics or the future of the Negro or some new surgical technique.

He was my friend, of necessity. You have to imagine, sir. Five weeks together on a small ship, and not knowing what we would find when we put ashore. Once we almost foundered in a gale and once we had to storm a village on the Mexican coast when they refused to provision us. Then, when the word came that we were off the Gulf of Fonseca and almost to Nicaragua, the tension alone was bad enough to sink us. And what would they have turned to but me to take their minds off that tension, if it had not been for Colonel Walker? No, whatever happened later, whatever the tragedy of it, he was my friend then.

I remember two of his officers, one from Mississippi named Hornsby and the other from Texas named Henry, who came to the rail beside me while we lay off the port of Realejo, waiting for word that it was safe to go ashore. Hornsby had a thick black beard to his waist and was the only man to wear a uniform on board—the rest just wore their denim pants and flannel shirts, but Hornsby wore his old army uniform from the Mexican War. He spoke as gravely as the Bible sounds and I've heard him say he was proud that was the only book he had ever read. He was tall and thin and straight as an ironing board, and though he had no love for any but the white race, he was a brave enough man, dull and dutiful. Tom Henry had a face like a horse, and homemade india ink tattoos the length of his arms. He drank a considerable amount and seemed to love fighting more than any man ought to. And killing. And baiting me.

It had rained for days, so that at times you couldn't tell the sea from the sky. Now we could hear the thunder again in the east and the native *bungo* canoes that hung about us put in for shore and our blood was heavy and irritated, dreading the new rain. Henry and Hornsby stood near enough so that I could hear them and Henry said in a loud voice, "Well, they don't look white to me," and pointed toward the natives in the *bungos*, who had tried to sell us fresh fruit.

"They Indians," Hornsby said, serious as a tombstone.

"Well, then they ain't white. But they ain't niggers, either."

"I've been told they's a tribe of nigger Indians here," Hornsby said.

Henry spit. "Could get goddamn confusing. I been told Indians think niggers is white people if they speak English."

"No," Hornsby said. "Even Indians couldn't think that."

"Nonetheless," Henry said.

"Nonetheless."

"I could do some things with that land yonder if I had me some niggers," Henry went on, and pointed toward the shore, which was flat and covered in mangrove swamps. "But if

8

them people think that niggers is white when they speak English, how am I going to get me any real niggers that'll stay convinced they niggers?"

"They'll know."

"No, no, they won't. Give 'em half a chance and they forget." He pushed away from the rail and looked toward me. "Ain't that right, Doctor? Give 'em a suit and a education and they forget."

"No," I said to him. "They don't forget."

"Well, that's a comfort. Because I don't reckon they's anything worse than a nigger who don't know he's a nigger. Do you, Doctor?"

"Yes," I told him. "A Texan who thinks he's a man."

"That's it," he said. "You done it. You dead." He pulled his revolver out, cocked it, and pointed it at me. Hornsby moved his hand as if to touch the pistol. Henry jerked it away and Hornsby shrugged. My own revolver was out of reach under my coat.

I won't say I was brave, sir. You see, I had noticed Colonel Walker moving up behind Henry before Henry ever pulled that pistol, so I waited for him to speak. "Captain Henry," he said, in that soft voice that got even softer as he got madder. "I reckon you're requesting a duel."

I saw Henry stiffen, but he didn't turn around. "Not with a nigger, Colonel, no sir. I ain't studying no duels with niggers."

"Then it's with me."

"Sir?"

"I need my surgeons, Tom. You commence to shooting them before we even make land, and I take it as a personal affront."

Henry didn't answer for a time. "Never saw it that way, Colonel," he said finally.

Henry loved him, sir. Like a dog loves somebody and won't cross him even though he'll kill another dog on sight. And in his own way, I think Colonel Walker loved Henry. And I

9

loved Colonel Walker, and I think he loved me—in his own way. That was William Walker, and don't ask me why yet. But when people couldn't love themselves, or believe in themselves, they could in William Walker.

I thought it was Mohamet's paradise at first. Oh, not the streets of that little port town, where the pigs and chickens and children shared out the mud among them. And not the barefoot honor guard in their dirty white pantaloons who marched up and down for us when we put into shore on the *bungos*. Nor the mud huts and ragged clothing (the children had no clothing at all—only straw hats on their heads and cigars in their mouths). No, that was all too close to the way I had been told my own people lived in the Southern States. And I wasn't unconscious we might be walking into a trap, either.

I mean the land, sir. No matter how poor the hut might be, it had flowers covering it like a wedding dress. Orchids grew wild in the trees. There were red flowers big as your hand they called bora-bora, and yellow flowers that hung thick as berries from bushes they called chilca, and morning glories on all the fence rails like bright scarves. It was so fertile that even the fence posts sprouted! As we walked inland, we saw trees called ceiba that rose straight up for hundreds of feet—their trunks were oyster white, with no leaf or branch at all—then broke out into huge umbrellas of leaves and limbs and Spanish moss. Macaws the color of an artist's palette sat in them and screeched at us, or dove and flashed in the sunlight. There were old haciendas along the road, spread out at the ends of long lanes, and fruit orchards stretching behind them as far as we could see. And in the cool air of the morning, before the rains came, we saw a line of volcanoes like lace on the horizon, sir, like the world was about to be created all over again. We were all poets that first morning, poets, black and white and Indian, in our souls. I could see it and I could hear it. Our spirits were light as the mist that still lingered in the green meadows, and even Colonel Walker seemed less wary and solemn than usual. The fat Indian colonel they called Chélon who had come along as our guide into León strummed a guitar as we rode, and kept up a string of jokes with the peasants along the road as if we were a holiday procession, and not what we were, with our rifles and bowie knives and pistols.

And from all those colors, we came into a town of only three: the white of the houses, the red tile of their roofs, and the gray cobbles of their streets. It was as likely a town as I had ever seen. It had a university and a great square cathedral in it, and houses with carved stone gateways that would have made the grandees of Spain jealous. I smelled food cooking in all the marketplaces—there were tortillas and bananas frying and meat roasting and porkskins boiling in fat—and crowds ran alongside us everywhere we went, babbling in Spanish and shoving things to eat at us. Women with high combs and black mantillas watched us from the green-barred windows of houses, and men who wore silver coins for buttons would ride close to us for a time, then race away down some side street or another to carry the news of our coming. Oh, if I could only tell you truly how we felt after those weeks at sea, to have come to such a place! It wasn't Mexico City, no, but surely Cortéz couldn't have felt less wonder than we did.

And I wasn't stared at. No one seemed to think it odd that I was in the company I was in. The skin of the Indians was nearly as dark as my own, and in the crowds I was certain I saw many faces that were more Negro than Indian. They were a people of a thousand shades of skin, and only the white men stood out among them, like the bland underbellies of fish.

But it wasn't good for long, sir. It all changed quick as a minute, quick as it took Eve to pluck an apple.

CHÉLON

Oye, compañeros. It's true, God forgive the ignorance of a poor, fucked, fat Indian with a stiff leg: I thought the gringos' ship ought to be made of gold, and the sails of silk— at least that. All morning on the way to meet them, I tried to make a song about them to carry back home (ask anybody —Chélon's our newspaper, they'll tell you, Chélon's the poor man's newspaper). But what can a Christian man rhyme with Walker in a Christian tongue? Who can even pronounce it: *Gualquer*?

The harbor pilot had seen them already and told me not to be surprised. Bears, he said they were, blond bears with beards and red shirts and floppy hats like all gringos wear, and sometimes they looked at you like you were a bug that they'd never seen before. Only sixty of them, but armed like Saracens, even the *zambo* doctor they had with them. And William Gualquer? Not as big around as your arm, Colonel, he said, like a boy in a communion suit. And even freckled! If he was a famous fighter it was only because he was too skinny to hit from more than five *varas* away. Then he leaned close to me and said, But when this El Gualquer orders them to jump, they jump. And he has gray eyes, Colonel, like the man in the old Stories. And then he pulled back and laughed, because we were Christians and members of the Democratic party and didn't believe in the Stories any more, even if we were *indios.*

"But he has eyes like in a picture, *mi Chélon,*" he said. "They follow you, even when he's not looking at you. I don't like his eyes. Go softly." And this time he didn't laugh. I ordered him to send the decent women in the port off into the

12

forest, and to make sure the whores were clean. Gringos liked that. They were ungodly clean.

I was prefect of Chinandega then, and a colonel of infantry, though God knows my leg was as stiff as it is now, and had been since a damned shoewearing Conservative's ball split my shin the year before at the seige of Granada. We kept up that siege nearly nine months and could have won it anytime, but the pureblood snots who came to run the army wouldn't let us. They held my poor barefoot Indians at the edge of the city, watching them get cut down like cane, because they couldn't make up their minds who was going to get what post in their shitty government if we won. Well, that was it, *muchachos*. I'd been fighting for the revolution twenty years, off and on, but that was it. I told my boys, go back to your fields, and I promised I would only call them up again if we were going to fight to win. I saw the straightnosed politicians and lawyers with their faces like paintings in a church take the army away from my friend, Maximo Jerez, who was the only one who really cared a fig about the people. And I came home to Chinandega where I knew I could wait with my *indios* for the time when the politicians would come to me. *Oye, Chélon,* our brother, I knew they would have to say to me one day. Bring your *indios*. We're going to take the land away from the scummy aristocrats at last and give it to them. We're going to give them the mules and the oxen. We're going to let them own the stores. We're going to teach them to read. They'll live like gringos or Englishmen, Chélon. That's the revolution. We need you for it.

I've been told by my mother who could turn people into monkeys and dogs, God save her, that everything circles and comes back, and that it would be our time again some day. But the politicians and lawyers sat on their assés in León and couldn't make up their minds, waiting for the gringos to come and then figuring how to get rid of them once they did come. (Don't worry, my friend General Maximo Jerez told me, the gringos are like the rain—they'll come, do us some good, and if we're lucky, go away in their season—and God protect us from floods.) And here was Chélon, getting older and fatter, turning into less and less of an *indio* from living like a pureblood, and the gringos came at last, in the rainy season. . . .

So I had put on my uniform even though I sweat like a pig in it and smell like a wet dog in the rain, and then put my bad leg and myself on a horse and rode through the mud to greet the gringos. And when I got there the ship looked like it would sink any minute, and the bearded bears ignored me or looked at me like I was a bug, and grunted at each other in a language that sounded more like boars rutting than Christians talking. I tried to make them a decent speech But El Gualquer cut me short—gringos never let a man do the decent thing—and started to ask me questions without even offering me a glass of brandy. The Transit Route—that's all he wanted to know about. Everything about el señor Vanderbilt's Transit Route, until I thought that thin head of his would split open with the answers I gave him and the man who spoke Spanish for him.

No Transit Route, I told him. Forget the Transit Route. El señor Vanderbilt hasn't paid his rent on it in years, and besides, the iguana-fucking Conservative shoewearers have got their friend, General Guardiola the Butcher, down from Honduras holding it with his army. The Butcher cuts off ears when he gets bored, my colonel Gualquer; you'll wind up soup bones, I told him. Forget the Transit Route. Go for the head of the thing, go for Granada. We'll mount another siege, then worry about the Transit Route after we've shot all the politicians and landowners. I tried to make some jokes then to see if he would offer me some brandy, but there wasn't a prick hair's worth of humor in him that I could find.

No humor, just the Transit Route. He didn't hear me. If we could get to the Transit Route, he could promise us everything we had always wanted. We'd have ships full of guns and plenty of gringo investors with money to build factories

14

and railroads and telegraphs and mines, and all my poor *indios* would have jobs and take their vacations in New Orleans or New York or San Francisco. We'd put macadam on all the roads, like el señor Vanderbilt had done on his already, and we'd have shops full of things from Paris that everybody could afford. Progress, he said we'd have, Progress and something called Sanitary Measures.

And all from the Transit Route.

I let him talk, *muchachos*. I liked the words. I had prayed for the words. But I didn't tell him that everything that makes sense doesn't make sense. And the next morning I took him and the bears into León to let him talk about the Transit Route with the shit-sausage politicians. And the morning after that I brought him back again, with all the politicians plotting and prancing like little dogs in the council chambers behind them, certain that if the Butcher didn't kill him they would have to. (All except my friend Maximo Jerez, who believed in Progress as much as el Gualquer did then.) I never saw a man make so many enemies so fast! They had all strutted and sniffed and told him what they wanted him to do, and he had ignored them. He wanted two hundred men to back him up, he said, and he was going to take the Transit Route. *Sí*, just like that. He was going to go down in his ship and fight the Butcher's army and take the whole Transit Route away from him. It was crazy, *compañeros*—even I knew it was crazy. And they hated him because if it worked, they would all look like the asses they were.

But me? I didn't volunteer to go with him then, did I? I had my daughters to take care of. Nobody has ever called Chélon a coward, but nobody has ever called him a fool, either.

If El Gualquer came back alive, he had been sent to save us. Not if he won, just if he came back alive—that would be enough. I would go with him where he asked me to. But God had to decide it. God might understand gringos. A poor fat, fucked Indian didn't.

BRIAN HOLDICH

I CAN NEVER find myself in the heat of summer like this, gentlemen, without also finding myself in Nicaragua. There was a constant buzz of insects—no, louder than a buzz. A shout of insects, when the air was still. And thunder that made the earth shake during the rainy season, which was when we set off on our first expedition. Thunder, and sheet lightning that lit the sky at night like cities burning, and rain that would suffocate you if you were fool enough to stay out in it.

I was twenty-three and fool enough to do most other things. I wanted to draw, for example. I wanted to be an illustrator for *Leslie's* or *Harper's* or such, and that's why I had gone out to California to begin with. But it was an age of heros, too—or the end of an age of heros—and I wanted to be a hero. My father in Alabama had sold his last two Negroes to get me in the university, and when that money ran out he wanted me to come back and take the Negroes' place, I believe. So with my head full of Homer and Virgil and Shakespeare and Scott and Byron and other nonsense, I went to California.

"You have read Byron, Mr. Holdich?" William Walker asked me the first time he interviewed me, when he found out I'd had a little university.

"Some," I told him.

"Are you aware that a proper reading of Byron reveals that the highest art is war? That death in a good cause is the finest poetry?"

"I hadn't thought about it much, Colonel," I said to him.

"If you're chosen to go with me to Central America, you'll be painting a far more noble picture than you ever could by making illustrations for a petty weekly. I intend to make myself and those who go with me immortal. Nothing less, Mr. Holdich. Immortal."

You have to understand, gentlemen, that everything was possible in those days. Sam Houston had proved it in Texas. We had all proved it when we took half of Mexico in that easy war. The only thing you needed was the right place. The world was endless; if you were an American and had the future on your side, the world was waiting for you, praying for you. Everything we did was new. You could still do things for the first time then, if you were young enough. So, no, it didn't sound strange to be told that I would be immortal. It sounded like a natural right, in fact. After all, would any of us have come to California to begin with if we didn't believe in the possibility of everything?

He took me because of the Spanish I'd picked up, and because I had learned to ride and shoot and use a sword tolerably well in the university. He made me his interpreter and told me I would be a lieutenant when we got to Nicaragua. I would be privy to things no one else would be. He gave me his permission to sell any sketches I made, as long as he approved them first. I jumped at it like a calf at a nipple.

I was twenty-three: you have to keep remembering that. The only thing I'd found in two years of California was a job selling mining equipment to Mexicans. Let that excuse some things.

They were afraid of us at first—they were afraid of us for a long time, in fact. And except for the fat Colonel Valle—the one they called Chélon—and the thin-faced general named Maximo Jerez, who was the smartest and most decent one of the bunch, they despised us after the first day. Oh, not the people—just the politicians and the generals, such as they were, who had something to lose. To the people, of necessity we were better than what they had. But the politicians and the generals had never wanted us in the first place, you see. Maximo Jerez and a friend of Walker's, a newspaperman from California named Byron Cole, had signed the contract for us to come down. And now Jerez was out of power, and Cole had given us up and taken off to the interior to hunt gold, so, in effect, we walked in blind. The rest of the bunch of Democrats in León were too afraid to tell us to go away, but the way Walker treated them the first day confirmed everything they wanted to believe about us.

They gave us the two hundred backup troops we asked for, all right. But what troops! Two hundred half-naked conscripts with old muskets that fired pieces of sawed-off iron window gratings because the generals claimed they didn't have enough ammunition to spare. Two colonels to lead them, one a surly half-breed who wouldn't say a dozen words to any of us, and the other a hatchet-faced lancer who called himself Mendez the Cock, and who started a monte game on the deck of the ship that lasted four days. By the time we put into shore near the Transit Route, he'd pocketed nearly all of what little money his troops had, and their spirits were low as slaves' on an auction block.

None of us knew much then. I don't believe even Walker himself did. We were Americans. They were greasers. That's all we needed to know. They tried to tell us in León that we were outnumbered ten to one, that the Honduran general they called the Butcher was barricaded in Rivas, a town we'd have to take beside the Transit Route. But we were in a hurry. We were off to become immortal, all of us, men and officers: sad Hornsby, loudmouthed Tom Henry, myself, Tim Crocker.

Has Tim Crocker been mentioned before, gentlemen? It's

possible he hasn't. We thought he was going to be very important to us then, since he was Colonel Walker's aide and shadow. He was no older than myself, dressed like the rest of us in denim britches and red flannel shirt, but he had perfect blond curls and the most beautiful face I ever saw on a man. Beautiful, I say on purpose. A face I'd use as a model to illustrate an edition of Ivanhoe. And he was not much bigger than Walker himself, but no one of us crossed him. He had been with Walker the year before when Walker had taken over Lower California, and had made that terrible march back across the desert. He was reported to have shot four deserters singlehandedly when Walker told him to, though none of us asked him about it, of course.

One was unimaginable without the other: Walker in his black suit, never smiling, Crocker marching beside him like a head boy at school. While the rest of us were whoring and emptying the liquor casks at the *pulperías*, the two of them would sit with a table between them, going over maps by candlelight or Walker writing, writing, while Crocker cleaned his two revolvers or polished his sword. No one questioned Crocker's right to that closeness, not even Tom Henry, who would have killed any living thing at the slightest word from Walker. What they found to talk about, I never understood, though since I was billeted beside them in the ship on the way down from California I knew they did talk. Sometimes late into the night I would hear the mumble of voices through the bulkhead.

Later Walker talked to me a few times, and he seemed to enjoy talking professionally to the Negro surgeon, Guy Sartain. And when Byron Cole finally caught up with us, Walker would talk to him about newspaper things. But aside from a man named Randolph, who came down much later, only Crocker seemed able to pull more than a sentence or two from him.

And it was because of Crocker that I learned how different

19

William Walker was from any other man I'd ever known, or have known since, or am likely ever to know. But that in good time.

We were four days going down the coast, where the land lay mostly flat and filled in with mangroves or reeds off to the east of us. We could see volcanoes and mountain ranges in the distance when the clouds cleared. We landed at night, in a cove where the sand stretched off flat and gray in the moonlight on either side of us, and the waves left a faint silver on the beach when they slid back out to sea. We had a guide who was to lead us through the jungle so that we could make a surprise attack on the town of Rivas in the early morning. We'd be done by noon, Colonel Walker told us. Once we had access to the Transit Route, we had access to men and supplies from all over the world. Without it, we were nothing. He talked about Destiny and protecting the weak and the rights of the strong and we cheered him before we got into the longboats.

But when I watched the two Nicaraguan colonels trying to whip their conscripts into line on the dingy beach, and truly realized that we were going to make a night march, slip up on a city, and try to take it with those, I felt fear in my belly like bad meat. I had never killed a man before. Most of us hadn't. But it wasn't that I was afraid of. That was abstract. It was the strangeness, the utter damned strangeness, the fighting with these men, and in this place.

I remember trying to concentrate on the clatter of rifles and the steady pounding of the waves behind me as we started into the jungle. But the waves disappeared and I forgot the clatter under the calls of night birds and the thrashings and shrieks from the brush beside the damp footpath. And when the moon vanished behind the gathering clouds, I would have given my mother's soul for a torch, gentlemen.

"Fixin' to rain," I heard Hornsby rumble somewhere behind me. "Them natives back yonder will melt off into the trees like sugar candy if it does. Mark me." I tried to picture him in the dark, scowling behind his great beard.

And from ahead of me, I heard Tim Crocker's sharp voice. "The order is silence, damn it, Captain." I tried to picture him, too, blond and pretty, walking beside Walker in his old suit that was black as the night. In my mind, I sketched them all, the long column vanishing into the jungle. Like a snake creeping up on something, I imagined them.

We drew up on a rise just above and to the west of the town of Rivas, waiting for morning. The rain had been light. But it had left enough clouds behind to make that coral sunrise as spectacular a thing as I had ever seen. The land dropped away in a greensward below us into the waters of Lake Nicaragua, which vanished into the morning distance like a sea. Rivas sat a mile or so inland. Beyond its red tile roofs, rising straight out of the lake itself, I could see the twin cones of a volcano.

Colonel Walker's eyes moved over that landscape, it seemed to me, as if it weren't land, but the body of a woman asleep. Then he caught himself, almost embarrassed—though I don't know that I could ever attribute that emotion to him fully—turned to Crocker and the rest of us, and took a deep breath of the morning air. "If I were still a newspaper writer, gentlemen, I would say the air is opium this morning. As I'm not, I'll say it's time to descend."

Colonel Walker started down the hill first, mounted on a horse we'd commandeered for him. Then the rest of us. The Nicaraguans were going to wait in the rear until we had got into town. They were supposed to come up to keep us from getting cut off, and bring in the supplies. I looked back at them one last time, bunched together at the crest of the hill, watching us go down into the woods. They looked more like children in linen pantaloons than soldiers. I was not comforted.

This is what I remember about the first battle of Rivas, as much of it as I can. I'll tell it as it comes to me and if any of it sounds odd to you, I'll make no excuses. It's how it comes.

It was somewhere outside town just as we came on the first houses that I forgot my body. I should have been tired, but I wasn't. I wasn't afraid anymore. I couldn't feel the twelve-pound weight of my Sharps rifle, nor my bedroll. My boots didn't seem to touch the ground. I was running before I realized I'd commenced to run. I was yelling with the others before I knew I'd opened my mouth.

When I saw the first fresh dirt of a barricade where the road passed the big, square main house of a hacienda, I knew that everything was wrong, but by then it didn't matter. *They're waiting for us, damn it, they've got barricades already*, I recall thinking, but I was running too hard to stop. And when the first native, wearing the same dirty white pantaloons as our own native troops except he had a white ribbon around his hat instead of a red one, when that first Conservative soldier stood up from behind the barricade, the only thing I could think about was an Alabama turkey shoot. The turkey pops up, you shoot, and he's gone. . . .

I shot, but I didn't feel the kick of the rifle. Colonel Walker's horse leapt over the barricade and swerved into the yard of the big, square house. He shouted for me to get the doors of the place broken in. Crocker and Henry and Hornsby kept on running, yelling for the main body of the men to follow them, heading for where the plaza ought to be. Nicaraguans with white ribbons stood up, took a shot, dropped their muskets, and scattered.

Everything scattered. Chickens squawked, and a mule in the yard near me brayed and reared up. Blood came spurting from its throat and it veered away among some banana trees, slammed into a rail fence, and fell. Two girls, servants I suppose, naked from the waist up, screamed and tumbled out of one of the house's tall windows. I remember the shutters banging against the adobe walls. From under the porch, a dog leapt for me as I pounded on the heavy wooden doors with my rifle butt. Somebody shot it, and out of the corner of my eyes I saw it go twisting away.

Somebody else, a hill-country private named Talmedge Warner, I think, got inside through a window and flung the doors open for me. The house was dim in the morning light that slanted in behind me. I can call it back well: blue knit doilies on the tables, rough beamed ceilings with a thatch roof, heavy dark furniture, two long rooms. It looked like a place to take off your boots and wait for somebody to bring you supper. I stopped. It was someone's home, you understand; I had never come into someone's home that way before. Then the back door slammed open and another man in a red shirt like myself fell through it. Before I could think, I jerked my rifle up, as if I'd come on a burglar I ought to shoot.

Somebody brushed by me and I saw it was the surgeon, Sartain. He didn't seem to recognize me. A horse clattered on the boards of the porch, and I heard Colonel Walker's thin voice shouting over the racket. "Secure this place, Lieutenant. Get the supplies in here. See that Dr. Sartain gets a surgery set up. This is our headquarters, do you understand?"

I turned to salute. The colonel's eyes were staring, almost fevery. Beyond him, Mendez the Cock and half a dozen of his Nicaraguans were dragging a horse from the hacienda's stable. Walker wheeled his own horse and rode off after Crocker and the rest, toward town, without looking back. I shook myself and jumped off the porch to see to the Nicaraguans with the supplies. And as I came around the corner of the house, I saw the road, empty of people as a church on payday, skins and boxes of ammunition and supplies scattered all along it, one single abandoned pack mule wandering off into the forest. Not a Nicaraguan was in sight, not a breathing soul.

Mendez the Cock galloped through the yard behind me on his new horse, lance lowered, red ribbon flying from it, the plumes on his hat flattened in the wind. He hit the road and spurred the horse toward the plaza. "Pray, bastards!" he yelled at the mud huts. "Mendez the fucked is here!" But just before he hit the first cobbled street, he turned off and headed toward the forest. I was alone.

And I understood the new barricades, the empty road, the trap. I may have been a fool in those days, but not that big a fool.

Then something whinged past me like a junebug and I felt little chunks of adobe spit at me from the house. On the roof of a hut across the road, I saw a hat with a white ribbon on it sink down out of sight. So that's a real sniper, I thought, just as if I was watching a magic-lantern show. Be damned, I thought, and dug the thing that had whizzed past me out of the wall. It was a hunk of iron grating.

Something splattered against my chest and I looked up. Guy Sartain was in a window, throwing eggs at me. "Lieutenant, for God's sake. Get inside," he was yelling at me.

Those are the things you remember, gentlemen.

I have no idea how long the next hour was, in spite of my watch. Somehow I managed to send the man Talmedge Warner and the half-dozen others Walker had left me to pick up what supplies they could, while the doctor and myself covered them. When one of the men took a ball in the shoulder, Sartain set up his surgery. "Oh, indeed, Lieutenant," he said to me. "Today we'll need a surgery. And a morgue."

All morning the firing kept up, now heavy, now light, from the town. Nobody came to the rear to report to us. Only once, in the early afternoon, Colonel Walker himself rode up and yelled in a window, "They've deserted, then?"

"Be in Costa Rica by tomorrow, Colonel," I told him.

"I want barricades," he answered me. "I can't get the rest of the men on. They're faltering. We may fall back."

He reined his horse around without waiting for an answer. He'd gone no more than a dozen yards when a sniper's ball caught its leg. It stumbled and Walker fell over its neck into the mud. He rolled to his feet, shook his head to clear it, then stared at the horse, which tried to stand but couldn't. He pulled out a revolver so big his hand barely reached around it, shot the horse, then started at a trot back down the road. The picture I have of him to this day is of a schoolboy, hurrying to class. I ordered the horse be made part of a barricade.

It was mid-afternoon when Tom Henry straggled into the yard. "Can't get nowhere. They all holed up in them little dirt houses, and ever time you move, there's half a dozen poking musket barrels at you. They was ready for us, God A'mighty ready."

"Where's the colonel?"

"A-coming. Crocker's got holes all in him and the colonel's helping him in. Near dozen of us is dead, I reckon."

The worst ones Dr. Sartain stretched out on what bed linen and cushions he could find. The others he laid as well as possible out of the line of fire on the dirt floor. Within half an hour they were all in, all but Crocker and Colonel Walker. And still there were no Conservative troops but snipers in sight.

And then I saw them, Colonel Walker supporting Crocker, the two of them hobbling along like boys in a sack race. Even as I ran out, I could see that Crocker's left arm was held on by his shirt more than anything else. His pants just below his hip were dark with blood, as if he had beshit himself, and his blond curls were matted to his head by blood. Still, with his good arm he raised his revolver and fired behind him. As myself and some others reached them, Walker loosened his hold on Crocker so that we could carry him. But Crocker fought away from my hands, teetered, and took a step back down the road toward the plaza. He was crying.

He tried to raise his pistol again, and then his face was gone. It burst open with a little *whoomp* when the ball hit it. I crouched to take hold of what was left of him, then let it fall. I couldn't bring myself to touch it. I'm ashamed of that.

Then Colonel Walker was beside the body. With the useless habit of a surgeon, he held its pulse for a moment. When he stood up, his eyes had lost none of that staring kind of feverishness they'd had. " 'Tis a pity," he said, nothing more. He waved us back toward the house. A couple of the men began to drag Crocker's body with them. "Leave it," Walker said to them, as if he was talking about a sack of sand. "We've got no use for it." The bad-meat feeling came back and rose to my throat. I tried to hold it in, then felt it burning my nose. I let it come out.

I said that it was because of Tim Crocker that I learned how different William Walker was from any other man I'd ever known, or would know. As best I could tell, he had loved Crocker. Then what to make of that moment? I don't know. Maybe that was his appeal, the reason we stayed with him: we understood that he would have treated us all just as he had Crocker, and he had loved Crocker. In some way or another that made him beyond us. We had to reach for him.

Not better than us, I said, gentlemen. Hear that. Not better, but beyond.

We held out through the afternoon, hoping for the cover of rain that didn't come. The house smelled like fresh-killed hogs, because of the wounded and the cauterizing that Guy Sartain was doing. The blue doilies were bandages now. The Butcher's troops kept their distance, since our rifles had a much greater range than their muskets. But they were there, flashes of white moving under the porches of adobe houses, drawing up in little bunches in banana groves, running crouched along fences and walls.

As the shadows of the banana trees grew longer, Colonel Walker kept those of us who could still shoot rotating among the windows. He was scrupulous as a church usher. Nobody served longer than anybody else, and all of us had time to rest. But the night was coming on. And at night no matter how long our rifles were, they would be useless as sticks.

The colonel himself kept pacing, avoiding our eyes. He moved from window to window, as if he were expecting a miracle to come in through one of them. At last he settled on a window that faced the road eastward. I put myself over beside him.

Beyond the road was a ditch, no, a large gulley. From where I stood, it seemed to deepen as it got closer to the forest. If we got to it, we had a chance to make the trees.

"Colonel?" I said.

"Lieutenant." He glanced at me, then went back to his watching. The spent greaser bullets kept up against the adobe walls steady as rain.

"You looking at the ditch, Colonel?" I said.

"I am," he said.

I waited for him to go on. He didn't. So I said, "Be dark soon, Colonel."

After a time, he said, "How many wounded can't run, Lieutenant?"

"Five, sir. Maybe six."

"How many are we all told?"

"Forty-eight, sir."

"Any notion of how many enemy bodies are out there?"

"More than a few. Seventy, eighty, I think."

He ran his hands through his hair. It was fine as a baby's hair. "They'll bayonet the ones we leave behind, you know."

"I've heard that, sir."

27

He sighed. "Lord God," he said.

That fevery look was gone from his eyes now, and he kept staring out the window. It almost seemed to me that he had forgotten where we were, that he was watching for the sunset to tell him it was time to let the house slaves set dinner. Sometimes I think he might have stayed that way until the Butcher himself knocked, if it hadn't been for the boy with the bottle.

We didn't even see him at first. Somebody yelled and I ran to the front window to see. There was a wedge of them running toward the porch, taking our fire and keeping on coming, shielding the boy until almost the very moment he hurled the bottle. He couldn't have been more than fifteen, brown as mud, and he threw the bottle so hard he lost his balance. None of us realized what was happening until it was too late, until we saw the burning rag hanging from the bottle and knew that it was on its way to the thatch roof. The boy stood still and watched it. I believe he saw it hit the roof before our volley cut him down. I'm told they've made a great hero out of him since.

The *whoosh* that came from the thatch as it caught fire seemed to slap Colonel Walker out of a sleep. While the men were yelling and dodging burning thatch, he called Hornsby and Henry and myself to him. "Charge them," he said. "When they scatter—and they will—veer off. Stay low in the ditch and keep together in the woods."

Then he went and spoke to each one of the wounded, low, so nobody else could hear. One of them, a boy from Vermont I believe, cried. The others stared at the ground. One counted a rosary. The last he tried to speak to was already dead.

For myself, I have no idea what I felt then. I don't recall that I felt like feeling anything.

Walker was first out the door. He went firing a revolver with each hand. We followed him and, just as he said, the Butcher's men fell back, confused. By the time they had recovered, Walker was in the gulley and the last of us was at least to the road.

As I jumped into the ditch, the man next to me fell against me. He was the son of a tailor from Manhattan, in New York, though I've lost his name. I shoved him away and he slid down into the mud. I stopped and saw a long rip in his back, where a ball had just hit him. In the novels that had taught me what I thought I knew about war, I would have dragged him along with me through the ditch. But I didn't. I left him in the mud and stumbled ahead to keep up with the others. I am ashamed of that, too, though even William Walker later told me it was the reasonable thing to do.

But I didn't do it because it was reasonable, gentlemen. Not at all.

TALMEDGE WARNER

I DON'T recollect much of the run, then the march through the woods. Just that the tree branches kept a-slapping at me like hands as I run, and the boys was wailing and bitching the whole way like whipped niggers. Colonel Walker wouldn't let none of them stop to cut me a crutch until he was sure the greasers wasn't following. I had did just fine staying back in that house with Lieutenant Holdich and that darkie doctor while the fighting was going on. But damned if I didn't catch my foot in a tree root in that ditch we run out into and there I was, a-hopping and a-hollering to try to keep up. It beat all.

The pain eased up at first with the crutch and the slow march, but when we come upon old Commodore Vanderbilt's transit road and the walking was easy and level, I seemed to hurt worse. Maybe because I had time to concentrate on it. I was damn certain they'd have had to leave me on the transit if it hadn't been for that man Dewey, and that's the part I want to think about least.

Dewey had come clattering out to us on the white macadam in the early morning on horseback to tell us that the little piss-ant port at the end of the road, San Juan del Sur, was all right to go into. He was a pinheaded sort, a slack-jawed drifter who had some kind of work there, and who you couldn't never have liked, except that he had seen my predicament and give me his horse to make the last three miles on. I knowed I'd of been waiting out beside the road for the greasers and their greased bayonets but for that.

But then Dewey got drunk and set fire to the native's barracks in San Juan del Sur, probably thinking Colonel Walker would be pleased. So it was his own fault to begin with but it still didn't make it no easier. I just wish the colonel hadn't come to me to settle it. He knowed damn well I owed Dewey.

We was already on board the ship before Dewey fired the barracks. But when Colonel Walker found out, he sent a party to arrest him anyway, though nobody could figure out just what for. Dewey run off, but didn't head for the jungle like a sensible or sober man; he taken over a boat, a little coaster that belonged to some mulatto. Well, the colonel had already ordered it took in tow before we found out that the mulatto's woman was on it too. Dewey stood her on the bow and hollered that he'd blow her tits off if Colonel Walker didn't cut him loose.

Colonel Walker didn't cut, but Dewey didn't shoot, either. He had at least enough sense not to give up his only protection. So we set sail with Dewey still in tow, cussing steady. I laid in the stern of the brig, praying for sleep without much luck. My foot was pumping pain like signal flares. To keep my mind off of it, I watched the woman on the boat behind us. She was a mulatto, too, young and with her hair down and no blouse on, like most of the women went around down there, which was right hard on me. She stood with her hands clenched up in front of her and looked to me like she was crying. I felt right sorry for her.

When the touch came on my ankle it was so soft I thought at first I was imagining it. The shock was to see Colonel Walker hisself, his face gray and wore out, a-holding my foot. "Dr. Sartain is sleeping, private. You'll allow me?"

"Yes sir," I said to him, as if he'd had to ask. I don't believe I'd never had no real doctor touch me before. I was glad the first time wasn't a nigger.

"Sprained," he said and pulled my leg toward him. I tried not to wince nor holler while he wrapped it. But his touch was gentle as a mama's. If he'd stuck with being a surgeon, I reckon he'd have been a good one.

"I need a man I can rely on," he said to me as he tied off the bandage. He looked back at the little coaster that bobbed along behind us. "It is a matter of honor. I've watched you, Private. I think there's not a better shot among us."

"What you asking me, Colonel?" I said to him.

"I want you to station yourself here on the stern until the man on that coaster comes up for air, as he will. Then I want you to shoot him."

I started to answer him, but stuttered and quit. By my own count, I'd killed four men the day before—even though they was greasers, the first men I'd ever killed. Now Colonel Walker wanted me to do more killing—an American, too, a man I owed. Like the man was a weasel that got in among the colonel's chickens. I shook my head.

The colonel's voice was almost lost in the wind, it was so thin. It put me in mind of something, of a snake charmer's flute I'd heard in a raree show in Kentucky once. "What will these people say if we let one of our own get away with pillaging, Private?" He was talking to me big as you please, just like I was an old friend of his, and here he hadn't said three words to me ever before. I couldn't make it all out, things about universal justice and protecting the weak, things I'd heard him say in speeches. But them gray eyes never left me, and all I could do was nod like he was making sense.

Finally he did say something that almost made sense. "If we act as if we're defeated, Private, we are" is what he said. And then he got up and walked off, like he'd stopped to pass the time of day.

I'd heard that all my life, and reckoned it was true enough. You weren't whipped till you acted like it. Well, I'd surely have said we was whipped when we run out of Rivas with our tails between our legs leaving the wounded to be bayoneted and burned. But here the colonel was telling me that if I shot this man Dewey for setting fire to some rickety greaser barracks, somehow or another that meant we wasn't whipped. I had to study on that.

I picked up my rifle and leaned back against the railing and thought about destiny and universal justice and being whipped and them things. The morning had turned off warm and the air on the sea smelled like fish. How did I feel about killing those men I'd killed back yonder in Rivas? I ought to feel bad, and I supposed I did if I thought that they might have families and such. But when I'd shot them, I was just glad it was them and not myself being dead.

Near dusk, Dewey leaned out of the hatch to reach a jug of water. I shot him. The puff of smoke blowed off in the wind almost as soon as it come out. Dewey pitched up onto the coaster's deck. The woman, who'd flung out her arms like she was a-begging me not to fire, grabbed holt of her shoulder, yelled, and fell down on her knees. I must have grazed her without meaning to. I did feel right sorry for her. Nothing was her fault.

Well, that was what it come to, that was how the first battle we fought down yonder in Eden wound up. Me blooding a woman and killing a American who hadn't done nothing. I'd studied on it before I shot, and have studied on it since. It didn't have nothing to do with universal justice nor destiny nor making like we wasn't whipped. It was the colonel so full of spite because the greasers had whipped us, so full of misery for that friend of his, and so needing to make out like he was above all that, too, that he couldn't help himself. Think on it. It makes sense.

And why did I shoot Dewey, then? A poor man has to make a place for hisself in this world. And sometimes he don't have but one chance. You got to make some choices.

RACHAEL BINGHAM ‖‖

August 27th, '55   Arthur believes in William Walker, like the others. We have a future here, he says. That he got shot in that saloon while we were waiting for the steam packet for San Francisco was a blessing, he says. He'll become an importer when the war is settled. Americans will pour in. Nicaragua might even become a State.

I don't want to be an importer's wife, I told him. I'm an actress—perhaps not a great one, but a good one. I'm only twenty-eight, I have time left, and I'm sick of flies and the smell of rotting garbage and war. And nothing but this diary to confide in. I want friends, other women to talk to. I want my life.

When I married him (is it possible that I was ever sixteen

and he thirty?) I know I was in love with him. But now, all that reminds me of that time is that when I poke around in the ashes they tell me there was fire there once. Oh, and I understand well what it means to have to say that! Tonight, I looked down the table at him, filling the new officer's glass and splashing wine on my last linen tablecloth, and I felt a chill, even with the tepid evening rain coming on again. He looks so much his age now, and more, with his hair streaked gray and his face all hollow and yellow. He's withering on his crutches, like a plant with a broken stalk.

He has been drunk since noon. We argued again today about going on to San Francisco, to the booking I know is waiting for us. I begged him to say we'd go, but he lost control of himself and I had to call the serving girl to help me calm him. What use is a crippled actor, he said. And then he told me that I can go whenever I decide to, but that it's him they want to see, not me, and he won't let them see him until he has the use of his legs back.

When he calmed, I tried to make him see for the umpteenth time how Walker has been sulking in his tent like Achilles for six weeks now and that there was seemingly no end to it. He isn't a hero anymore the way he was when he came back alive in spite of the fact that those generals, his "allies," tried to trap him. Nobody seems to really want him here but he won't go away. His men are locusts. They run up huge debts and mostly stay drunk and kill each other in stupid duels out of boredom.

The rains are soaking our souls. I wonder if the sky has ever been blue anywhere. There is malaria and breakbone fever and cholera and typhoid and I fear if I hear the dead cart rattle by once more I'll scream. Everybody says that if the Conservatives don't decide to come north out of their capital—such as it is—and hack everybody to pieces, then the yanqui-haters here in León will.

Can't he see that we are moulding here? Can't he see that

there is a terrible kind of kettle boiling over? Can't he feel it, the way I can?

He can't, and after tonight's dinner, I doubt that he ever will.

The new officer who was here tonight was introduced to me as Byron Cole, the man who had negotiated Colonel Walker's contract in the first place. Apparently, months ago he gave up on Walker and went off hunting gold in the jungles. He rode in last night muddy and full of ticks—and just before we sat down for dinner tonight, Walker made him a major. I can't imagine Byron Cole fighting anyone. He's a chubby trader, a promoter of things, a gentleman's horse dealer; I would cast him as any of those, and give him lots of funny lines to go with his good laugh. He's like the rest of them, all miscast.

Like William Walker, who sat on my right and fingered that little gold cross he wears, the one he'll never talk about. (Could there have been a woman somewhere in his life? I can't conceive it.) Who sipped light wine and stared around at everyone without saying anything or smiling (have I ever seen him smile?), for all the world a lizard on a stump. Who ought to go away and quit filling these men full of ideas that they're living in some awful kind of poem, so they can all go home. So that I could perhaps even go on with this game I've been playing about falling in love with Brian Holdich—if that part of me where falling in love comes from could ever stop feeling as withered and paralyzed as Arthur's legs.

And if Brian Holdich weren't five years younger than I am. And if he weren't as bound as on getting himself blown gloriously to pieces in this muddy place as the rest of them. And if the whole notion of falling in love here weren't utterly improbable anyway.

I've never been unfaithful to Arthur, though I don't think he believes that. I don't know whether I could be or not, but I know I have a right to. I've been nothing but needs, a whole sheaf of needs for months while I've done nothing but attend to Arthur's. Whatever is owed, I've paid.

Even poor Chélon was here tonight, doing his best. Every time one or another of Walker's officers made a toast, he'd join in with the here-heres like he knew what it meant. I feel sorry for him. Some of our people treat him like one of those characters from a comic sketch in a newspaper, but when Arthur insisted that we spend money we don't have for tonight's dinner to welcome Byron Cole, Walker sent word that he would particularly appreciate it if I invited Chélon. I wasn't able to imagine why then. Sitting between that Bible-thumping, prophet-bearded Hornsby and that tattooed horse, Tom Henry, the old thing was as out of place tonight as an apple in an onion bin.

Well, I know why now. Walker wants to use him, just as he used my house and hospitality tonight. Maybe Byron Cole's coming pushed him out of his sulk, or maybe he's been mulling this over for all of the past six weeks. I don't pretend to know where things come from in him. He's a well I can't see the bottom of—the bucket goes down, the bucket comes up.

The bucket came up full tonight, full of talk about being weary of waiting, about "characteristic American love of action," all sorts of nonsense and catch phrases that got applause and toasts and table poundings until I thought I'd stumbled into a west-side political rally. A new army was what it was all about, a glorious new army. Volunteers only, that Chélon is supposed to round up for them among the Indians. A "people's army," Walker calls it. No more waiting for the politicians to make up their minds about anything, no more depending on the generals to arrange for conscripts to desert. A new army and "techniques of modern warfare" and training and white officers and then off in their leaky ship to take Cornelius Vanderbilt's Transit Route again. No more bothering with taking cities—just the Transit Route, then they'll have all those ships from New York and California running back and forth with recruits and supplies.

Dear Lord, I thought as I watched them whip themselves up (Brian Holdich held back more than the rest. I was pleased with that.)—not a thousand dollars among them and they're going to just take property away from the richest man in America without asking, run it for him, and he's supposed to treat with them and be grateful. Dear Lord, I still think. I watched Walker manipulate them in that voice that always reminds me of gray snow, and Chélon's face glow with wine and some sort of transport that was closed to me as he hung on to the snatches of translation that Brian Holdich managed to get through to him. They weren't fools, I knew that. So they had to be madmen. I was serving dinner to a pack of men who belonged in chains in a madhouse.

When the toasts started again and the cigar fumes got thick as factory smoke, I had to get out. Arthur would keep them drinking with him all night if he could. I made an excuse and slipped away. They all toasted me, but they all looked relieved, even Brian Holdich. Well, let him be. What, after all, is there to myself and Brian Holdich? Some Sunday picnics when it hasn't rained, always with other people around. Exchanging chapters of Mr. Dickens' new book in Harper's. Feeling at ease, that if I ever needed to talk to him he would sit himself in that kept-in, Southern way of his and actually listen. Pooh.

I came back here to my bedroom and my brandy and the smell of orange trees. I tried to read, then sew, then gave up and watched the night moths dive into my candle and listened to the thunder until I heard the voices of the first to leave, Holdich and Chélon and Walker. I met them in the entry hall

37

and showed them out, Chélon bowing like a humpty-dumpty and Walker clicking his little heels like a French count. Brian Holdich took my hand.

For a moment, I thought I might tell him to come back and I would meet him in the garden for a glass of brandy. But I didn't.

As he left me at the door, I felt a rush of panic. I was alone in the house now with Arthur and his mad drinkers. Again. I came back here to write and bolted my door.

I think I would feel better among the Nicaraguans. I don't dislike the ones I know or think of them as a separate creation, the way Walker's people do. I get along with the women here excellently. They organize no armies. There is a devil in the guts of men that I will never understand, nor accept. Never.

August 28th, '55 As I read over what I wrote last night, I'm not sure I like myself. I sound carping and cynical. I don't think I've been that way before. It may be that I'm afraid. I've been afraid a good deal lately, last night more than ever. I believe they truly mean what they say about organizing a new army, and if they do, only God knows what will come of it. All I know is I will be caught up in it, whatever horror it may be. If I'm to survive, I must watch William Walker, and learn him.

CHÉLON

AND SO I went, *compañeros*. El Gualquer had come back alive from fighting the Butcher, and that was a sign, so I went. I rode out to my boys in the fields and in the woods where they were hiding from the conscription, and I told them the day had come. And what I told them and what I sang to them, they believed. Their mothers trusted me and showed me the caves and clearings where they had hidden their sons. And when I had found two hundred of them, as El Gualquer wanted, I hid them in the woods together from the conscription, and the gringos came there to teach them.

No more sleeping in gutters, toe to toe across the cobbles, I promised my boys. No more whips. No more sieges that nobody wins, God plague the filthy purebloods. It was our army now, an army of *el pueblo*. The transit road was the first thing, I told them, and then the rest would come. The gringos had already brought the road and the giant steamships that docked at the two ends of it. There would be railroads next, and telegraph. They would build factories and bring money to us. There would be jobs. People would eat. We would all be rich as gringos, or nearly. And then the gringos would dig their canal where the transit road was, as they'd promised. And El Gualquer would even see that el señor Vanderbilt paid his rent on the Transit Route at last.

I promised them those things because El Gualquer promised them to me. Not to the politicians and the generals, the way all the other gringos had done, but to me and to my *indios*. To us, the way the man in the Stories had done.

The boys had only two weeks, but they got good. And not only because of all the things the gringos taught them about loading and shooting, and retreating and charging the right way, and respecting discipline because you were treated like men and not like filth. No. This time there were no angle-nosed, high-assed Spaniards to meddle. This time I picked the officers, *indios* like myself, good men I'd served with before. Like Chinaman, who had been with me when we cut the shoe-wearer colonel in two at Granada. Even like Mendez the Cock, who would steal the calf out of a cow's belly but who was the best colonel of lancers in Nicaragua when he had a fight he thought he could win.

And when we left, the generals tried to stop us but the politicians stopped *them* when El Gualquer threatened to blow up León if they didn't. Did that bother me, *compañeros*? Did I feel like a traitor? A little. But not for long, and not to my *indios*. I had been fighting for the revolution for so many years, and nothing had changed. Who could invent us a new country, after we had failed? Who could bring the circle back around at last?

El señor Vanderbilt's paved road shone for us in the moon-light like a silver snake from the Stories. Nobody had been waiting for us when we landed at the end of it, at San Juan del Sur. Nobody had tried to stop us when we started walking on it. I listened to my horse's hooves on the pavement and to the boots of the gringos ahead of me as loud as a pack train and thought what a noisy world the gringos made. Behind me I couldn't hear my own men's bare feet at all.

I looked over at the outline of Mendez the Cock, asleep on his horse beside me. Night marches. Ay, God. How many night marches had I made? I was too old and my leg hurt like the fires of hell were in it and somewhere was Guardiola the Butcher with three times the men we had, gringos and *indios* together. Ay, God.

I remember how loud the gringos' boots seemed to get

after dawn as we approached the end of the transit road and the village, Virgin Bay, where the Transit Company's lake steamers docked. Was it just that we had left the hills and that the stillness of the open ground made them seem louder to me? No. It was more than that. It was the silence everywhere.

I knew it shouldn't be so quiet; it was morning, the people in the village should just be getting up. There should be chickens and hogs and dogs and children. But I heard not a sound, not a sound but the boots and the waves on the lake.

I had been here only once, years ago before the Transit Company came. It had been a mudhole village of a few fishermen's huts made out of reeds then. Now there was a warehouse big as a cathedral, and a wooden hotel next to it with a wide porch and a balcony. Around both of them ran a wooden palisade, like a little fort. And beyond those, a big two-story house and a dock into the lake. And all of it empty as a moneylender's soul.

The huts were still there, only there were four times as many of them now, scattered all across the road from the gringos' buildings. And they were empty too, house and yard.

El Gualquer and the man who spoke Spanish for him drew their pistols and rode up toward the warehouse. I spurred myself up beside them. I remember I heard the wind from the lake moving around the big building like music. At the porch El Gualquer shouted something. After a moment, a gringo without much hair stepped out.

"Col. William Walker?" he said—that much I could understand. For the rest, I understood that the man smiled like a nervous man does and shook his head and pointed around at the forest, then shrugged a lot. I didn't need to understand more. He didn't know where the Butcher was, and the people had gone to hide in the forest.

It was the boots, *compañeros*. They had never heard so many boots before as the gringos wore, all marching together.

After those three had talked together awhile, the man who spoke Spanish turned to me and asked me what I thought.

"I think we should have breakfast," I told him.

After all, men who carry the weight of so many boots, so many bedrolls, so many pistols, so many knives, so many clothes when they go off to fight must have gotten hungry, no?

The gringos made their fires and cooked their beef and boiled their coffee. My boys broke out their cheese and mixed their cornmeal with lake water for *tiste*. El Gualquer didn't eat—I never saw him eat. He planned. I never saw a man who planned so much, either. He paced along the lake, climbed the low hill beside the village, squatted behind fences and sighted. Sometimes when he squatted, I thought his hat was going to swallow all of him.

We set pickets along the road, and the people from the village came back in dribs and drabs from the forest. They shoved their hogs and led their milk cows and carried their chickens. I was pleased. I spoke with the men and teased the women and let the children touch the plumes on my hat and the brass buttons on my coat. They should know that there was nothing to fear from us, that we were going to make a new world together with these blond bears. It was a fine day to start everything new on, I decided, with those good people in that good place. The morning opened like a flower, like the morning glories that trailed up the village fences.

Here's a drawing. The man who spoke Spanish for El Gualquer and who I think was my friend, Brian Holdich, made it that morning. He sat with a pad of paper on the embankment by the lake and made it. See, there are the great double volcanoes on the island of Omotepe in the lake in front of us. I watched him make it and he gave it to me. It's good, *caballeros*, but it's not the thing. The thing was better. There

42

was a mist that morning and the lake was gray as the ocean, the sand on the beach so gray it was almost black. Later, in the sunlight, I knew the waters would turn a deep blue, and you could see sails and canoes on them, and beyond the bay the jungles would hang over the water, as deep a green as the lake was blue.

I've heard that the lake, which the Spaniards call Lake Nicaragua but we *indios* have another name for, is over a hundred miles long. It's a sea, in truth. Yet it's gentler than a sea. I think there must be hundreds of calm little islands in it, all green, where sometimes you can spend days on end with no other sound than the small waves of the lake and the parrots and macaws.

I watched a plume of smoke, or it might have been a cloud, drift out across the waters from Concepción, the bigger volcano on the island. Trees rose half way up it like a skirt. You've done well here, God, I thought. Chélon approves, God. I stretched out in the long grass and listened to the sound of Holdich's pen and the waves and the wind in the palm trees. It was hard to find that ease, I thought, when you were fat and fifty and had a bad leg. I drifted away toward sleep.

The first shots came to me as if from a great, great distance. Two quick ones, a picket firing at a patrol and being answered. Musket thuds, not the sharp sound of gringos' rifles. Then a long string of thuds like fireworks on a saints' day. But I knew the distance wasn't so great; the shots were only muffled by the jungle. A woman in the village behind me screamed. I struggled to get up, my *maldita* leg caved in, and I sat down again. Then Brian Holdich's hands were under my arms lifting me up, and my eyes found El Gualquer on the porch of the hotel. He stood perfectly still, watching the transit road, while all the others with him pointed and shouted like mule drivers.

All right, I thought. Here it is, God. It's been a long time, God. Let's see about it now, God.

. . .

That day breaks up into bits and pieces for me, *compañeros*, into flashes, like a bottle smashing in the sun. We had the center, and the gringos took the high ground on the flanks. Their long rifles could reach the shoewearers from there, and our muskets couldn't (the shoewearers' muskets couldn't reach the gringos, either, but we didn't think of that then— we were proud to have the center).

The shoewearers came at us first in waves, I remember that. Their shitty officers in black uniforms rushed ahead of them, waving their swords like they were trying to slice a path in the air for the men behind them. And every time a wave of them came, I heard the sound of my own men's muskets speed up like a drum tattoo. After a few waves, they didn't come again.

Then they tried from the sides, but the gringos rushed out at them with pistols and yells like no Christian man makes, and they threw their guns away and crawled for the bushes, no matter how much their mounted officers beat them with whips and swords. Even their poor conscript corpses smelled like liquor from the *aguardiente* they'd had poured down them. But all the details of the battle? How can I give you details? There were so many battles before that one and there have been so many since, how can I make sure I'm not mixing them all up?

Once I remember I looked at the sun and saw it was afternoon. My leg had long since gone numb. The sweet air of the morning had turned to sulphur, and my sweat drew gnats that closed in around my head like a net every time I stopped moving. When I rode into the woods I found dead shoewearers tied to trees. It had come to that already.

Yet every time I counted or asked Mendez the Cock how many of the boys were dead, the answer always came back *none*.

44

"That's a sign," I told him.

"That's training," he told me.

Here's a thing I haven't forgotten. It was late, because the shadow of the Transit Company warehouse lay almost completely across the white road. I was with Mendez and my friend Holdich at the edge of the woods by the road, and Mendez pointed toward the palisades around the warehouse. El Gualquer was coming out to us. He was walking through the crossfire on open ground, all by himself. *Madre de Dios!* I thought, just like a whole pissing army weren't there to shoot at him. Every now and then he would stop, raise up his pistol, and fire.

And then they hit him. He spun around, grabbed at his throat, and sat down with his legs spread out under him like broken sticks. I started toward him behind Holdich as best I could. Sweet God, I thought, not now! Now when we're so close. But before I had gone a dozen steps, El Gualquer was on his feet again and waving us away. He staggered, then came on. I saw a dozen of my men hiding in the grass cross themselves.

When I turned back, I saw another man, *compañeros*, alone like El Gualquer, but sitting in the middle of the transit road on a great mottled horse. He was dressed in a long flowing shirt of red and black checks and was too far away for even a gringo rifle to reach. I strained to see the man's face, but I knew already who it was. I could make out the mustaches that curled up behind his ears, and that was enough. I had seen the face once before, in Honduras, when I was in exile with my General Maximo Jerez. I knew the face was flat and pockmarked. I knew its chin sloped like a pig's. I knew it was a face that had no right to be so ugly and live among Christians. It was Santos Guardiola, the Butcher, and he sat still as a statue in a plaza, watching us.

I pointed toward him when El Gualquer reached us. *"El Carnicero,"* I said. El Gualquer stared at him a long time. Then he took his hat off and made a little bow toward him.

The Butcher still didn't move, and for a moment I wondered if the syphilitic bastard was still alive. But at last he reared his horse and plunged off into the forest.

That was the last time I ever saw him. Did El Gualquer ever see him again? I don't know, but if what I've heard is true, he must have, God help him.

El Gualquer opened his mouth to speak, but nothing came out. He touched his throat. There was a red mark the size of an egg on it, just above a little gold cross he wore. He spat, whispered something to Holdich—some order, I imagine— then turned away from us.

As he made his way back across the field toward the warehouse, I looked to my men. They watched him walk away with their mouths open. I knew that in a month every *indio* in Nicaragua would know the story. El Gualquer is not afraid of bullets. He was hit at Virgin Bay but he didn't bleed. He is the one from the Stories.

Half an hour later, it was done. We charged and the Butcher's army melted away into the forest like rain. Afterward I rode up the transit road for two miles looking for signs of them. Nothing, nothing but the empty *aguardiente* demijohns they'd liquored up with, scattered like cannonballs that had missed their mark. Once you got past the dead shoewearers near the village, no sign of a Christian soul. *Cristo Rey*, I thought. Half my life I'd waited for something as miraculous as this, and now this silence, this weariness was all that was left of it?

I turned back to the job of shooting the wounded prisoners. It was a messy one and I never cared for it. Mendez the Cock would do it. He liked it, though this time I supposed I would have to keep him from chopping the feet off them first, the way he'd done at Granada.

I rode past my man Chinaman on the way back. He was

already at work with a detail of men burying the dead. In the late light, I remember thinking that the shovelfuls of earth they threw looked like heavy grain they were winnowing. Further on, some gringos were unloading the Butcher's personal supply train. They were into his liquor already. That was another thing the Butcher wouldn't forgive, fuck his humpbacked mother.

Mendez was beside the lakefront, away from the new campfires. He had a dead chicken tied to his belt and sat against the trunk of a ceiba tree, flicking his knife into a plank he'd propped up. He hadn't bothered to wash the dust off his face, or have his uniform brushed. He looked up at me and went back to flicking his knife.

"Have you seen to the wounded shoewearers yet, *viejo*?" I asked him.

He flipped his thumb toward the warehouse, like this.

"Not buried yet?" I said.

"Not dead yet."

"That should have been done quickly."

He gave me a little laugh. "Go look for yourself." He threw the knife so hard it split the plank. "The *zambo* doctor's treating them."

Six kinds of shit! I thought. The world was knee-deep in shit and now Mendez was heaping more on. "Where are they?"

"I told you. El Gualquer's orders."

He looked up at me and I could see he was serious. "What in God's name for?"

He stood up and wrenched his knife out of the split plank. "I think, *mi Chélon*," he said, "I think because that's the way El Cid would have done it."

"Eight kinds of shit."

"Ten kinds," he said.

I let my horse take me to the hotel, as slow as he wanted to. So, I thought, El Gualquer had his Transit Route. So. We didn't shoot prisoners anymore. So. We'd just run off the most dangerous son of a whore in all Central America—with only two of my men killed in the last charge. So. This was the way the new world began. *Plin!* Just like that.

I should be jubilant, I knew. Maybe tomorrow I would be, when I wasn't so tired. Ahead of me on the hotel porch the gringo officers were toasting one another. Let them, I thought. They weren't tired; they'd only been at this killing business two months. I'd been at it all my manhood. I wanted it to be over, like the night marches. I checked the porch for El Gualquer and didn't find him. No, he wouldn't be celebrating. Like me, *compañeros*, he knew it wasn't over yet.

The night was coming on quickly. Already the lake was vanishing. There would be rain in the night; I could smell it. A huge gray moth fluttered past me toward the lantern on the porch. My guitar would be waiting in my room instead of a woman.

I remembered Job, and understood the poor bastard. When, oh Lord? I asked as I swung my poor throbbing leg up the first step of the hotel.

Soon, I heard a voice say from the darkness that was gathering. *Soon, my faithful fat servant, soon.*

It had damn well better be, I answered. I'm tired.

GUY SARTAIN

QUICK AS a minute, I said, sir. It all changed quick as a minute. Oh, not the place. In those three weeks of September that we sat in San Juan del Sur after we chased the one called the Butcher back home to Honduras, the land never stopped being Mohamet's paradise for me. I sat on the hills above the town, and I don't think I had known a greater peace. Down below me the bay lay still as sleep between the green hills. And it was a green that fairly glowed, like a firefly. I even had a woman there, and the pleasure of the woman and the pleasure of the land have become so entwined for me that they seem almost to be the same now.

No, it wasn't the land that changed. It was that no place is paradise when you begin to know too much about it.

Tom Henry had been right on the ship, you see. The natives thought of me as a white man, and the white men thought of me as a Negro. They settled the problem mostly by making me invisible. That way they didn't have to solve me. I was considerably lonely, but I learned things.

Here was our situation. We had the Transit Route, and with every ship that came we had more recruits. And there were plenty of native deserters from the Conservatives who wanted to join us, so at the end of those three weeks we nearly doubled our forces. Colonel Walker still held that he was only doing what he was contracted for by the government in León, so the people there had no choice but to treat us as heros.

They put on great fireworks displays for us, and made sure we heard about them. They gave the ones of us who had come down in the first fifty-seven a name, the Immortals, and made us all officially part of the Nicaraguan Army. The American Phalanx, we were, *el falange Americano*. It was all taken quite seriously, too.

They were desperate to appease us, no matter what silliness they had to resort to. The truth, of course, was that in that country of warlords the colonel was doing as he pleased. But he was a lawyer, too, as well as a surgeon. He was not at ease unless everything he did *sounded* legal. That is part of the American genius, I have found.

I had no quarrel with him yet. He took no conscripts, raided no lands to provision us. (Not that he had to, since the landowners were all too glad to give him provision in exchange for our protection.) I was still his friend. At table, he always made sure I was seated with the other officers, though often only he and Lieutenant Holdich, who was his aide now, spoke to me. Most of the time, when I could do it without offending him, I asked to eat alone. He seemed to understand that. He loved solitude, I think, and did not begrudge me mine—though I know he failed to see the difference between our two kinds.

We had far less time for our talks than we had had on board the ship, and I missed them. But when we talked, he seemed to assume that he and I had more in common than our studies. We were set apart, he told me. Once he said that his sensibilities were as sure a mark on him as the color of my skin. A few times he talked about his boyhood, how he spent much of it reading aloud to his mother, who was sickly, or how he suffered from the cruelty of other boys in school, who called him such names as *missy* and *honey*. On those times I was embarrassed. I think he understood well enough how greatly such things had shaped him; it wasn't any ignorance of his that embarrassed me. No, it was because I knew that he was telling me those things because in his heart of hearts he thought I was invisible too. He would not have wanted to hear them from me. I didn't want to hear them from him, but I had no choice.

I was embarrassed when I went among the Nicaraguans, too. I had spent my time well and learned a fair amount of Spanish by then. Some of them talked about us as if we weren't men like themselves, as if we were special sorts of creatures who had to be carefully studied and imitated. Others of them hated us, and said we were monsters who had to be destroyed. So I was embarrassed because, although I knew what they thought about us was false, I didn't know what to tell them was true.

And there had been the killing and the drunkenness and the duels and the arrogance. No, that was not paradise. And I was the one they called to set it right, though they would not speak to me at table. How was it, I wondered, that Colonel Walker's life had been so devoted once to the saving of lives, and now was given over so greatly to men whose job was killing?

But it was not my place to dwell on such easy ironies. I had sufficient of my own. I worked and waited and took what pleasures I could and willed myself to trust and believe as much as possible. Like most of the others, I had no place else to go, no one else to believe in.

The difference was, I think, that I knew it.

BRIAN HOLDICH

I WAS THE one who translated the captured dispatches for Colonel Walker, and I thought nothing of them at the time. They said nothing of value I could discover, nor did the colonel's answers give me a clue they meant anything to him, either. They were from the Conservative government in Granada to their own commander-in-chief, a man named Ponciano Corral. After the Butcher went home to Honduras, this Corral took over and holed up in the town of Rivas to watch us, you see. The dispatches only begged him to finish us off quickly and come back to Granada. The Conservative garrison to the north in Managua was half dead of the cholera, the dispatch said, and the people in Granada were terrified that the Democrats would come down from León to attack and there would be nobody to defend them.

The colonel sent the dispatches on to Corral. And he put a note of his own with them. Nothing of interest to me here, he said. All I can see is that your people are suffering. Why don't we communicate with each other?

Then the next day, we were given the order to prepare to march. He told none of us where—unless it was his friend Byron Cole—not even me. And I was his aide, gentlemen. We went so quickly that some of the boys had to leave their laundry behind, and I myself had to leave a letter to a woman in León half finished on my desk.

That was in early October of 1855. I have no notion what Colonel Walker was planning before those dispatches came. I don't know that he was planning anything. I think that if anyone had tried to plan most of the things that happened to us in Nicaragua, he would have been locked away. If there is such a thing as destiny, as the colonel always claimed, we rode it like a racehorse, rode it to the very end.

We marched in the daylight this time, toward the lake along the twelve miles of the transit road. There were near four hundred of us, I believe, with close to a hundred left behind to see after the Transit Route and make sure Mr. Vanderbilt's blue-and-white stagecoaches full of passengers and his wagons full of specie and supplies got through without molestation. When we saw which way we were going, the bets were that we were going to try to draw this Ponciano Corral out of his hole in Rivas and have done with him.

But the bets changed when we passed by the road to Rivas. We kept going, toward the lake.

It was already after dark when we got to Virgin Bay, at the end of the road. We camped, but Colonel Walker ordered no campfires be built, which didn't set well with the men. The transit agent for the place, a bald man named Cushing, invited the officers to have supper and a whiskey. We did, except for the colonel, who didn't take strong spirits. We sat on the hotel porch after supper, I recall, and talked amiably enough about the end of the rainy season and how much easier it would be for troop movements then, and of the famine that would come because of the war. None of us mentioned the thing that was most on our minds. We knew Colonel Walker would tell us in his own good time, and until then we had damned well keep our mouths shut about it.

"I understand your lake steamer is due to dock at nine this evening, Mr. Cushing," Colonel Walker said at last.

"It is."

"I will need it for a time."

Cushing sipped at his brandy awhile. "I beg your pardon, Colonel?"

"I will do everything in my power to see that no harm comes to it."

"That steamer, Colonel, belongs to Mr. Cornelius Vanderbilt. It is the property of a United States company."

"I am aware of that," Colonel Walker said, that Tennessee voice of his as level and cold as ice on a pond. He was staring off into the distance, I recall, as if Cushing was talking to him from behind a curtain.

"It is under the protection of the United States Government, sir," Cushing went on.

"It flies the Nicaraguan flag, Mr. Cushing. International law gives the Nicaraguan government the right to requisition it in time of war."

Well, Cushing thought a little bit, and his face got more and more troubled. He opened his mouth to say something once, then shut it again. When he finally did get the words out, his voice was as formal as an Episcopalian preacher's. He was considerably afraid, I took it. "May I remind you, sir, that you are leading an army of revolution against the legitimate government of Nicaragua."

The colonel stood up. His face was flushed and as near to angry as I think I'd ever seen it. "That is splitting hairs, sir," he said, and his voice got softer and colder. "Within a week, I will represent the only legitimate government of Nicaragua. Mr. Vanderbilt will appreciate my reasoning when the time comes." He put down his coffee cup and stepped down off the porch. "In the name of the people of Nicaragua, this village is under martial law. If you or anyone else attempts to leave it between now and tomorrow noon, he will be shot. My apologies."

And he meant it, gentlemen. Let there be no doubt.

The bets changed again then. It was San Carlos we were heading for, where the steamer put in at the mouth of the river across the lake. We were going to take the whole Transit Route, all the way to the Atlantic. A few of us tried to pump Byron Cole, but he only smiled and told us what a good country lawyer Colonel Walker had been.

The steamer was on time to the minute. We had it before the captain even knew we were on board. We put the passengers and their baggage into Mr. Vanderbilt's twenty-six coaches and sent them on with a guard detail. So far as I could tell, none of them realized a thing was going on. The women turned their heads away from us and the children touched our beards and stared at our revolvers just as they always did.

This is something I remember. One of the passengers, who was a fat man in a swallowtail coat, stopped in front of the hotel porch a minute. "Ain't much chance of getting a look at that terrible Walker we been hearing so much about, is there?" he said.

Colonel Walker stood beside me. "I'm Colonel Walker, sir."

"Well, damn my eyes, Colonel. You're a right puny thing, ain't you. I'd expected eight foot tall and breathing fire."

Byron Cole thumped his chair down onto the porch back in the shadows. "He is, friend," he said. We laughed the fat man to his coach.

We boarded at dawn, four hundred men and two horses— one for the colonel and one for old Chélon and his bad leg. We were far too many for the boat, but we took almost no supplies. We had orders to keep the men absolutely quiet. I recall that everything smelled like engine grease and fresh varnish, an American smell that I'd missed.

When the paddles on the side of the ship commenced to

move us back away from the dock, I could feel the tension in the air like the mist from the lake. I was in the cabin with the colonel, keeping a pistol on the captain. As we set out onto the lake, I watched the wake glisten behind us and pick up the colors of the sunrise. They're as clear to me now as the color of my own eyes.

When we were a fair distance out on the lake, the captain said to Colonel Walker, "I have to take a direction, Colonel."

"You'll set a course north, captain." Colonel Walker said. "Please stay as far offshore as you think safe."

"North, sir?"

"North, sir. Toward Granada."

TALMEDGE WARNER

WELL, WHEN them greasers on the boat found out we was a-heading north toward Granada, they carried on and whooped and hollered so much that we had to whip them with rope to get them to shut up. You'd of thought it was Resurrection Day. I reckon they had it in their heads that they was going to rape and pillage, but they didn't know Uncle Billy Walker.

By then we'd got to know some of them, and on the whole they wasn't bad. We steamed all day, and they mingled in with us and some of us give them tobacco and showed them how to spit right, and they give us cigars that some of the boys chewed. I was nervous, but not too much so. It was like a sight-seeing boat. I never seen so many islands, and I wouldn't have minded getting set up on one. You could grow piss if you wanted to, I reckoned. I'd get me one of them

wicker rocking chairs like they have down there and one of
them native women that I wouldn't let eat so many beans and
get fat like they do, and I'd be set up. A man could tolerate
greasers fine if he got used to them. If they'd left us alone, we
could of been good for them.

Toward dusk, we passed a volcano they told us was called
Mombacho, and that meant we was near about to where we
was going. And then just at evening, with canvas over the
windows so our lanterns wouldn't show, we seen the outline
of an old castle breaking the shoreline and the lights of a city
making the sky glow behind it. It was Granada, they said.
The Paris of the Isthmus, the colonel told us. Paradise on
earth, he said.

It couldn't have been more than three or four miles past
the city that we turned in toward shore. It was good dark by
then, and the shore was the darkest part of it, I recollect. We
anchored, and the colonel sent two men swimming ashore
with a cable. It was quiet as a held breath, not a thing for
the Lord hisself to hear but the swimmers a-splashing and
the boilers a-hissing and somewhere somebody a-praying
low. Then when the cable was tight, we slipped two iron life-
boats into the water. We was going to pull them along the
cables like ferries, so there wouldn't even be no sound of oars.

The night moved on toward midnight while we were working. We unloaded steady, quiet, and quick. The moon kept
scudding in and out of clouds, and I almost wished it would
go ahead and rain so the dark would settle in for good. I
stayed behind on the boat to help unload the colonel's and
Chélon's horses, which was the last to come off. Once they
got into the lifeboat they bucked and neighed and clanged
their hooves against the side of the boats till I was sure they
heard us all the way up to New Orleans. But the woods stayed
quiet, and when the rain finally did commence, it was like
you'd throwed a wool blanket over the world.

When we set off into the woods, it was like we was stumbling through dripping laundry. The colonel stayed in front,

56

but old Chélon kept a-riding up and down the line and every time he brushed past me I could smell his wet horse and hear him a-muttering to himself. Only three miles or so it was to the city, like I said, but there was four hundred of us, single file in the dark and I could have swore we marched to China. The boy in front of me shit his pants. I could smell it.

Just before dawn down there, the dark changes. It's not really sunrise yet, but there's this kind of half-light that comes before daylight. The rain stopped then, and the morning sounds started up: bugs buzzing, birds waking up and a-chattering, things crashing off in the bushes. The wet woods smelled like loam, like Kentucky after plowing. My clothes was soaked and itched me worse than the ticks I had.

When real dawn come, the trail widened out. We passed a cane hut where this naked little child, still half asleep, watched us pass by the door like we was still part of his dream from last night. And then beyond that there was an orchard, and past that a cotton field. And past the cotton field, in the haze of the morning, huts, fences, streets, walls, towers . . .

We poured through them little narrow streets yelling like fiends. Way out ahead of us the colonel hollered *Charge!* and jumped his horse over the first empty barricade amongst the huts there on the edge of town where the Indians lived. I picked out Captain Hornsby, who was so skinny and tall he could have been a guidon, and followed behind him. People was running out of the huts and hollering and dropping things like the demons of hell was among them. We run them down, knocking plates out of their hands and cigars out of their mouths and throwing our bedrolls away so we could run even faster.

And then the huts stopped and the town itself took up, and that's when the bells and fireworks commenced. Ever church bell on earth, it seemed to me, and skyrockets like the Fourth of July shooting up from ahead of us. God Almighty damn, I thought. Here it's Rivas all over again; here we are trapped sure as gophers in a corncrib, and I'm dead, damn I'm dead.

Captain Hornsby slowed up and Lieutenant Holdich, who spoke Nicaraguan, come up beside him and they grabbed ahold of a boy who was running by. Lieutenant Holdich jabbered at him and the boy tried to say something but couldn't get nothing to come out until the lieutenant slapped him. Then he jabbered something back and the lieutenant laughed.

"Translate, by thunder!" Captain Hornsby hollered with his long black beard flapping like a buzzard's tail.

"Celebrating," the lieutenant said, and he couldn't stop laughing. "Celebrating whipping the barefoots up north somewhere yesterday. By damn, they're having a party!"

Old Hornsby, who was mostly sober as a stump, let a grin sneak up on him then. "And here comes the hangover, by God," he whooped, and loped off toward the next barricade.

Well, the drummer boy was a-drumming, we was running and yelling, and the people on the streets was diving for cover. Only time anybody tried to stop us was a couple of soldiers in a church tower shot at us and missed, and Tom Henry taken a half dozen of the boys and rooted them out with revolvers. Every time we scrambled over a barricade there was another one ahead of us, empty as the one behind, all through them narrow streets. And then there was this broad boulevard in front of us—and no more barricades. Just this boulevard, with one fat native in a frock coat running down the middle of it yelling, "Save yourself, save yourself!"

And at the end of it all, there sat the plaza. Just there, empty but for some dogs, with this big stone cathedral throwing its long morning shadows across the dirt and them smoking skyrockets on the ground. Ahead of me, I seen Captain Hornsby draw up at the edge of the church and look around him like he was lost. I caught his eye and stopped too, and seen he was as set back on his heels as I was. A priest run out from the cathedral, seen all of us bearded men a-throwing ourselves behind posts and carts around the plaza, screamed something, and scuttled back inside.

That was it for the bells and the fireworks. Here and there from side streets I heard a rifle echoing or a musket thudding, or a yell, or a woman screaming. But aside from that, the whole town had got silent as death. Even old Chélon's greasers, when they come running up, stopped and stood still. It was like everything had turned into a picture.

And then something moved, at last something moved. He come out from under the covered porch of the cathedral, drab as a storekeeper, and walked toward the center of that plaza. I reckon I'd lost sight of him, trying so hard to follow behind Hornsby. He was all by hisself, walking slow as judgment, and I couldn't get shut of the notion that he was about to commence to recite something, the way I'd seen actors and such do when they walked out on a stage. Nobody else stepped out there with him, like we was all hypnotized. Then, just about square in the middle of the plaza, he pulled up. Oh, I can see it clear as day—he turned full circle, his great eyes running over the cathedral and the government buildings and the fancy-carved houses and the stores, running over them like he was taking inventory.

Then Captain Hornsby stepped out into the plaza, then Byron Cole, then Lieutenant Holdich and Tom Henry, and then the rest of us, a-coming out from behind our carts and posts. Somebody started to sing "Hail Columbia," and then somebody else taken it up and it spread amongst us all, echoing off them stone buildings like a camp meeting in a valley. I was near to bawling. Old Chélon come charging past me, whooping and waving his saber above his head. And then somebody hefted the colonel up on their shoulders and some of the other boys joined in and they was dancing him around like he'd won a race at a fair. And all the time, old Chélon was a-riding round and round the plaza, while his own men tried to grab his stirrups, and one of our boys commenced to hopping a jig, and it was the greatest day I had ever seen, bar none, praise the Lord.

Well, and that was it, that was how we taken Granada, less than half a hour and not a breathing one of us killed except a greaser drummer boy and I don't think that counts. I didn't recollect then that there was nothing else like it in history, nor nobody else like Uncle Billy Walker, of Tennessee. I still don't.

But wait. I say we was all celebrating. That's not true. There was one of us who wasn't.

That darkie doctor was standing off by hisself under the porch of one of the stores on the plaza there, watching us like we was a medicine show. Nobody else seemed to pay attention to him. I broke off from the rest of the boys and went over. I felt right sorry for him. It wasn't his fault he was who he was.

"Great day, ain't it," I said to him.

"Oh, yes," he said. "A great day." He looked pleased enough.

"You ain't celebrating?"

"No," he said. "I'm waiting."

"What for?" I asked him. "It's all done."

"No. No, I don't believe it is," he said to me. "You see, Mr. Warner, Colonel Walker just stole himself a country today. *We* did. I think," he said, and pulled him out a cigar. "I think I'll wait and see what we do with it."

No sense in putting up with that, I thought. I knowed what *I* wanted to do with it. But then I was white, and understood such things.

PART TWO

GENERAL WALKER

We notice in some of the newspapers which have been received here by the last arrival from New York, that some of the letter-writers in Nicaragua affairs are evidently disposed to make themselves merry at the expense of the gentleman whose name stands at the head of this article. We presume, however, that now, as success alone is the only criterion of merit admitted in that quarter of the world by newspaper paragraphists, the tone and style of correspondence on this subject will materially change when the intelligence of the final pacification of Nicaragua shall reach them. We who have witnessed the stirring scenes and taken part with him in the exciting drama which has been exhibited and enacted by the American Phalanx, know something more about the real merits of the man and his cause. . . .

Sharing without hesitation or reserve, in all the privations of his men, giving up his horse to any one who seemed to suffer from tender feet or fatigue, sitting at the same mess and preferring the plainest dishes, he has endeared himself to his command as a true republican gentleman, who acknowledges no distinction except those which superior virtue and character bestow. . . .

As a man, and as a General, he has exhibited equal amiability and republican simplicity of character towards those who have met him in a friendly spirit, as also to those who have encountered him with arms; and to all that conspired against his authority, stern justice, tempered with humanity.—In his military career, his strategy has been more than equal to the crisis, and for the first time in thirty-four years of almost perpetual war, has Granada fallen, and that too, by so unexpected and sudden a surprise, as almost to make it a bloodless victory. If from great and honorable motives, by fair and praiseworthy means to perform great deeds, influencing the happiness of an oppressed people, and controlling the destiny of a country as important to the world in its position and resources as Nicaragua, entitle a man to the appelation of "Great" in the sphere assigned him by Providence, then is General Walker entitled to it. Let those cavil and carp who cannot appreciate.

THE EDITORS
El Nicaraguense
Granada, October 27, 1855

In entering the room where General Walker was to receive us we would hardly believe that the little insignificant-looking person before us was the man who had shown such great talents as a military leader. . . .

"Letter from a Young Washingtonian on His Travels"
San Juan del Sur, November 29, 1855

WILLIAM WALKER ▫▫

Trujillo, Honduras: 1860. The voices seem to come to him
from a great distance; he sees the faces from a great height.
It is as if he has to snatch at the voices as they are being
blown past by the sea wind, to make out the faces in the
shadows the flat evening light leaves on the stone floor and
walls. It wasn't this way then, when he took Granada. He
thought for a time he had lost his solitude forever, until he
found that you could buy solitude with greatness, the way
his mother had bought it with sickness.

He doesn't need to make out most of the faces. They aren't
important. He thought they were then, but everything, every
detail of the life of every petty politician and schemer in
Nicaragua and in Washington, was important to him then.
He was creating a country where none had ever existed; he
was bringing order where there had been only chaos. Did
they realize, did any of them realize how radical the trans-
formation had to be?—not just the state, but family, labor,
every thread of the fabric had to be respun, rewoven until
the harmony of the new order was perfected. Destiny had
given him that time and that place like a laboratory. Each
breath he took was important, every word vital. The ex-
hilaration was like nothing any but a few on earth had ever
known.

And he was creating William Walker, General Walker,
Uncle Billy. Before Nicaragua I was what I had to be. In

Nicaragua, I became what I could be. I became what the voices and the printed words said I was. They made William Walker; I made them make him.

Listen. Let them talk.

GUY SARTAIN

THEY CALLED Granada the Paris of the Isthmus, sir. But I have been to Paris, and it was not. They called it the Gibraltar of Central America, and it was not that, either—though God knows I would hate to have had to take it with a siege. What it was, was this. It was a stone and adobe town of about twelve thousand people, less than half of what it had been before the latest fighting began. During the time we were there it reached almost thirty thousand people again, because of the peace. I credit William Walker with that. I do not know if it will ever reach that population again. And I blame William Walker for that.

It sat at the foot of a long, green plain that swept down to Lake Nicaragua like a drainboard. The beach stretched away from it in an arc to the north and straight toward the southern horizon. A huge volcano, called Mombacho, which you could see at the ends of streets from everywhere in the city, rose just to the south of it. All around it, and especially to the east in a quarter called the Jalteva, the Indians lived in thatched huts on mud paths and streets. Beyond those, the plantations and orchards began, which you could reach only by narrow lanes in the forest. I walked and rode those lanes many times while we were in Granada, and came to love their solitude and cool green peace like no place else I have since been on earth.

It was not Paris, no, but it was a beautiful city in some parts nonetheless, a city of aristocrats. There were houses in it that would rival those I have seen in Segovia, with carved stone façades and polished tile halls. Gold altars glowed in the candlelight of its six churches, and the Indians had worked the wood and stone into designs that France herself would approve. In its dim shops you could find British woolens and French perfumes, books from Madrid and New York, music boxes from Geneva, inlaid pistols from Massachusetts—even silks from China.

At dawn the streets would begin to fill. From a thousand paths the Indians seeped in with baskets that hung down their backs from straps around their foreheads. Melons, copal, cacao and coffee beans, squash, corn, green beans, pork, beef, rabbit, iguanas, turtle eggs, yams, homemade sugar candies, bananas, mangoes, tamarind, oh, sir, the marketplaces of Granada, the sickly sweet smell of them, with all those wonders spread out on cloths for pennies— sir, that hunger could exist, that the Indians were yellow-eyed from jaundice, full of ringworm and open sores and fever. . . .

There were even Negroes in Granada. Slavery had long been abolished in Nicaragua, and these were free men, from the Mosquito Coast. They spoke English, most of them, but I did not get on with them. Even they thought I was a white man. I treated their diseases and their snake bites and rat bites and their wounds from machete fights, and sometimes they paid me with a chicken or some potatoes, but when I met them on the streets they took their hats off to me and did not invite me home to meet their wives and daughters. I was at last fully a white man to all but the white men. I perfected my solitude in Granada.

When the poor saw that we came with an army of Indians,

and that Chélon was leading them, they rejoiced. They brought us gifts. They knelt and touched the coatsleeve of William Walker as he passed. They told me stories that they were half ashamed of about a feathered god with gray eyes who promised to come back one day and restore them—even Chélon did not seem comfortable denying it. We could have had anything from them, anything we asked. And there was so much we could have done for them. Would we have done those things, given enough time and peace? I don't know. I'm a Negro. I've lived all my life with promises any fool could see ought to be kept.

But right then, the promises were so close I could almost reach out my hands and touch them.

IRENA O'HORAN

THEY PUT him up in my house when he first took the city, just as they had put the idiot of an American Minister there when he first arrived. My friends have made me the unofficial whoremistress for the gringos, that's what I told them. No, it's because you speak English, Irena, they answered me. Your grandfather was an Irishman, which is almost the same as a gringo. The gringos like you. You can understand them and watch them. So I said, all right, but then you'll have to listen to me when I tell you about them. This time you can't say to me I'm a woman and to keep my hands out.

And why should I not have had Walker in my house? He was a man, though not much of one. If he stayed in the country, *pues*, why should I not have him? I could put up with him if I had to. Surely his cock would be so small that I wouldn't even have to feel it if I didn't want to.

I gave him and his translator the north wing of the house, and I brought him his tea and his cheese and his bread, which was almost all he ate, like a monk or a mouse. If he spoke to me at all in the beginning, it was to say, "Thank you, señora," "This is very thoughtful, señora," "Good evening, señora" . . . señora always, as if I were a score of years older than him, and not just two or three.

Ay, but he was too busy for conversation with a woman then—not in the city three days and he found poor Luz Cuadra's dead husband's printing press and started himself a newspaper. He called it *El Nicaraguense, The Nicaraguan*, and we all nearly retched when we realized that he was calling himself and his pack of *pistoleros* Nicaraguans. When I asked him why he was in such a hurry to set up a newspaper, you know what he told me? "Nothing truly exists in this century, señora, until it has been recorded by the press." As if my country itself didn't exist without his newspapers!

Well, I existed, whether I was recorded or not. But not even my friends thought so, did they? Did they listen to me when I told them not to offer to make him president of the country? I had only known him two or three days then, but I wasn't stupid. Why should he want it? I asked them. You'll look ridiculous. Who would recognize a government like that? You're offering him counterfeit money.

But who else? they said to me. Somebody has to be president. The barefoots up in León have made him a general. The Indians and the peasants are mad about him: they think he's Christ our Lord come to make Indians white and peasants rich. And who protects us? Who was the man who said he would shoot anyone he caught looting or molesting any of us? Who told us that we could keep our haciendas? Who is the only one who stands between us and Chélon and that Indian army of his? If the barefoots can make Walker a general, we can make him a president.

And if not him, they said, then who? Chélon? Maximo Jerez, God protect us?

Don't we have an army still? I said, trying to make them ashamed. Isn't Ponciano Corral still down in Rivas with our best men? Don't we have a good garrison up in Managua between us and the barefoots in León?

They were worse women than any woman I've ever known. No, no, they said—would you have Ponciano Corral come and attack his own city, attack *us*, to drive the gringos off? We'd all be slaughtered. I thought they would piss down their legs.

So they got poor Matito Mayorga, who had been our Minister of War and was the only cabinet member too simple to run away, and they came to my house in a great delegation. I gave them tea and we all went out to look at my vegetable garden and they offered William Walker the presidency. And he turned them down, of course.

Don't be too hard on them. They thought they understood what he wanted. They thought that they could save themselves by bringing him gifts, like the Indians, that he was only another *caudillo* who would come and go, and that our lives would keep going on as they always had. But they were only guessing. In truth, we all were. He was our first gringo.

"Now," I told them. "Are you satisfied?"

"No," they said. "We still don't have a president."

"Then offer it to General Corral," Walker told them.

"*Our* General Corral, Don Ponciano Corral?" poor Matito Mayorga asked, simple as ever. "For the pity of God, why?"

"Isn't he a capable man?" Walker asked him.

"Yes, yes, of course," Matito stuttered out.

"You need a government of National Reconciliation. Shall I explain it to you?"

"Oh, no, señor," Matito said. He was beaming, and he looked at me as if he were saying, *see, see*. This gringo is no radical. What does he want to have to do with Indians, really? *We* are his people.

But I knew. Walker had just done the most arrogant thing I had ever seen a man do. I wanted to spit. He had offered the presidency to Ponciano Corral because it really didn't matter to him who was president. He was buying us off, keeping us happy. Ponciano would bring his army in from Rivas, and the war would be over for good. Walker understood that the barefoots up in León were as afraid of him now as we were. If they objected to anybody he wanted to name as president, then *ya*, there it was! He could turn on them, with us behind him, without blinking, no? He had the power, all of it. What could anyone do to him? Ponciano wouldn't attack his own city. And the Democrats wouldn't attack Chélon and their own troops.

But again they didn't listen to me. Why didn't they? Because when everybody is afraid, nothing is clear but staying alive from one day to the other. I didn't have a family. I didn't think the gringos would kill a woman. So maybe I wasn't afraid enough.

"Ponciano," I wrote Corral. "Don't take it. It's a trick."

How Walker ever talked that idiot of an American Minister into delivering the offer to Ponciano in Rivas personally, I'll never know. I suppose he used the right words, the way he always did. That was what made him so dangerous: he always knew the right words. But the Minister went, and we waited, most of us terrified that Ponciano would say no, me terrified that he'd say yes. Why? Because as long as he was down there in Rivas with his army, there was hope—for something, somehow.

Ponciano wasn't always a fool. He was just not clever, and a little slow sometimes. I had known him since we were children together. When we were younger, we thought for a while we might get married, but neither of us wanted it very much. He was a fine figure, though—not a more handsome man in the country, when he was in his full uniform on a horse. He owned the best fighting cocks, and was good to his *peónes*, and I don't think there was a more popular man in

71

Granada than he was before the gringos came. We don't have theater here, no famous actors and actresses. We make do with generals. Even the peasants worshiped him—and he didn't have to be a genius for that.

But when the word came back that Ponciano had turned the offer down and put the American Minister in jail, I think I breathed for the first time in two days. He hadn't been a fool, not this time. Matito Mayorga and my friends trembled in their frock coats, but I served Walker his tea. I gave him the news and a lump of sugar, and I saw nothing at all on his face. He was that way. He'd sit and stare at you and you never knew whether something terrible was going on behind his eyes, or nothing at all.

"Well," he said. "We'll find somebody else." Just like that. You slab of bacon, I thought.

That's what I mostly remember about William Walker's first week in Granada, that and the hammering from the gringos starting to put everything back together that had been destroyed in the fighting last year, and the way prices went up and the rum supply went down. And the whores came out.

His second week, God sent him a gift. God did, or the devil did—it was all the same to him. He used it, and we were lost.

By then he had relaxed a little—as much as he ever relaxed. At night, nearly all night I could hear him across my patio, his pen going and going until I thought we'd have to kill all the geese in Nicaragua to keep him supplied with quills. He would be up at daylight, and he and that translator of his, Holdich, would talk about the day. Then one of the guards who were always outside at my street door would come and knock and say that this officer or that officer was there to see him, and then they would all talk. By the time anybody but a peasant was ready to get up, he would be on his way to his office—which was in the Government Palace, where our own people used to be.

Once, after he was gone, I went to his room with the maid to see what he stayed up all night scribbling. In a week, he'd written enough for a book! He wrote everything, articles for his newspaper, letters, orders, proclamations, journals, plans for things like, oh, mining and mapping expeditions, new docks, lighthouses, buildings, roads, railroads, factories. Have you ever seen the way a little boy makes up countries? But it was my country he was making up.

Still, peace was good—I could ride out to my hacienda in the country and not worry that it wouldn't be there when I reached it. And he hadn't shown any signs of wanting to take anybody's hacienda yet, the way his Indians wanted him to do. Sometimes he would ride with me—to learn the country-side, he said. I asked him questions and he did the same to me. I think he was beginning to trust me a little bit, and yes, I was flattered, even though I knew what he was.

I wasn't ugly then. Oh, I was a little wider than I'd been when I was twenty, and I had a little mustache that I had to pluck now and again, but I'd had no children to spread my hips and wrinkle my breasts, and I never have had that flat *chata* face that the Indian women have. I didn't have to look for men, I'll say that. I could have married if I'd wanted to.

But whenever that one's hands would touch mine, helping me down from my horse, or brushing against me on a narrow path or in a hallway, he would pull back like I was full of thorns. "Excuse me," he would say, as if he had stepped on my foot.

Once I asked Holdich, who was always drawing things and who seemed like a good enough man, I asked him if the general had any *novias*, any lady friends.

"No," he said. I think I embarrassed him.

"Has he ever?"

"I think so, señora."

"Here?"

"No. In New Orleans, I understand."

"A long time ago?"

"It must have been."

"And what happened?"

"I'm told she died."

"How?"

"That's all I know, señora." He was very uncomfortable.

"You don't ask him about it?"

"No."

That night, toward the end of Walker's second week in Granada, I went to his room early with his tea. When he came in, I was waiting for him. All right, I thought, you're not the first general who's come here to my house. Let's see how *you* do.

He stood in the door for a little while and then stepped to the side, as if he expected me to leave.

"I brought you your tea, *mi general*." I said to him.

"Thank you."

"And some sugared rolls."

"Thank you," he said again. "I never eat at this hour."

"Oh." I waited for him to go on, but he didn't. I was beginning to feel foolish. I was taller than he was.

"I'm very sorry to hear about your *novia*," I said.

"Señora?"

"In New Orleans."

"Who told you that, señora?" His eyes were the color of rain clouds, and they got larger when I took a step toward him.

I shrugged. "Is that from her, that little cross?" I reached up to touch it.

He took another step back and bumped against the door. For a moment his eyes met mine. They made my stomach sink, but I kept on. "Shall I help you off with your coat, General?"

I don't know what I expected. Would he hit me? Tell me to leave? Sit down, drink his tea, and talk to me? I don't think

74

for a moment I believed he would touch me, start undoing the eyelets of my bodice. I don't know what made me keep going.

But what he said to me was this: "Señora, I don't have the strength."

No man had ever said *that* to me before. I stared at him.

"Good evening, señora," he said. I stared at him some more, and what I saw in his eyes was hate or fear, something terrible anyway.

When I came across his man Holdich in my patio, I could have slapped him.

Later that night, his gift from the devil came. I've prayed to God many times since then that what I did to Walker in his room that night had nothing to do with how he used the gift. But I think it did.

Here's how it happened. Just after I got back to my own room, my girl came running in with her eyes the size of mangoes and told me there was a cannon firing out on the lake, and that everybody on the street was in a terrible panic and getting ready to run for their haciendas. Ponciano! I thought. Ponciano's got a boat and he's coming to drive the gringos out!

But then I thought, no—if you're going to attack a town, you don't announce you're coming with a cannon. Not even Ponciano would do that.

So I put on my shawl and went down to the lake. By the time I got there, half the town must have decided there was no danger. The docks were packed, in spite of the gringos' curfew, and one of the Transit Company's lake steamers was trying to tie up. It fired off its cannon one last time and the people on the dock cheered. The boat's lights were gleaming out across the water, and its boilers were hissing, and when the cannonnade stopped—I swear to you—I heard a brass band.

A lake steamer? I thought. A brass band? *Madre*, a lake steamer from the Transit Route shouldn't be here anytime, much less in the middle of the night acting like a gypsy circus. Poor Matito Mayorga came up in his housecoat, wiping his bald head and looking puzzled and worried. I stayed up on the hill above the water with him so we could see, and when the gangplank flapped down, I thought, dear God, the gringos are Your own fools for sure.

They had torches. First off the boat came a one-armed man with a beard, then two overfed men in blue army uniforms leading two overfed gringa women in dresses and bonnets as dark blue as the men's uniforms. Then the band, a half dozen scraggly men with their breeches too short but their horns gleaming in the torchlight like candlesticks, tooting and stumbling through the people on the dock. Then a file of men who were trying to march and not doing so well, all of them with beards and wearing red flannel shirts and floppy hats like Walker's men, all of them armed like gunboats. And then behind those, timid as new puppies, people I took to be the regular passengers on the boat, who looked around them like they'd stepped off onto the moon.

My people and the gringos too were yelling and waving like crazy people, and I'm certain not one of them had the slightest notion why. *I* didn't.

When the one-armed man got just beside where I was standing by the church at the top of the hill, he threw his hand up in the air and everybody stopped behind him like a train. And there was Walker, his jaw so tight I thought it would crack. He looked over at me, then looked down the hill at the crowd and the band and the torches like he was smelling vomit.

"You're Parker French," he said at last. His voice was so small I could hardly hear it.

"Parker French," the man bawled out, and saluted with his one arm. "Reporting for duty with the first California volunteer regiment."

Then the men behind him threw their hats up in the air

and whooped like mules, and the whole ridiculous parade took up again before Walker could answer.

Well, before it stopped that night, they'd marched around the plaza half a dozen times and I think even Ponciano down in Rivas must have been awake. Finally, they got Walker to come out on the balcony of the Government Palace to make a speech. Just as he tried to start, the band decided to play one last song, which I now know to be a song the gringos call "Yankee Doodle," and if there's a sillier song I don't know it. But he listened to it, and when they were all done, he must have been so mad at the whole night, he gave the shortest speech I ever heard him make. His voice was like glass, and I can remember every word he said, because I knew they were all directed at me, to insult me.

"Fellow citizens and soldiers," he said. "This is perhaps the first time such music has been heard on the plaza of Granada. Let us hope that it may be heard through future ages."

And then he went home. I sat awake in my bedroom until dawn.

Pues, and how was that Walker's gift then? This way. You see, that Parker French had recruited a lot of men for Walker in California, and those were the men who were with him. He wasn't much—a gambler and some kind of petty politician, I think. But I was told that he knew people, people with money. Some even said he brought down a trunk full of gold for Walker, and that was why Walker didn't want to punish him—but *quién sabe,* who knows? Maybe that's a story to throw on the trash heap with the one about how Walker stripped all the gold from the churches and buried it. I don't believe it. Gold didn't interest him.

Anyway, when Parker French got to Nicaragua, he heard

that Walker was in Granada and decided to give him a present. So when he got on the lake steamer, he made the captain take him all the way across the lake to the mouth of the river to the Atlantic. He was going to be a hero and capture the fort there for Walker. *Bueno*. But he didn't do it. He was such an ass that he'd forgotten to bring enough powder and ammunition and had to retreat.

We didn't know about that until the next day when another Transit Company steamer came into the dock. On it there were a dead gringo woman and her dead baby. That was how Walker knew he had a gift. Our people had seen this second steamer coming toward them and thought it was Parker French on his way back. So they shot a cannon at it, and killed the woman and her baby. And whose fault was that? Who had taken a steamer full of passengers across the lake to attack the fort to begin with? Oh, but Parker French was a gringo. Parker French had friends. Parker French could recruit gringos to fight.

So who did Walker decide to shoot because of the dead gringo woman and her baby?

Poor Matito Mayorga, of course. My friend.

HON. JOHN WHEELER

THE MAYORGA business was regrettable, clearly. But you will understand, my friends, that General Walker was not acting as an American citizen. He was an officer of the Democratic Army of Nicaragua at the time. As United States Minister, I had no jurisdiction whatsoever. Everything that General Walker did as a member of the Nicaraguan army was strictly the internal affair of Nicaragua.

But as policy, I must confess that General Walker's actions in the Mayorga business were brilliant. His eyes were always set firmly on the future. As he himself told me, when I went at the request of a woman of Granada to intercede on behalf of Mayorga, "Those who see only present sorrow, and not the thousandfold greater sorrows misplaced mercy can bring, are not fit for public office." I thought it cold of him at the time, but I soon came to change my mind.

Since Mayorga was the only member of the Conservative government still in Granada at the time it was natural for General Walker to hold him morally responsible for the deaths of the American woman and her child. Parker French *was* a scoundrel, indeed, and I regretted as much as General Walker that he felt it necessary to have dealings with him. But how could French be held responsible for something he had no way of foreseeing?

And I will add this: General Walker's sense of fairness was absolute. Two days before the incident of the lake steamer, one of Walker's own men, an Irish boy named Patrick Jordan, had been brought to him on a charge of killing a Nicaraguan in a tavern brawl. So that there would be no question in the minds of the Nicaraguans as to the equality of the American element's justice, General Walker ordered that Jordan be shot on the same day as Mayorga. I cannot fault him, my friends, nor can any fair-minded man among you.

I attended those executions, my first in that country. They were both unpleasant affairs, more like sporting matches than solemn events. From early morning a crowd gathered in the plaza, and staked out claims to good vantage points. Food vendors set up their stalls and wagons, and children and dogs kicked up great clouds of dust. I will forbear to give the unhappy details; suffice it to say that Mayorga died with a great wailing from his relatives, and poor Patrick Jordan took on and called for his mother so, that he had to be given brandy and bound to a post. The crowd seemed satisfied, the more so since General Walker ordered that Mayorga's body be left where it lay in the plaza until sundown. But I returned to my family in as black a mood as I ever recall.

Enlightenment, my friends, enlightenment is the duty of the American element wherever it finds itself. I have been accused by many of being a partisan of William Walker. That is not true. But I have always been a partisan of enlightenment, and if William Walker was its bearer, then so be it. And who would not be a partisan among a people, childlike though they may be, who make celebrations of public executions? Or whose notion of religion is to take a figure of Jesus Christ, place a priest's hat on his head, twine his hair with yellow flowers, and parade him behind a band of music through the town on a *jackass*. If William Walker's methods seemed harsh at times, how much harsher was the alternative: barbarism.

By that one execution, my friends, how many lives were saved? For it accomplished what years of war, thousands of deaths, could not. The very evening of the execution, General Walker sent a message to Ponciano Corral informing him of the execution and advising him that the full leadership of the Conservative faction in Granada was being held hostage against the civilized behavior of Corral's forces.

And the next morning, General Corral sent notice that he was prepared to surrender the entire Conservative army to William Walker.

However much I may have been fond of poor Matito Mayorga—and I was—however much I may have been moved by the pleas of his friends, the fact is unalterable: after thirty-four years of almost ceaseless war, peace descended on Nicaragua because of his death. It is the great tragedy of Central America that the government that I represented did not allow me to take the steps that would have made that peace permanent for all time, and ensured the regeneration of a decadent and barbarous continent.

I do not consider it a breach of my official neutrality that I attended the drawing up of the peace documents any more than I did when I had delivered an offer of the presidency of the nation to Ponciano Corral earlier. How could it not be in my government's interest to pursue peace in Central America, at whatever the personal risk to myself? That President Pierce and Secretary of State Marcy did not see the truth of that has grieved me many times since.

However, let me assure you that a more generous victor than General Walker never existed. As was his habit, he sat silently for most of the session and only nodded in agreement to each term of the treaty that General Corral suggested. I may say that the document is almost wholly of General Corral's composition. Nothing in it could cause objection in the most republican of minds. Elections were to be held in fourteen months. In the interim, a gentleman of General Corral's own faction was to serve as president—a collector of customs about whom no one seemed to have strong feelings one way or the other, named Patricio Rivas. And as his Minister of War: General Corral himself.

Throughout, General Walker's conduct was absolutely correct in insisting that he was only a servant of the government in León, and that nothing could be agreed upon without his government's approval. Whatever his position of power, his conduct was absolutely correct; let me emphasize that. How can he then be faulted for insisting on the two clauses he added to protect the hard-won rights of the American element? Only two, out of the entire document: that he be named commander-in-chief of the armed forces, and that nothing in the treaty should hinder as many Americans as wanted from becoming Nicaraguan citizens. And yet even those seemed to upset General Corral to the extent that he had to be prevented by cooler heads from leaving the conference.

Had it been within my power, my friends, I would have recognized such a government at the very moment General Corral put his pen to the document creating it. What treachery, what horrors might the world have been spared!

TALMEDGE WARNER ||||||||||||||||||||||||||||||||||||||||||||||||||||||||||||||||||||||||||||||||||||||||

THERE'S NO question to me looking back now but that Uncle Billy knowed what he had in mind and what would come of it—and that's why he made such a show out of the day of peace.

I was a sergeant by then and they put me in charge of the boys that was getting the celebration ready. Them people down there don't believe nothing is real until you put on a big spectacle about it, see. Still . . . I didn't like the notion. Uncle Billy and Corral had got together and signed the peace thing a week before, so why this? Why did Corral have to come a-marching right into Granada with all his conscripts? Couldn't he just leave all them half-naked natives down there in Rivas or wherever and come in by himself? We could have had just as big a to-do. And me and the boys wouldn't have had to spend half a week sweeping spiders and things out of their quarters for them, like they was company.

Not to mention that I didn't like the notion of having all them shoewearer troops crawling all over town, no matter how many treaties they'd signed.

But you see, that was Uncle Billy's plan. That was just what he wanted.

We was careful. All morning of the day they was to come in, Captain Henry and me seen to squads of our boys and Chélon's natives that searched everywhere for arms them shoewearers might have hid. I didn't trust nobody in Granada. It wasn't like up in León, where the people was always giving us dances and things to eat: down in Granada we had to stand guard on all the street corners day and night. You could feel them hating you like fever. Once they even tried to kill Uncle Billy, but they wasn't much better shots at that than they was on the battlefield. Oh, some of them made speeches about how we had come to liberate them and such, but the rest wouldn't have anything to do with those.

Then there was Chélon's natives to worry about. They didn't like being nice to them Granadans, no more than if they'd been snakes. Since they'd drawed up the peace, old Chélon himself had been huffing and puffing around on that bad leg of his until I thought he was going to have a apoplexy. One day he drug a couple of them shoewearer muckle-demucks into Uncle Billy's office and demanded that they be shot for looking at him wrong, and when Uncle Billy set them free, Chélon came near to taking straight off back home. There wasn't no more chance of peace amongst them people than that Baptists would start saying mass.

But me, I kept my mouth shut and my eyes open and nailed up them speakers' stands and hung them flags for the celebration like I believed it all. I had me two hundred and fifty by-god acres a-coming when my enlistment was up, and I reckoned that if I played it right I might wind up with a right smart more. Most of the boys said we was going to commence taking them shoewearers' haciendas away soon. Figured it was owed. We hadn't been paid nothing yet. And being one of the original Immortals, I ought to be right up there in line.

Come about noon that day and I was nervous as a whore in church. Runners kept trotting up with reports: Corral and his troops was on the road into town; they was in the suburbs and people was throwing flowers at them; they was heading up onto the main avenue to the plaza. Captain Henry'd chose me to be part of the American honor guard, so I had me a good place to see from up on the porch of the cathedral. I recollect looking over at our boys drawn up on the far side of the plaza with their long blue rifles a-glinting in the sun, and I felt better. Then I looked at Chélon's natives lined up along the avenue, some of them in pieces of old American or British uniforms they'd scrounged up, and I even felt good about that. They was doing fine: not a one had took a pot shot at Corral's natives yet.

When I seen the first dust from Corral's men in the distance, I thought, maybe it'll work. Wouldn't that be real good? Wouldn't it be good if everybody wound up getting on with one another after all? Down below me, a brass band was a-tooting and tuning, and I could see off in the side streets that restaurants was unbarred and open again, and when the brass band got quiet I could hear pieces of guitar music starting to come out of some of them. Everywhere up and down the streets serving girls was flitting in and out of houses getting ready for all the suppers and fandangos that was planned for the evening. I seen old John Wheeler flailing his arm and practicing his speech on the speakers' stand, his sidewhiskers ruffling in the breeze. Then I seen yonder in the distance the first part of the shoewearer army, their officers in their black and gold uniforms and their horses a-prancing, and I heard the boys choir in the cathedral behind me commence to warm up, and the priests in their fine robes stepped out on the porch, and I thought, oh, yes sir, wouldn't it be good.

. . .

But I knowed better, truly. I never seen so much brotherhood in my life as that day, and so I knew I ought to be suspicious. That long column of shoewearer soldiers drawed up in the avenue, dust rising into the breeze, and Corral and his officers rode on out into the middle of the plaza like they had won the war. The band was blaring and our boys shouldered their rifles and fired off a salute and the flags was flapping, and that Corral was right near the splendidest thing I'd ever seen. He had more braid on him than his men had ticks.

But he wasn't smiling. Oh, no. Not a bit.

Nor was Uncle Billy. I first seen him coming out of the dark inside the arches of the Government Palace, no more than a dark spot himself. He stood for a second or two in the sun, like he was taking inventory again. Then the other officers come spilling out behind him in as wild a bunch of uniforms as you could imagine, not a single one the same, and I swear I thought I could see Corral's nose wrinkle. When Uncle Billy and him hugged, Uncle Billy looked like he was going to smother in all that braid. Oh, and they was a pair all right when me and the other boys in the honor guard marched them up the steps to the cathedral, and the priests started flapping around them like old women: Uncle Billy no more than shoulder high on Corral, nearly having to trot to keep up.

They've told me since that Corral tried to trick Uncle Billy right there in the church—gave him a Catholic cross to kiss when they swore to abide by the peace treaty they'd signed. Corral was sure Uncle Billy wouldn't do it, but Uncle Billy did. Captain Henry told me later Uncle Billy said he knew right then the war wasn't over so far as Corral was concerned.

I don't know about that. If he didn't know till then, why would he already have planned what happened later that night?

I was on guard at the big fandango at the house of the woman where Uncle Billy was staying. We all called her

Niña Irena, though she had a proper name, I reckon. It was a real blowout: a great long table full of food and liquor, guitars twanging, and everybody dancing fandangos while the poor people and Indians hung in the open windows and clapped and the moths sizzled in the candles. Whatever else, them people knew how to have a good time. And most of us figured Niña Irena had made this evening even more special because she was trying to get her teeth into Uncle Billy.

Toward the end of the evening, Captain Holdich come up to me and told me to go out in the patio and stand guard in front of Uncle Billy's door because they was going to have a meeting. I did, and before long Uncle Billy come out with old Chélon and this other man I'd seen hanging on him all day, a greaser in a good suit who had a big high forehead and a frown. I knew I'd seen him up in León, but I couldn't mind his name until Captain Holdich whispered to me that it was Maximo Jerez. Dog, I thought. That's a muckledemuck for you. They ain't going to be playing cards in there tonight.

When General Corral and the old man they'd appointed president come along a little later, I knew for sure it wasn't no social meeting.

They must have stayed in Uncle Billy's room a hour. Every now and then somebody's voice would get loud (never Uncle Billy's) and I'd worry I was going to have to run in and commence shooting. But mostly I smelled the oranges and jasmines and listened to the music and wished I was an officer and inside a-dancing—so when General Corral come busting out of Uncle Billy's room fit to be tied I jumped a foot. And when Uncle Billy come to the door and watched him stomp off without calling him back, I knew the brotherhood business was over.

As Captain Holdich told it to me, in there that night Uncle Billy had slicked them all. First Corral got the news that he was going to have to serve in the cabinet with Maximo Jerez, who he hated like sin. That was Uncle Billy's sop to the barefoots up in León; I reckon that old man who was president was so scared he would have appointed a anteater to his cabinet if Uncle Billy had told him to. Corral hollered like a stuck pig. But the real killer was this: Corral found out he didn't have a army no more! See, Uncle Billy was commander-in-chief now. So he said that as long as there was peace, there wasn't no need for conscripts. Just volunteers, and he was fixing to send all the conscripts home. And that army of Corral's that was sleeping peacefully with our boys and Chélon's natives guarding them? Conscripts, all conscripts.

Praise the Lord! Never seen a snake-oil salesman pull it off cleaner. All that braid on Corral didn't help him nare bit.

IRENA O'HORAN

WHEN I GOT to Ponciano, it was near dawn. He was still in his uniform from the ball. I found him in his sitting room with one of his daughters; she had been crying, and I think he may have been drunk.

"Ponciano," I said to him. "Remember your daughters. Listen to me again. Wait, bide your time. Be a man, not a fool."

"It's too late, Irena," he said. "I've taken care of it. Go home to bed."

"Ponciano!" I said. "Don't give him what he wants. Don't give him another gift."

"Go home to bed," he said.

He was a fool.

CHÉLON

I CLUTCHED the letter to me that night like a prayer book. I remember that it was a night that choked your breath off with the wet air. I sat and held the letter and smelled the odors of garbage from the street, of rot and flowers, and I thought, thank you, God. You've sent me this, God. You've sent me a letter vouchsafing me justice, God, for all the cows the pureblood filth have stolen from me, for my poor brother they killed at the walls of this very town, for all my poor shit-upon people. Rejoice, You are saying to me. Rejoice at last!

"You got this from Corral's hand? Himself?" I had asked the man who brought it to me.

"From his hand."

"Can you read?"

"Yes, *mi coronel.*"

"Read it."

He leaned over to the candle, trembling like a man with a palsy. "It is addressed to General Santos Guardiola, señor, President of the Republic of Honduras, Tegucigalpa."

"You told me that."

"*Sí,*" he said, and squinted. " 'My Esteemed Friend,' it begins. 'We are in a terrible, terrible, terrible position. Remember your friends. They have left me with the clothes on my back and I await your help. It is necessary that you write friends to advise them of our danger, and that they go to work actively. If they hold off even two months it will be too late. Remember us and the offers you made us. I salute your wife; you have only to command your friend, who truly esteems you and kisses your hand.' And there's a postscript, señor. 'Nicaragua is lost, lost Honduras, San Salvador, and Guatemala if they let this thing gain body. If they come quickly, they will find allies.' "

"And the signature?" I said to him.

"P. Corral, Excellency."

"You know the writing?"

"It's his. I know it."

And that was what came from being able to read and write. It was the night of the Day of the Dead, *muchachos*, the night before All Hallows. In the cemeteries that night the dead were awake, filling their bellies on the food their relatives had left for them. I saluted my poor brother and all my poor dead *indios*.

We had celebrated the peace that day. The ass had sworn in front of all of Granada and before God to defend the peace. El Gualquer had seen to that.

I walked outside to the patio and splashed cold well water on my face to drive away the fumes of the rum punch at that whore's ball. El Gualquer would be up at dawn. I sat down in the hot dark of the patio and waited.

It was an execution like the country had never seen since the Spaniards came. El Gualquer had given Corral his choice: court martial by us, or by the gringos. Corral thought the gringos would never dare convict him. He was not a very smart man. When the gringo officers convicted him, they recommended mercy to El Gualquer, but El Gualquer *was* smart. He said no. When you've caught a snake, do you keep it in the house with your children?

The people began to show up at dawn. My *indios* came in their pantaloons and black dresses, with their children and tortillas. The rich sent servants with whips to stake them out good spots. I had a good seat, right on the balcony of the house of my General Maximo Jerez, which looked out over the plaza, over everything. All morning we sat and watched the parade that went in and out of the Government Palace—the American Minister, priests, Corral's daughters and their grandmother—all of them to ask for mercy. Mercy! I thought. Where's the mercy for all the poor people and *indios* the shoe-wearers have worked to their graves? God will give the *cabrón* whatever mercy he deserves.

By noon the plaza was almost full, and still Corral's daughters and his mother hadn't come out of the Palace. I was nervous, and who wouldn't be, *compañeros*? I could hear the rumors going up and down the street below me—Corral had escaped, El Gualquer had changed his mind, the shoewearers were going to rise up and free Corral. Any of those could have been true, or all of them. I took a drink from the brandy flask that Mendez the Cock had in his lap, the flask he had been drinking from since breakfast. When I offered a drink to my General Jerez, he shook his head and said, "I hope to God Corral has some of that."

My General Jerez had barely said two words together all morning. He had hardly spoken to a Christian soul since he heard the sentence two days ago.

"You sound sorry for him, *mi general*."

"I am," he said. I felt a little ashamed of the way I had been thinking, but not much.

"His wife is dead, no?" I said.

"The cholera."

"They say one of his daughters is mad because of it."

"So they say."

"And his lands, *mi general*, will the government take them like Mayorga's?"

"No doubt."

Mendez the Cock reached for the brandy flask. "Will El Gualquer take them, you mean?"

"No, *hermano*," I said. "I don't mean that."

"Are you interested in them? Eh? Forget it. He'll sell them to gringos in New York, like Mayorga's."

I didn't like to talk to Mendez when he was drunk. I turned back to my General Jerez. "So the daughters will be left with nothing."

"*Sí*," he said.

Mendez finished the flask. "That'll cure madness quick," he said. "Poor people can't afford to be mad."

I sat and listened to the noises of the crowd for a while. I wanted to be down there that day, seeing that my boys did everything as it should be, but today was the gringos' day. A gringo named Tom Henry, who was the most terrible one of them, was going to lead the firing squad, and all over the plaza the others were pushing with their long rifles to keep the people back. Their eyes kept moving everywhere. My friend Holdich had told me that the gringos themselves didn't like the idea of shooting Corral.

"God help Ponciano Corral," Mendez said all of a sudden. "He made a fine figure, that one did."

"Be quiet," I said to him.

My General Jerez leaned forward so he could see around me to Mendez. "Why are you a Democrat, Mendez?"

Mendez shrugged. "Because I'm from León, and I'm an Indian. Everybody who's from León or an Indian is a Democrat."

"Just that?"

"Is there more?"

My General Jerez sat back. "Poor Nicaragua."

"I'll tell you something, *mi general*," Mendez said. "There are only two ways to rule Nicaragua—with silver, and with a whip. I think my fine-nosed gringo general is learning that now. But what he's not learning is when to use one and when to use the other. All he knows is the whip. And, fuck his mother, I think he enjoys it. It's the only shitting passion he's got. At least Ponciano Corral is a man, *mi general*. At least he has a prick."

He tried to take another drink out of the flask, but it was empty. "I don't like the gringos. Another year of this and

91

we'll be asshole deep in them. Maybe they think that if they pile enough of them on us we'll sink into the earth, like carrots, eh? Do you believe in all those things El Gualquer says, *mi general*? Is that why you're in his cabinet?"

"I don't know. I want to see."

Mendez snorted. "Like Corral wanted to see? Me? Tomorrow I'm going home to León."

"Go," I said to him.

He put his feet up on the wall of the balcony and looked at me. "Poor Chélon," he said. He was no good when he was drunk, no good at all. But he was a wonderful fighter, and there were many things I had to forgive him for—up until the last, and then I couldn't forgive him at all. I couldn't forgive any of them.

It was two o'clock before Ponciano Corral finally got to see the people in the plaza who had been there since first light for him. El Gualquer came out of the Palace first and got on a horse. Then some gringos heaved the old man who was president up on a horse beside him—his name was Patricio Rivas, like the town, and because his name sounded like Upside Down—*patas arribas*—we called him that. I think he was one of those children my mother, God be kind to her, turned into a rabbit. They kicked through the crowd to a place close to the wall of the church, where people were executed in those days.

My General Jerez went into the house, and Mendez put his chin on his chest and went to sleep, or pretended to. I kept watching.

Some more gringos broke a path for Corral's people. One of his daughters was crying into the arms of a man who must have been his father. The other daughter looked around her like she was in a bazaar. She jerked her head like a chicken and twisted her face into puckers, and I knew that must be the mad one. Neither of them could be over fifteen, near the ages of my own daughters.

Then, with one of my boys beating a slow drumbeat to lead

them, a squad of red-shirted gringos made a hollow square with Corral and a priest in the middle of it, and started across the plaza. Their feet threw up little puffs of dust that reminded me of the souls that the Stories said came out of people's mouths when they died. I've always looked for those souls when I see people die; God willing, someday I'll see one and know what shape a soul is.

Corral had a bright blue broadcloth coat on—I remember that because I thought what a sin it was to waste such cloth, but why would a shoewearer care? The people from Granada wailed when they saw him, and my own boys hooted, but Corral didn't look. A priest whispered in his ear as they walked. He didn't seem to notice that either.

The closer Corral got to the church wall, the louder the wailing from the women grew. From the day of my mother's funeral fifty years ago I've hated the sound. It was a sound like a jaguar makes at night, a sound only women can make. Guns I don't mind, but that sound—no. Even El Gualquer's horse reared and backed away, and a cat jumped from the roof next to me and ran.

They stopped not twenty *varas* from the balcony. On the porch of the cathedral, Corral's family clutched at each other and reached out their arms toward him. Their women were wailing too—except for the mad girl. That one kept up her puckering and her jerking, like a chicken, and *saben*, she was the one I felt the least pity for.

As Corral stepped up to the wall, the gringo Henry took his shoulder to turn him around and make him kneel, the way it should be. But Corral shook him off like he was a beggar who had grabbed his arm. The priest whispered something to Henry, and Henry shrugged and walked away. Corral backed up to the wall. He wasn't blindfolded, and I saw him give the priest a bad look when the priest started whispering in his ear again. That's not for me either, *compañeros*— no priest dribbling in my ear when my time comes—so I understood. Then Corral looked up and saw me on the balcony. And you know what he did? He spat. I understood that, too.

The drum beat again then, but faster, and if Corral had any last words, he wasn't going to get to say them. And when the drum began with that beat that we all knew, a stillness spread out from it through the crowd. Henry raised up his sword.

"Ready!" he yelled.

Except for the mad girl, the women in Corral's family buried their heads in the grandfather's black coat. They were like birds. El Gualquer kept his eyes on Corral, and I wondered if he was waiting to see his soul come out too. Upside Down Rivas looked at his horse's mane.

"Aim!" Henry said. All across the crowd now, people—the decent people—were turning their heads away, but I had to keep seeing. I crossed myself.

And then Corral stepped away from the wall! No! I thought—the *pendejo* is going to run.

"Fire!" he shouted. "Fire!"

The drummer looked at Henry and stopped his beating. One of the riflemen lowered his rifle, then jerked it back up. Walker kicked his horse and started through the people. I thought he was coming to give the order himself if Henry didn't. Henry saw him, too. "Goddamn it, fire!" he yelled.

When the noise of the rifles exploded, *ay!* the plaza did too. I saw little bits of Corral splatter on the wall just behind his back and little puffs of adobe go up, but he kept standing, not at all surprised, even though he slumped back against the wall. And when he fell at last, and I saw his back, all that fine blue broadcloth streaked with whitewash and ruined with holes, and dark spots spreading out on it. I thought, fuck me, I forgot to look for his soul.

Then El Gualquer reined his horse around and Upside Down Rivas followed him, and the wailing set up again from the women. But not just the wailing this time—now they were screaming, too. The people pushed against the gringos, but the gringos pushed them back with their rifles.

I stood up. I didn't want to see any more, but I couldn't leave the balcony, *compañeros*, I had to keep seeing, all of it. I had a lust to see it, God forgive me.

Corral's blood spread out from him on the sand, and the sight of it seemed to give the people more strength. They broke the line of gringos. The women in their black dresses, some of them on their hands and knees like dogs, hit at each other with their elbows and fists to be the first to get to the body. They shoved handkerchiefs at the bloody sand, at the holes in Corral. They were going to take smears of him home like saint's relics. *Carajo!* How can I let you see it?—I only saw little bits of the rest, like the little bits of Corral on the wall. I saw black dresses flashing like fish in a school, I saw a knife blade hacking off locks of Corral's hair, I saw his leg rise when they ripped pieces of his pants off, I saw handkerchiefs, more handkerchiefs.

Not like that, I thought, I didn't want it that way. I fired my revolver into the air. Nobody noticed it. They rolled Corral away from the wall and I couldn't see him anymore in the black dresses. My rejoicing was cold as a stone in my chest. I fired my revolver until it was empty, then threw it at a fucked, lame dog who was slipping behind the women toward the sand with blood in it.

Before I went in for brandy, I saw Corral's family beating at the backs of the black dresses—except for the mad daughter, who was standing by herself in the shade of the cathedral porch. She looked up and puckered her face at me.

We buried him in a grave without a stone, the way El Gualquer wanted.

BRIAN HOLDICH ||||||||||||||||||||||||||||||||||||||||||||||||||||||||||||||||||||||||||||||||||||||||||||||||||||

IT WAS A spectacular season, gentlemen, by the time February came around. The rains had left off for the most part three months before, right around the time we executed Ponciano Corral. Whole days passed when only a few gypsy clouds came along and stirred up the blue of the sky, or when a warm shower or two fell only long enough to clean the air. The sunsets stretched from horizon to horizon, and when there were clouds, the sky was full of great brushstrokes of coral or magenta or pink. I would ride as far into the country-side as I could in my free time—of which there was consider-able since General Walker had learned to do most of his own translating. I filled sketchbooks almost faster than I could talk the steamer captains into supplying me with new ones. After the great migration from Granada that Corral's ex-ecution had caused, the country slowly came back to nor-mal, more or less. The fields sprouted, storekeepers brought their stocks out of hiding, workmen drew their wages—such as they were—the smugglers went back to work, and Gen-eral Walker settled into a routine of dawn to midnight work that seemed to content him more than I had expected any-thing would be likely to.

Not that everything was fine, you understand. There were sufficient who said that it was all too good to last. Hadn't President Pierce called John Wheeler on the carpet and taken back the diplomatic recognition he said we had no right to? Weren't Conservatives all over Central America whipping one another up into a fit of gringo hating, and threatening us with everything from war to the curse of God? Hadn't Maximo Jerez resigned from the cabinet in a huff and gone home to León because General Walker wouldn't go start a holy revolution in every country in Central America for him? Hadn't the whole damned cabinet resigned at one time or another (except for a man named Parker French; only God and General Walker knew how that one wound up in the cabinet). And wasn't General Walker monkeying with the devil by setting up commissions to investigate the Transit Company and sending dunning letters for back payments to old Commodore Vanderbilt? I hardly paid attention. I think I had less sense then than when I'd signed on. I was full of myself. All I believe I knew was that I wasn't having to kill anybody anymore, that I was a captain now, that I'd turned twenty-four the month before, and that I was having a damn fine time.

I must have given a score of interviews to reporters since the fall of Granada. Every paper that the steamers brought— from San Francisco, New York, London—was full of nothing but General Walker and the American Phalanx. You'd have thought we were the only thing happening on earth, war in the Crimea notwithstanding. The papers said that there were rallies for us in New York and St. Louis and New Orleans, and that there were riots at the docks when a steamer left for Nicaragua. And no matter that the government tried to stop the ships from leaving—they might as well have tried to swat swarms of bees with straws.

All over Nicaragua, the sounds you heard most those days were hammers and saws and carts rumbling by full of adobe bricks. The General Walker Hotel was open for business on the plaza in Granada by then, and full. The new dock that one of our work crews—in uniforms that I designed—was building at Virgin Bay was nearly done. At the dock, you took the new schooner, the *General Walker*, to any point on the lake without fear of pirates. Lighthouses were going up, survey teams were hacking their way through forests all over the country, roads were being drawn up, mining expeditions were out, books were being written. Our newspaper, *El*

Nicaraguense, was being quoted all over the world, and had even taken to printing love poems some of the boys wrote on the front page. I sold two sketches to *Leslie's Illustrated,* and thought I was on my way. We even had a proper school after a time, a place called the Academia Walkerania, run by a Mrs. Rachael Bingham and her husband. He was a cripple and not good tempered, but I recall her as a fine woman, though I wasn't well acquainted with her.

There were always balls, and new immigrants had commenced coming in with their families. The houses of the shoewearers who had run off when Corral was shot were filling up with American women and children, while their men were off setting up offices and stores and shops on plazas all over the country—mechanics and merchants and importers and investment brokers and the like. We had four good American restaurants in Granada alone. I heard American songs in all the villages I rode to. John Wheeler's son had got up a Young Pioneers society, he called it, and they drilled and held parades. With every ship that came along, the brass band we had got bigger, and even held concerts in the plaza on Sundays.

The spirit of American enterprise, I recollect that *El Nica-raguense* said once, would wait for nothing. And of course I believed that.

Well, then, peace hadn't done much for making Granada peaceful. And fancying that I was of an artistic temperament, that was why I spent as much time away from the city as I could. There were over twelve hundred Americans in the country by then, we figured, more than eight hundred of us in the army, and most of those were in Granada. There were duels, liquor, womanizing—too much for even General Walker to control now that there was no fighting to put the fear of God into the men. The general's brothers—James and Norvell, I believe they were—had come into the army, and Lord knows they were as bad as the rest. Just too many recruits of the wrong kind, you understand, boys from the

Bowery in New York, hooligans right off the wharfs of New Orleans. You took what you could get.

Not all bad, of course. Never let anyone tell you that we were an army of rabble. I spent an entire afternoon once arguing about the translation of Thucydides with one recruit. On sentry duty another night I ran across a boy, younger than even I was, writing a sonnet. We had two senators' sons at one time or another, and more than one of our boys died leaving a considerable estate. I believe that all in all it was the most unlikely mix of men I've ever been among, even more so than in San Francisco.

And each steamer that landed brought more unlikely ones. I remember a man calling himself Colonel Billy Wilson got off the *Uncle Sam* from New York one week with a trunk full of nothing but linen shirts—stood on the dock and laughed while he threw them to every white man in sight, then took the next steamer out when he saw there was no more fighting. We had a whole company of Frenchmen in the army, another of Germans, and enough Jews to have already rented a building for a synagogue.

Or the Cubans. Dear Lord, there was a crew. A man named Domingo de Coincoura had shown up with two hundred and fifty recruits from New York, all officered by Cuban exiles. De Goincoura, I understand, was a friend of Commodore Vanderbilt, and had struck a deal with General Walker that, when Nicaragua got on its feet, the general would go help him free Cuba from the Spanish. I didn't put much stock in that happening, I'm sorry to say. De Goincoura had sworn thirty or so years before not to cut his beard until Cuba was free. It was turning gray when I met him, and hung down somewhere around his knees.

And there was the cholera. Not an epidemic, but it was always there, stalking one or another of us. Never a week passed that we didn't lose half a dozen or so of the boys, and God only knows how many natives. And not a damn thing you could do to stop it. You kept clean, you made sure you washed your food and knew the well your water came from, and you prayed. But every day that passed another man would begin to vomit, to beshit himself in the street, then his skin shrank up and turned gray, he begged for water, and went into convulsions and that sleep he never came out of. You've doubtless seen it yourself—it's a filthy way to die, and I'll never get used to it. I stopped my ears every time the dead cart rattled by.

Poor Guy Sartain had done his best, but it overwhelmed him. Even after another surgeon from New York—a white one—came down and the two of them got a clean and orderly hospital set up, the deaths didn't slow. Nothing would slow down death in that country.

If I had to say when it all began to fall apart, I would pick that month of February, 1856. But if I had to find the first crack that led to that fall, I would have to go back to Christmas of the year before, when a man named Edmund Randolph got off the *Northern Light* from San Francisco.

I've mentioned Randolph, though I imagine you don't recollect. I'll tell you what I know about him, and that's what he told me himself. He was a lawyer. He had known General Walker as far back as New Orleans, when the general couldn't have been more than twenty, and I believe the general first read for the law in his office. There was something about a woman that both of them had known, but I never found out just what. He was the reason, so he said, that the general had first come out to San Francisco—claimed the general had followed him out. Then, he said, he was the one in San Francisco who had got the general involved in politics to begin with, had defended him when the government tried him for taking off and attacking Lower California in '54, had got him out of jail when the general wrote some newspaper articles about corrupt judges, and had raised most of the money and men for our own expedition. The last part happened during the time I was in San Francisco, and I know it to be true enough.

As I look back, he was everything the general wasn't. He was a handsome man, tall and a good talker and a gladhander. Women took to him. He dressed like a lord. If General Walker could have been anybody he pleased, I think he would have been Edmund Randolph. . . .

In any case, by February General Walker had moved out of Niña Irena's house. The general was living in a little room next to his office in the Government Palace—nothing but a cot, some maps and books, a desk, and his big clock made the place different from the storeroom it had been before. The general and Niña Irena weren't getting on then—she was very nervous around him, it seemed to me—but her house was the best accommodation in Granada, so Randolph got put up there. I had kept my room with her, and had gotten fond of her.

I had just given my mare to my *mozo* and was going into my room for a bottle of liniment to rub her down with when I heard the general call to me from Randolph's room. Randolph had a fever at the time, and the general was sitting next to his bed with a sheaf of papers in his hand. They seemed to be in uncommonly good spirits for two men in a sickroom.

The general handed me a few of the papers and said, "Captain, I'd like you to put these into Spanish for me. I don't trust mine sufficiently."

"Yes sir," I said, and began to read them over to be sure I could make them all out. Well, they were full of whereases and heretofores and to-wits, but as they began to make sense to me my heart sped up. Because, you see, those papers announced the unmitigatedly damnest thing I had ever seen in my life—it still is, when I think about it.

These two men, in a hot, whitewashed room in Granada, Nicaragua, were going to nationalize the Transit Route! Were going to take it away from Commodore Cornelius Vanderbilt, the richest and most powerful man in the entire damned United States. Repossess it, like it was a horse. It was all there in those papers, dated the next day and ready for the signature of old man Rivas.

My mouth must have been open, because Edmund Randolph laughed. He had a gold tooth, I recall. General Walker got up and brought Randolph a dipper of water, like he was his nanny. "Well, Captain," he said, with his back to me. "Go to."

Why didn't I get on my horse and take the first coaster I could find to Panama, like a sane man ought to have? Because as I said, gentlemen, when you were making a new world, everything was possible.

Well, old man Rivas took on like that decree had been a gift from the Magi. He shook every hand he could get hold of, had two glasses of wine, and declared that William Walker was a new Bolívar, a new Washington. Nicaragua was taking its national treasure back again, he said. No more foreign domination. Prosperity had come at last. They'd have a railroad from Granada to León. The jungles would be full of plantations managed by scientific Americans. They'd have telegraph, pumps, an icehouse!

That lasted one day. The next morning, the general gave him the rest of the papers he'd had in that sheaf for me to translate.

You see, Nicaragua didn't have the Transit Route after all. A company in San Francisco that Edmund Randolph worked for had it, an outfit called Morgan and Garrison. Had it on terms that even I could see were twice as good as Vanderbilt's had been.

Old man Rivas pitched a fit beyond anything I would have thought him capable of. Said we'd have to shoot him to get him to sign, that we were selling the country. I think he knew better than to turn the whole thing down, but he haggled. He wanted such and such a provision taken out, these words changed, this amount raised. He even met his cabinet without Walker once.

The general bore with him for a week, cajoling and changing one provision or another to suit him. I think at last he hinted that he might have to shoot him after all, and the old man signed. And that seemed to be that.

The decrees went out on the same day the *Uncle Sam* landed. There were two hundred and fifty recruits on the *Uncle Sam*, sent down to us free by Cornelius Vanderbilt. There was a letter on it too. Vanderbilt offered to send down all the men we needed, and to give us loans and transport our guns.

That Cuban who was a friend of Vanderbilt's, de Goincoura, cried in the general's office when he heard about it.

WILLIAM WALKER ||||||||||||||||||||||||||||||||||||||||||||||||||||||||||||||||||||||||||

I WILL NOT have Edmund blamed!

What I felt for Edmund Randolph was not of a character to be expressed by words. He had been my support, my refuge. In those last days in New Orleans when I watched Ellen's pure face withering before the violence of cholera, his voice and his hand were there to comfort me. He introduced me to Ellen. When all others were against me in San Francisco, he defended me. When they laughed at my Nicaragua plans, it was he who made them possible. His ideals were mine; I dedicated my mission in Nicaragua to him as much as to myself.

I had no certain knowledge of the reason for his coming: nothing had been planned out in advance between us. But whatever he asked, I was certain I would not hesitate in doing; not only because he was my friend, but because my faith in him was such that I knew he would ask nothing which would not benefit William Walker's cause and destiny.

Even now I can only half believe that he, too, was capable of betrayal—the betrayal which self-interest that does not recognize itself brings. I do not doubt that he loved me. It is only a matter of vision.

COMMODORE CORNELIUS VANDERBILT

WHAT THE little bastard needed was men—men and arms. He could have had all the money he wanted as soon as he created a reasonable business climate down there. I knew that; I could have seen to it. I even admired him—after he took my Transit Route away from me, I was still willing to deal with him. I told my man de Goincoura that, but he spit in de Goincoura's face. Randolph, Edmund Randolph, that's the only man he could see or hear. I don't know what was between them, except that one must have been as big a fool as the other.

I'll tell you what I think. I think what he wanted was a damned little feudal kingdom down there. He hated me because I had money, and the future of this century belongs to money. But no, he wouldn't accept that. He wanted to live in a damned book. He knew I hated Morgan and Garrison. He knew they'd tried to manipulate my stock the year before while I was off on the goddamn European cruise. What did I tell them?—I won't sue you, I told them, the law is too slow: I'll ruin you. Is that the lot he wanted to throw his in with? Well, if he did, he got it.

I have no idea if he knew what he was up against, but I did. I'd had my people out down there ever since he showed up—down there and in Washington. As worked up as the natives in all those other countries around him were—I can never remember them all—what in hell did he think they were going to do when they heard he'd cut off his best supply of men? Sit down to dinner and wait for him to figure out another way to get men in there?

If Morgan and Garrison had any ships, I didn't know about it, no matter what kind of promises they made to him. And they surely as hell weren't getting any of mine.

I do know he'd heard of the British Empire. And unless he hadn't read a newspaper in the past twenty-five years—if he was that old—he knew that they thought Central America was as much theirs as Ireland was. Send in a couple of gunboats and they could get anything they wanted, without the expense of colonies. I know for a fact that almost precisely at the time he took my Transit Route, the British struck a deal with one of those countries—Costa Rica, I think—to send them down a shipload of rifles. So he had the damned British Empire on his hands too.

But I'll tell you the one thing he had that was more important to him than any other country in the world. His stock was high. Every jackleg in America thought he was a goddamn genius. He had investors falling all over themselves: anybody with an ounce of sense could see that a North-South war was coming in this country, and was looking for a place to get out to or send their money to. Why, there was a fortune waiting for anyone who had a safe place to supply both sides from! And what in hell did he think bucking Cornelius Vanderbilt was going to do to his stock?

Even if I'd wanted to let that go by, I couldn't. I had stock to keep up, too, by God. He'd gotten too big for his britches. Somebody had to come up with a way to split him out of them, and I sent to work on it. As I say, I don't know what Morgan and Garrison promised him, but I thought at the time it had better be the moon.

Or maybe it didn't have to be. I'll tell you why. I sent some of my people down to check up on him, who he was, where he'd been. Here's a story one of them got out of his brother. When he was a boy, he didn't amount to much—kept his nose in a book and was a runt. So the other boys chose him to tease, as was natural. He'd wait for them after school, then pick out the biggest one of the bunch and light into him. Knowing, of course, that he was going to get hell beat out of him but not being able to stop himself. Now what does that story tell you?

And here's another one. I'm fond of it. I think it's the perfect story for the man. He had a woman in New Orleans— engaged to her. One of the finest-looking women in New Orleans. But you know why he took to her? I'll lay any man odds: it wasn't because she was a handsome woman.

It was because she was deaf and dumb. Now what do you think about that?

PART
THREE

RACHAEL BINGHAM

April 15th, '56   It has been almost four months since I've
felt the need to write, ever since Arthur and I left León and
came here to Granada. I've had a kind of life in those four
months—and now I'm fearful, truly fearful, that even that
life is about to be over. I have every reason to think so. There
is war again. Walker's Phalanx is preparing to march in the
morning. Though it's nearly midnight, I hear them outside,
with their mules and shouts and boots. Their torches are forever flashing through the cracks in my shutters. For days
they've been getting ready, and Granada has been a madhouse. It's the custom here for the people to open the great
doors that lead into their houses in the cool of the evenings,
and gather together in rocking chairs on the sidewalks to
talk. But no more. Since Walker's men have been rushing
through the streets at all hours, they keep their doors and
their shutters closed and locked.

There has been an invasion, but beyond that I have no real
knowledge of just what is happening. When I try to find out,
I get only the most general news. I'm treated like a child by
Walker and his men—all of the women here are, as if our
lives weren't to be affected in the least by what is happening,
as if we weren't going to live or die because of it. I'm reduced to picking up snippets of things from Brian Holdich,
or hearing them through a Negro, Guy Sartain, who is
treated to only slightly more confidence than I am. He's a

109

gentle and intelligent man, and since Arthur and I have been here in Granada we've become friends with him, much to the displeasure of many of Walker's officers.

Well, Walker's officers who don't like it can all go hang laundry! I'm not that new Major Thompson's wife, who lives next to us and keeps me awake all night screaming while he beats her. In New York, I had what friends I wanted; as long as I'm keeping our school going here and doing all the work that should be done by a man, I'll choose my friends like a man.

Why, they even blame a woman for their war! There's a native woman named O'Horan, who Walker lodged with for a time. As soon as they took over the Transit Route, Walker claimed he caught her outside Edmund Randolph's chamber, listening to them plot. To make it worse, Randolph said in public that she had been trying to seduce him to get information, and Walker ordered her placed under house arrest. Like anyone with the least sense, she ran away. And now, of course, they're claiming that she's the one who carried the news about the Transit Route to the Costa Ricans. Guy Sartain tells me his connections in town say that's nonsense, she's hiding out on her hacienda, but it's not convenient for anybody to believe that. Oh, they'd love to have somebody like her to blame their troubles on. For myself, I liked her greatly.

As best I can discover, our new circumstances are different from any other that have ever been—here or anywhere. We have been declared war on—not Nicaragua, just the Americans—by Costa Rica. For all I know, every other country in Central America is ready to join them, but the Costa Ricans are here already. Walker sent men down across the border to keep them out of the country—mostly his Frenchmen and Germans—but they broke and ran when they saw how many of them there were. And now the Costa Ricans are braver than ever. They're almost in Rivas already, and somehow Walker is going off tomorrow to get there before them and protect the Transit. Truthfully, with the talk that

Walker has been putting out making Costa Rica and all the others part of some kind of United States of Central America with him at the head (he hasn't said he'd be head of it, but of course that goes without saying), I'd try to run us away, too.

And yet he's my only hope. Our only hope. Without him, there would be such a slaughter here that none of us would ever escape. I'm tempted to actually pray for him—and yet every time I see him I'm repelled by him. I've never known a man I had such a fascination for, and was so afraid of, and disagreed with so violently. The bizarreness of that overwhelms me—though I know that everything that's happened in Nicaragua since last June is utterly bizarre.

At first, when he and his men came down, I decided that what I had to do was watch them—pull back from them and watch, because I knew that my life and Arthur's might depend on that. And then when they left León, I realized I missed them. I could talk to them! Not about much, but at least they were Americans. And now since we've come to Granada and there are a fair number of American women here, too, I know how desperate I would be without them. Guy Sartain says that too; even though there's so little in common between him and the other Americans, he would be lost without them.

So we're both bound to them, will suffer or be happy because of things they do that we have no control over. Slaves are like that, I tell Guy, but he shakes his head and says no, no there's a difference.

I think it's because of Walker that I've been sleeping with Brian Holdich.

At first, I thought I was falling in love with Brian. Or I used that as my excuse. That part of Arthur was dead to me because of his "accident," and probably always will be now.

After Arthur was shot, I recited to myself everything I'd been taught about womanly self-sacrifice and sick-nursing and the satisfaction those would bring. That was a lie. I think what I've discovered in this place, where we're all supposed to be starting over, where nobody is who he was, is that nearly everything I've been taught about being a woman is a lie.

I was the one who invited Brian Holdich into my bedroom. I had asked him to teach a Spanish class in the school (it was Arthur's idea to call it the Academia Walkeriana, not mine) and he began to stay over for dinner from time to time. One of those nights when Arthur had passed out and I'd put him to bed, I simply invited Brian to my room. I don't think he knew what to make of me or the invitation, but he came. And he's been coming back ever since. I don't think I knew quite what to think of myself, either. But I'm glad I did it. I've felt almost whole since then. If Brian is killed tomorrow, I'll do it again, with someone else.

For a long time I kept wondering when I was going to start feeling guilty. I don't wonder now. I didn't even feel guilty when Arthur found out. I can see him sitting there before my bedroom door with his thin yellow chicken's legs hanging down from that wheelchair he had the natives make, while Brian and I stared at him from my bed as if he'd been a ghost in a bad opera-house play—and I can pity him with all my heart as he sat and cried, but *I will not feel guilty.*

We haven't spoken about it since that night, and I know that what he's done is, in his fashion, given me permission. I pity him even more for that, but I know there's nothing I can do about it, nothing at all.

I'm certain now that I don't truly love Brian, not the way I loved Arthur when I married him. He says that he loves me, and I don't tell him he shouldn't—because I want him to love me. I haven't hurt him, and if I can help it, I won't. Is there any harm in being loved?

But as we've gotten closer, I am discovering something

112

that horrifies me. When we talk, I want to talk about William Walker, not ourselves. It's almost as if Brian is a window glass, with Walker on the other side. And here's what frightens me: I don't want to think of William Walker as a *man*. Now I look at that little gold cross he wears and I begin to wonder, who was she, what kind of woman could have made him love her so that he's never taken another since?

At dawn I'm going to watch the Phalanx leave, with the other women. Then I suppose we'll come back here or go to one of the other women's houses and talk about how it would be spring at home, or how the price of everything decent is so outrageous in this place because it has to be imported—anything but what's on our minds. We can do that, or we can take lovers, or we can pray, or we can walk the dirt floors of these great galleries of spider-hung rooms we live in and wring our hands. And that's all. In two days, a week, we may wake up to mobs of howling Nicaraguans and Costa Ricans. If I only knew more!

Is there a more perfect torture than this waiting? And yet, if by some miracle Walker does manage to save us this time, whose war will it have been, where will the medals go? What can they ever understand about waiting? I'd a thousand times rather face Costa Rican muskets than the thoughts in this diary.

TALMEDGE WARNER

WELL, THERE WE was fixed up good in Granada, and this damned mess started. There was whores a-standing in line for us, we eat good, and I got to see the country a right smart:

113

Colonel Hornsby was military governor down in one province, Byron Cole up in another, Chélon in another, and so on, and me and a couple of the other boys was always riding off to one or the other of them with dispatches. You know, parts of it down there up in the mountains put me in mind of Kentucky, where there was meadows and horses grazing and creeks and woods, and I wanted me some land there so bad I could taste it. Uncle Billy said he was a-going to set the whole country up like a military outfit, and I knowed that would do me fine—I might even wind up with a town to run.

Truth to tell, there was a couple of problems, but I didn't really pay them no nevermind then. Uncle Billy could deal with them. The steamers wasn't coming in like they had when Commodore Vanderbilt was a-sending them down, so we wasn't getting the new boys like we ought to. Then they told me Uncle Billy had sent that Parker French off to Washington as ambassador just to get shut of him, and half a dozen states had men waiting to arrest him for one kind of fraud or another the minute he stepped off the boat—none of which done Uncle Billy's reputation much good back home. There was some that said Uncle Billy was commencing to make all kinds of mistakes a man like him just oughtn't to, but I never believed it. If Uncle Billy didn't know what he was doing, then nobody did. I *had* to believe in Uncle Billy's luck, see, because it was mine, too.

No, what got me in a uproar was the three thousand Costa Ricans that had come into the country already, with six thousand more on the way, they said. And God only knew where anybody was at. We taken off down to Rivas after them, didn't find them, got hold of a rumor the Guatemalans and Hondurans and such had come into the country from the north, went a-flying off up there only to run into old Chélon with the news that there wasn't no more invasion happening up there than dogs can fly.

Well, no sooner did we get turned back around again than the news come that the Costa Ricans had burned up everything at Virgin Bay and then had dug in at Rivas like badgers.

So there we was. Nothing to do but set out a-marching back down south toward Rivas, which we'd just left, except now it was full of Costa Ricans, and we was so wore out from all that running back and forth that we couldn't hardly think. That's the way it was down there, trying to fight. Nobody really knowed what was going on anywhere, and the natives would tell you whatever you wanted to hear because they was afraid of everybody. Whether all that running up and down was Uncle Billy's fault, there just ain't no telling. See, you got to be a genius or a damned fool to try to fight a war in Central America. I still believed Uncle Billy was a genius. But sometimes it was hard.

Well, on the way back to Rivas, Captain Henry sent me off to see that the supply wagons was leaving like they was supposed to, and by the time I got all the mules and greasers straightened out, the rest of the boys wasn't where I'd left them and I went after them in the wrong direction. I figured they'd head out down toward Virgin Bay and come up the transit road toward Rivas so as to sneak up on the Costa Ricans. So that's the way I went.

By the time I got to this little town on the lake a little ways before Virgin Bay, called San Jorge, I knowed it wasn't our boys that had come through there. I had to slip past Costa Rican patrols on both sides of the place, and the people I seen as I went through the town was walking around in a daze. More than a few of the houses was still smoldering, and I could smell the corpses burning in them. At this ditch on the edge of town as I rode out of it, there was two dead children, a boy and a girl, with flies hanging over them already. Whatever you could say about us, that wasn't Uncle Billy's work.

But I'd started that way, and there wasn't no going back. I come over the little hill before Virgin Bay at dusk, my horse lathered and me cautious now as a squirrel. In that evening light, the people moving in the village looked like ghosts. At the foot of the hill, I come across a bunch of them throwing dirt up for graves, and when I looked off to my left where the dock we'd built had been, I couldn't see nothing but a few black pilings sticking up through the water, and the beach everywhere was full of burnt timbers. Where the Transit Company manager's house had been there wasn't but a rock foundation and a circle of burnt-up bushes and grass around it.

When I got close enough to see who the graves was being dug for, I seen that a good dozen of them bodies was white people like me. They was all in civilian clothes, and I recognized one of them as a missionary preacher I'd met in Rivas. That wouldn't do, I thought. Wait till them New York reporters get hold of that—might be the only good thing to come out of this for us.

Over at the Transit warehouse, the loading doors was swinging back and forth in the breeze like shutters. It wasn't natural, no sounds but the creaking of them doors and the waves and the wind in the trees and greasers' voices from the village real low, coming and going on the wind. I kept riding, looking for signs of all them straggly cows and razorback hogs and chickens that had been everywhere last time I'd been there. They was all gone, every one.

So in the last of the light, I rode out along the transit road. Then at a crossroads just outside Rivas, dark caught me for good. Off toward Rivas I could see the light from Costa Rican picket fires. So I went a ways into the wood and lay down to sleep with the mosquitoes and chiggers and spiders, and I thought about things.

It had been near six months since there'd been any killing like I'd seen back there behind me. I'd reckoned it might be over. But while I was a-whoring and having a big time, there had been all these things going on everywhere else—down in Costa Rica, up in New York, over in England—things to do with presidents and queens and rich men that I'd never have thought about in a thousand years. And all them dead people I'd seen that day? They was dead because of those things.

I looked up at the trees. They was so big they seemed to go all the way up to the stars, and I felt about as little as the spiders and the chiggers underneath them.

Then I shut my eyes so I couldn't see no more. Tomorrow or maybe the day after I'd have to commence killing again.

I found the rest of the boys in the morning just as they was hanging a spy they'd caught. They let him die slow, and while he was twisting there, Uncle Billy told us what we was going to do. This spy had said that the biggest muckledemuck of all, the president of Costa Rica himself, was holed up in the plaza in Rivas and that all their arsenal was stored there with him. So that's where we was going—us from one direction, Chélon's people from the other so as to confuse them. The boys looked like they was more ready for sleeping than fighting, but Uncle Billy was as wide awake as morning and made us another speech, so we went.

Everything started out like it was supposed to, us a-hollering and a-charging at them, and since they was conscripts who hadn't never seen gringos coming with revolvers before, they scattered. But then me and some of the other boys captured this little brass cannon. Well, we was excited. All the shooting and the horse's hooves and the sweat and a considerable of *aguardiente* to drink, and we just wasn't thinking. We was so proud of ourselves we decided we was going to find Uncle Billy and give it to him. So we tied some lines to it and went dragging it off down the street, and when the other boys seen us they took hold of it too, and before ten minutes was up I guess there was a good hundred of us

117

capering around it and hollering for Uncle Billy and acting like pure fools.

By the time Uncle Billy and Colonel Hornsby and Captain Henry and the rest come along and broke us up, the greasers had had time to figure things out and had pulled in so tight around the plaza that we fought right into the afternoon before we got to it. They was everywhere—up on roofs, in windows, in doorways—and the boys was falling all around me. Well, when we finally got hold of the plaza we was too exhausted to spit. And what did we find? Nothing. Their president had snuck off, and the arsenal was empty as a poor man's Christmas stocking. And where had everything and everybody snuck off to? To all sides of us. We'd fought all day just to get ourselves surrounded! Remember what I said about fighting down there? And about what a mess it all was? There you are.

Then what was we going to do? For the longest time Uncle Billy just stood and looked around him, like I had seen him and Captain Holdich do the first time we was in Rivas and fixing to run. He done things that wasn't necessary, like have us count the dead bodies (we come up with near a thousand), and put the greaser wounded up in the shade in case Sartain could get to them, and try to find friendly civilians we could give guns to. But there wasn't no civilians because I reckon they'd been through this enough times to know to go hide when they seen it coming. Everything stunk to high heaven and I kept my eyes on him, worried.

Toward night, he told us what we was going to do. We was going to dig. We was going to spend the evening and night tearing holes through them two-foot adobe walls to make a tunnel to get behind the Costa Ricans. And that's what we done. We used gunpowder when we could and hammers and rifle butts when we couldn't. Right through people's parlors and bedrooms we went, like moles, making an awful red dust that near choked us and ruined all the people's clothes and furniture. When the light run out, we used candles. Some of

118

the boys was always running off to some empty *pulpería* or another and bringing us back liquor, but that didn't help long. Even Uncle Billy's brother Norvell got drunk and went to sleep in somebody's bed. Come about two o'clock and we hadn't gone more than two or three blocks, and no matter how much Uncle Billy stood over us and told us how we didn't have no choice but to keep going, we quit. Just stopped and couldn't go no more.

I think even Uncle Billy seen it was hopeless after a while, and he wasn't one for believing anything was hopeless. So he told us we'd struck a "paralyzing blow," and that we'd best be gone when daylight got here and all them Costa Ricans come after us like we had gone after them. So we wrapped up the horses' hooves to keep them from making noise, made stretchers for our wounded out of the clothes of the dead greasers, and we went creeping out just before daybreak. The loudest sound we made was old Chélon a-cussing. I don't believe he thought much of our paralyzing blow.

That was how the mess wound up. That was when we all commenced a-whispering to ourselves that Uncle Billy's luck had run out—and ours. A quarter of us was dead, there wasn't no steamships to bring us reinforcements, and the Costa Ricans had whipped us and kept Rivas. Now all they had to do was wait, and before you knew it, all those other countries down there would be on us too, like flies on green meat. Time, all they needed was time. And that's what they had. I wouldn't have give you a plug nickle that a blessed one of us would be alive in a month.

Well, why did we do it? Why did we stay with Uncle Billy through all that? He'd got us in some damn messes, and he'd got us out of them. But this one was the worse one of all: we had a town, walked out of it, then fought our way back into it just to get ourselves trapped and have to go sneaking out

119

again. A man with an ounce of brains would have give up and gone home. But, you know, here was the funny thing. Not all of us, but most of us, thought that Uncle Billy Walker was the closest thing to Jesus Christ there was on earth. We didn't mind that we hadn't been paid, nor that we didn't have the land we'd been promised yet, nor that he got us killed without blinking an eyelash. You know why? Whatever we done, Uncle Billy could make it sound like we was going straight into heaven or the history books because of it. It was hard to walk away from something like that. It made us somebody we hadn't never thought we could be.

CHÉLON

IN JUST THREE weeks, only three weeks, the miracle happened! I went to church because of it; I made Padre Vigil, the gringos' own favorite priest, get up from his dinner table and confess me. I was a faithless, *pendejo*, ignorant Indian, and God had to know I realized it.

Hadn't I doubted? When we crept out of Rivas in the night like chicken thieves, hadn't I called Chinaman and my oldest *veteranos* around me and told them to get ready to go home and defend their families? Eh? Hadn't I taken my guitar and sat like an iguana under a rock and waited for the Costa Ricans and the Hondurans and the Guatemalans to destroy us? Didn't I doubt like the rest that the gringos were God's fists?

God and Science and Hygiene had done it for El Gualquer, no matter what anybody said. If I could have found priests of Science and Hygiene, I would have confessed to them, too.

He knew. When we went into Rivas and then left it again, he knew what would happen. He knew that the ignorant Costa Ricans didn't know anything about Hygiene. He understood that all we had to do was kill enough of them and then wait for them to throw the bodies in their wells, and when the wells were full, to leave the rest in the streets to rot. And that then God would be so disgusted he would send the cholera. He knew all we would have to do was to sit in Granada and drink sweet water and wait.

I told Padre Vigil that, and Padre Vigil told me I might be right. He even smiled at me.

But no, *compañeros*. He shouldn't have smiled. God's vengeance is terrible. He sent the worst kind of cholera ever seen on earth, so that you could smell the vomit and shit and rot from a mile around Rivas. And even that wasn't enough. When the news got back to Costa Rica that we had killed nearly a thousand of their men, and that over a thousand more had fallen down dead at their posts from the cholera, God sent a rebellion to them. And when what was left of their army went home to put it down, they died so fast beside the road that their officers couldn't count them. Five hundred they buried on the beach at San Juan del Sur alone while they were waiting for their ships, and for months afterward their bones stuck up out of the sand like dune grass. And then it spread on the ships that took them home, then all through Costa Rica until only God's own scribes know how many thousands of them were dead because they had challenged El Gualquer.

The truth is, *muchachos*, that I don't know if God meant it to go that far or not. I think even He might have been surprised.

El Gualquer didn't change. He took all the Costa Rican sick and wounded they left behind and put them into his own hospitals and let his *zambo* doctor treat them, no matter that the filthy Costa Ricans bayoneted every gringo prisoner they could get their hands on. My friend Holdich told me that even

121

the men from the newspapers in England wrote home that El Gualquer was a fine Christian because of that. I think El Gualquer knew that, too, would happen. He understood God and newspapers.

I told Padre Vigil everything, and asked him if he believed in the Stories. He kept smiling at me. I don't think he cared very much. I think he was too pleased that El Gualquer had appointed him the new minister to Washington to bother about God anymore. He went back to finish his dinner.

And why should I bother, either, I thought. God was pleased with us; I was pleased with God. Maybe we could let each other be now. Maybe we could start the new day at last.

I walked out of the church, and the rain was falling in great sheets. It was cutting gulleys across the dirt in the plaza and pouring off the roof tiles like ropes. I always liked to be home in the rainy season. I liked to sit on my porch and play my guitar and in the night feel my wife in the bed and listen to the clatter of the rain on the roof. I liked to plow, and to watch my daughters sew, and sing with my poor *indios* in the woods. I liked to count my cows.

I would go home now, I thought, and wait for the time to come when I could ride a steamboat to San Francisco. I would be a happy man.

But miracles don't last long the way they used to. Politicians and generals don't believe in them. Their noses are too straight and their hair is too fine, and they can read.

Upside Down Rivas, rabbit or not, wouldn't come home to Granada after God's victory. He said he wanted to stay in León so he could watch out for the Guatemalans and the Hondurans who would probably come down from the north any day. *Mierda!* El Gualquer was in Granada, that's why he wouldn't come home! They couldn't forgive El Gualquer for taking the Transit Route away, no matter how many victories he won. They couldn't forgive him for taking haciendas from the shoewearers and selling them to gringos who

122

knew how to use them. They couldn't forgive him for being a gringo.

So no, I didn't get to go home in the rainy season. Somebody who knew the politicians and the generals as well as I knew them had to stay with him, and I did.

Here's what they were scheming—scheming even while we were waiting in Granada for the cholera to do its work. They wanted elections, though it was months before they were supposed to come. They claimed that it was because they wanted to do what El Gualquer said they should do, to bring the country together. But I knew: they wanted their power back. And then they could go back to fucking my poor Indians again.

Bueno. So when the Costa Ricans went away, El Gualquer called me in and said, Chélon, get your *indios* together, and I'll get my Rangers and my Cavalry and my Rifles and my supply wagons and we'll all go up to León and see about things. We'll send a message that we're coming to find out about all those Hondurans and Guatemalans they keep claiming are getting ready to attack.

I told him, the politicians are sharpening machetes up there, my general.

They'll sharpen faster when we leave, he said to me, and I think he almost smiled.

So in the first week of June we went up to León. And when we got there they gave us the greatest celebration in the history of Nicaragua.

They met us at the edge of the city, all the politicians and generals and rich people. And on the way into town, they bounded around us like goats—they bowed and waved their hats and the fireworks boomed and the skyrockets whistled from the street corners and the church bells made a noise like the day of resurrection. They made us speeches saying how good it was of the great General Gualquer to come and let León show its gratitude and stop all those rumors that

123

His Excellency the General of the Armies was really on the side of the shoewearers in Granada. They said how wonderful it was that all these excellent new Nicaraguans from the great neighbor in the north had come to drink their liquor and eat their food and fuck their women. . . .

Me, *muchachos*? I like a circus too. I like it when women throw flowers at me as I ride past, and I like flags and banners and guitars and trumpets and poets reading poems about me and choirs singing to me in churches.

But I don't believe a circus is real.

I didn't go to the banquet they gave for El Gualquer that night. Since I sweat in my uniform like a pig, I didn't want the purebloods to have the chance to look down their noses at me. I know what I am, and I know what they are, and I don't need to prove it the rest of my life.

But there was no sleeping. Everywhere people were out on the streets drunk and yelling *vivas*, and I sat in that cavern of a house they had given me—a house I wouldn't have been allowed to come in the front door of when I was a boy—I sat there like an old maid, sweating and fanning and pouting, and I wanted company.

I wanted to see Mendez the Cock. I wanted to sit with another fucked *indio* and drink brandy and play monte. I didn't care that he was probably mad at me, from the time we shot Ponciano Corral. I wanted to see Mendez. I wanted to talk to him about the times before the gringos came.

I recognized the woman who came to the door at his house —no, I recognized the French robe she had on. Last time I was at his house there probably had been another woman in it. "Where's Mendez, little sister?" I said to her.

She was holding a candle, and the hallway was dark behind her, and she looked afraid. "He left, señor," she said to me. "*Se fue.*"

"And where did he leave to?"

She shrugged.

"Is he in León, little sister?"

"No," she said.

I took a step toward her, and she looked even more afraid. "Then where is he?"

"He left this morning, señor."

I took another step. "Where?"

"He said Honduras, señor. North. I don't know."

She backed away from me into the dark hallway, a darkness like a tunnel. I knocked the candle from her hand and it guttered out in its own wax on the floor. In the darkness I could smell her, and I knew she could smell me. "You do know, little sister. Why did he go to Honduras?"

Her voice was small. "Some men from the government came in the morning. They had a pouch with papers in it. He said to me that he had to take the papers to Honduras. God protect your soul, señor. I don't know any more."

I knew my general Jerez wouldn't stay at the banquet late. His house was only two blocks from mine, and when I got there his candles were still lit. His servant girl took me to him in the courtyard. He was still in his dark suit with his gold watch chain, in a rocking chair beside his wife. She was sewing and listening to him talk and seemed glad when I interrupted. My general Jerez didn't seem glad.

He called for some wine, and after a time his wife left and I said, "I went to see Mendez the Cock tonight, my general. I'm troubled."

He rocked, then cleared his throat. He was the godfather of my daughters, *compañeros*, and he was afraid to talk to me. "Which side do you stand with in this thing, Chélon?" he asked me.

"Are there sides between us now, my general?"

"There are sides. Let me put it that way," he said.

"I stand for Nicaragua and the Democratic party, then. I always have."

He rocked some more. "Do you remember I said once that the gringos were like the rains: if we were lucky, they came and did us some good, then went away before they drowned us?"

"I remember."

"They've been here almost a year. We're drowning, Chélon."

"And without them, Don Maximo?"

"I want elections," he said. "If enough of the gringos stay to make sure we abide by them this time, we can make them work—enough of the gringos and your *indios*." He thought a little while. "Maybe we've seen that there are worse things than each other now."

"How many of the gringos?"

"Two hundred. We'll ask him tomorrow to send all but two hundred of his gringos home."

Poor Don Maximo, I thought. "*Veo*," I said. "I see."

"The Costa Ricans beat him in Rivas, Chélon. He can be beaten. *We* can beat him. He'll know that. He can't turn us down."

"I was in Rivas, Don Maximo."

"He was beaten, Chélon. Believe me. All he had was luck."

"With your permission, my general, not luck."

"Then what was it?"

I looked at my general Jerez in the candlelight. His forehead was so high that it would slide onto his face if his eyebrows weren't there to hold it up. His nose was as long as a Spanish priest's, and his skin was as pale as the palm of my hand. I searched a long time for a piece of Indian in him, but I didn't find any. I loved him, and I was sad, *muchachos*. I couldn't tell him about the things I knew. "Have you turned on him, then, Don Maximo?" I said.

"The man is dictator of my country, Chélon—of your country. Sweet God, he's not even of your race!"

126

"No," I said, even sadder. "He's not. Does everybody want him to go now?"

"You don't."

"No, my general, I don't."

"Why, Chélon? Why?"

I watched two birds fight in an orange tree, and took my time. My general Jerez had the finest orange trees in León. "If El Gualquer sends most of his gringos home, after the elections you'll send the rest away. Then I don't care how many elections we have, we'll fight among ourselves again. And if we fight, who fights? My *indios*, and the poor people. Even you don't understand that, my general. You've never been an *indio*, and you've never been poor. With your permission."

"Then you'd rather have the gringos in control than Nicaraguans—any Nicaraguans?"

"Remember, my general, before the Spaniards came, my *indios* were the Nicaraguans."

"The time of the Spaniards is past, Chélon."

"Is it, Don Maximo?"

My general Jerez leaned his head against the back of the rocker. He looked very tired. "Then we know which side you stand with."

"What will happen if El Gualquer doesn't agree to send his men home tomorrow, my general?"

"I can't tell you that now." He was tired, but he was angry, too.

"Is that why Mendez went to Honduras?

"Don't ask me anything more, Chélon."

"Would you call the shoewearers in Honduras and Guatemala in against *me*, my general?"

"The reasons I want Walker to go are much, much different from the shoewearers'. They don't mind a dictator. They just can't forgive Walker for not acting like one they can understand."

"But if you had to, you would fight beside the shoewearers to get rid of El Gualquer?"

"There are reasonable men among the Conservatives." Conservatives, he said to me, Conservatives! I shit on "Conservatives."

"And what would that make you, my general?"

"A patriot, I hope."

I rocked hard and let my weight carry me up out of the rocking chair. My stiff leg jabbed at me like a stake, but I didn't care about pain then. "I'm less troubled now, Don Maximo." I said to him. "I thank you."

"That surprises me," he said.

"No. You've taught me something. And *indios* learn slow sometimes, my general."

"Learn what, *mi Chélon?*" The anger had gone from his voice now. Nothing but the tiredness was left.

"That there's not a hen fart's worth of difference between Democrats and shoewearers in this fucked country. My poor goddamned *indios* will wait five hundred years for a real revolution from either one of you. With your permission, Don Maximo."

So when El Gualquer made his announcement the next day, I knew he had to. I knew that the politicians and the generals had their machetes sharp, and were gathering around him like the women in black dresses had gathered around Ponciano Corral when we shot him. I had told him they were going to ask him to send most of his gringos home, and I knew that he had been up all night thinking. But what can I know about the things he was thinking? Did he understand how much they couldn't forgive him for? Or did he care? Or had he been waiting all along for them to give him a reason to make his announcement? It didn't matter to me. If he had asked what I thought he should do, I would have begged him to do what he did. And when he did it, I understood at last what the miracle at Rivas had been about. God is not very precise sometimes, *compañeros*, but he does his best.

They told him they wanted to send most of his army away, and he told them he was going to call the elections they wanted. And that he was going to run for president of Nicaragua. *Sí*! My little gringo was going to run for president of Nicaragua.

What more was there for me to doubt? El Gualquer believed in miracles too.

And so the celebrations in León stopped; the poets burned their poems and the women closed their shutters and we took our wagons and mules and men and went back to Granada for the elections. And I set to work helping God with his miracle. My poor *indios* weren't allowed to vote anyway, so what did I care if my boys had to roust out the landowners and merchants and see that they voted right? Or if we handed in some numbers that showed how they ought to have voted, even if they didn't. Oh, we couldn't tell El Gualquer about that, no, but he knew. He knew everything, always.

I think my general Jerez knew, too, and Upside Down Rivas. As soon as the vote was counted, they went riding off to hide in the forest and sent word to Mendez in Honduras to call in the Hondurans and the Guatemalans and the Salvadorans and, if they could have, God's angels, too. And they started conscripting Nicaraguans again, and there we were. In just four weeks, it was like it used to be. One government up in León that said it was the only real one, and another about to be inaugurated in Granada, and foreigners everywhere.

Except, *santos*!—now it was all backward. Upside Down

Rivas was president in León, and he was a shoewearer. And El Gualquer was about to be president in Granada, and he had been brought by my Democrats to get rid of the shoewearers in Granada. And me? There I was in the south among the shoewearers while my family was trapped in the north among my own people, likely to be chopped up into pieces.

The day of El Gualquer's inauguration, I sat in my hot uniform in the fancy cage of a house they'd taken away from a traitor to give to me, and the more I thought about the situation, the madder I got, and the madder I got, the more I had to do something. But what could I do? I couldn't shoot any shoewearers, since they were inaugurating El Gualquer. I couldn't shoot any Democrats, since I was a Democrat. God knew I couldn't shoot any gringos. After all those years of fighting, I felt more helpless than I ever had in my life.

So what did I do? I took my saber out of its scabbard and I killed the only things I could. First I hacked up the pictures of the shoewearers who had built the house. That felt so good that I went to work on all their blue china plates and jugs, then on the shelves and the carved tables themselves. And then, with the greatest pleasure of all, the leather books they had. I made sure that each one of the things, filled with the laws and lies that had got me into this situation, would never be read again. At least I could do that.

I had started to hack the whitewash off the walls when I noticed my man, Chinaman, watching me from the door, with all the serving girls from the house behind him. I was drowning in sweat and gave a last hack at the wall to show them I didn't care. But I did care. I had left Chinaman behind me in León, where my family was. I hadn't seen him in a month. He gave a little bow.

"A good job, *mi coronel*," he said to me.

"Where's my family," I asked him, when I could get my breath back.

"Safe, *mi coronel*."

"Safe where, damn it."

"In your house in the country, señor. They are under protection."

"Did you see them?"

"Colonel Mendez allowed me."

"What in hell has Mendez got to do with it?"

He looked away from me. "They're in his charge, Excellency. When he came back from Honduras, he wanted to claim your lands since you are a traitor, but my general Jerez wouldn't let him. For the time being, the general says. So Colonel Mendez is in charge of your family and your lands until you come home."

I swore at him and slashed at a mahogany commode.

"With permission, *mi coronel*, General Jerez says he wants you to come home. He says if you will come home and stop being a traitor and stay under house arrest and not fight along with the gringos when the time comes, he will let you keep your lands and your family. He says he will guarantee that, even though there are soldiers from Honduras and Guatemala and Salvador everywhere in León now. I think he thinks that if Your Mercy knows that Colonel Mendez is in charge of your daughters you'll come back quicker. He says to tell you that he has much regard for you. They let me come to tell you that."

"How long do I have?"

"They will give you one week, Excellency," he said to me, and he was ashamed to say it.

Outside the house, I remember, the gringo's brass band started to play for the inauguration. They were so loud they seemed to rattle the pieces of broken plates and pots that were scattered all around me. The serving girls behind Chinaman threw their aprons up and ran away toward the music. I thought of my family in the house in the country, of my daughters sewing while the cicadas made the last of those long *reeeee-er, reeeee-er* songs they make in the morning,

131

while Mendez the Cock sat on the porch and watched the mimosas in the wind, and watched my daughters. One week, I thought. The new day is beginning, and I have only one week. It shouldn't be this way, I thought.

"God damn it," I said to the mess around me.

It shouldn't have been that way. It should have been so simple. I had waited so long.

GENERAL WALKER'S INAUGURATION IN GRANADA

SPECIAL TO THE NEW YORK DAILY NEWS

GRANADA *(from a Letter Writer in Nicaragua)*:

If there are wars and rumors of wars in other regions of Nicaragua, a traveler to this ancient city would not have felt them today. Granada put all her finery for the elevation of General William Walker of Tennessee to the highest office in the land. Banners and flags waved from all the houses of substance here, and the streets echoed to the music of a dozen different sorts of bands, while the native populace lined the avenues and filled the balconies in a demonstration of the kind of abandon that only races of tropic latitudes can muster for their public occasions.

The day's celebration began with the grand inaugural parade along the main avenue to the city's plaza, led by a company of General Walker's redshirted rifles and followed by the presidential band and all of the native and American dignitaries from that portion of Nicaragua recognizing General Walker as its president-elect, including United States Minister John Wheeler, in his full American colonel's uniform. Firework displays and other illuminations greeted the parade at every street corner. The ladies of Granada spent the night before covering a grand staging with flowers in front of the cathedral in the plaza, and it was here that the parade had its terminus, for a midday of speeches, in which General Walker was hailed as the new Washington, the new Bolívar, the new Cromwell, hero of the battle of Granada, hero of the battle of Virgin Bay, hero of both battles

133

of Rivas, and savior of Nicaraguan Democracy.

The general himself endured the ceremonies impassively, and watched the crowds with eyes that seemed to this correspondent to be as blank as the sun which broke through the clouds overhead. He is a red-faced, freckled man who was dressed for the occasion in a flannel shirt and the dusty suit of a grocer. When called upon to do so by the Bishop of Granada, he dutifully kissed the Bible and knelt before a gilt crucifix to swear his oath of office, but seemed otherwise unconcerned with the historic significance of his role as a North American who was becoming president of a republic of Central America.

Upon taking the oath of office, he made a speech which was interrupted often by hoorahs from the American element, and *vivas* from the native. He spoke with some heat against civil commotions and intestine broils, invoking the idea of order frequently, and promising the utmost freedom of speech, action, and education, concluding with praise of free trade and progress. He ended by asking divine assistance, without which, he stated, all human exertions are but as bubbles on a stormy sea, and afterward he received a twenty-one gun salute and much cheering and throwing of hats into the air.

Following the inauguration, he led the procession through the crowds to the cathedral to receive the approval of God's emissaries, which proved for this correspondent to be the most impressive ceremony of the day. Two companies of American Rifles with trailed arms, their boots thudding and echoing among the arches of the ancient building, took up positions along the walls of the nave. Bats swooped down among the crowd of spectators, which included reporters from a dozen foreign newspapers, and the scene was as dim as if it had transpired within a cave. President Walker himself was given the Bishop's chair before the altar, a high, carved, and gilded affair, covered with a canopy of cloth of gold and padded with rich, brocaded cushions that gave it more the appearance of a throne than a mere chair. Mr. Walker is of such short stature that his feet did not touch the ground when he sat in it, as if he had been a child. This fact was widely remarked upon by those reporters unfriendly to the event.

When the president was seated, the Bishop ascended into the pulpit and chanted the Gloria, while another priest stood before Mr. Walker with a large silver censer, swinging it, and covering him in the smoke of burning incense in order to bless him. The president appeared to vanish entirely into the smoke, and to this correspondent he seemed to be more nearly one of the pagan effigies of old from this place, than the modern president of a republic.

When the Bishop had completed his offices, a band composed of harps and marimbas and guitars and trumpets began to play, and the choir began to sing a Te Deum in what undoubtedly was withal the strangest display of religious admiration the eyes of the many members of the American element in the crowd ever witnessed. . . .

The inaugural banquet was attended by all of the president's officers, including three new generals he had created for the occasion, and by most of the native functionaries of his government. Also in attendance were several representatives of American business interests, most of whom announced their intent to launch new bond rallies in the major American cities upon their return, in order to benefit the new government. More than fifty toasts were counted, although the president refused to allow more than light wine to be served because of his dislike of intemperance; of these, the most odd, as explained to this correspondent, was offered by one of President Walker's new generals, a man named Hornsby. Calling upon the soubriquet of affection Mr. Walker's enlisted men have given him, General Hornsby stunned the gathering by offering a toast to "Uncle Billy," at which many were afraid the president would take offense. Instead, the toast occasioned an event which it was claimed is the rarest that many who have served with Mr. Walker from the beginning of his expedition had ever witnessed: Mr. Walker laughed. . . .

PART
FOUR

HON. JOHN WHEELER

HONEYFUGGLERS, my friends. Word-splitters, politicians without a sense of possibilities. And, I am ashamed to say, my countrymen.

I maintain and will support the clear fact that, had my government acted with foresight and intelligence, William Walker would not have been forced to take the course of action he embarked upon after his ascent to the presidency of Nicaragua. First, had my government put itself squarely behind General Walker's mission from the beginning, the native element would not have been so emboldened as to rise up in insurrection against him, and he would not have found it needful to seek the presidency of the country at all. It was not necessary that he be president: with the authority of thirty million American citizens behind him, he could have regenerated Central America as an influence alone. But when he saw the straits in which he would find himself had he not assumed absolute power, he had no choice but to embrace that power, for the good of his men and the American element's progress and safety.

Now, I was fully aware when I went to him after the inauguration, and passed on the glad news that Washington had recognized the government of Nicaragua, that Secretary of State Marcy had extended his recognition without the knowledge that General Walker had assumed the presidency. But on the one hand, I had frequently been admonished simply to act as an agent of my government, and to take no initiative in interpreting my instructions. And yet, when I did obey the letter of my instructions and recognized General Walker's government, I was blamed for *not* interpreting the minds of my superiors. And when the recognition I extended was withdrawn upon the arrival in Washington of the news that Patricio Rivas was no longer president of Nicaragua, who was left in the most embarrassing position?

Honeyfuggling, my friends, and although I question the wisdom of President Walker's response, I assign him no blame for it. He had, in effect, been declared an outlaw by the government of his native land, and had no recourse but to seek support elsewhere—as he did, in the following manner.

His first step was natural: to turn to his ancestral land, England. He sent a Cuban named de Goincoura with a letter to Her Majesty's Government begging recognition and repudiating the notion that he sought any ties with the United States. Unfortunately, de Goincoura disobeyed his instructions and stopped in New York to confer with Commodore Cornelius Vanderbilt, for whom it had long been suspected he was a cat's-paw. Vanderbilt, a man without principle, offered a loan of one-half million dollars to President Walker's government if President Walker would betray his friend Edmund Randolph and return the Transit Route to his control. Furthermore, Vanderbilt presented what purported to be proof that Mr. Randolph stood to make a fortune from the new ownership of the Transit Route.

Now, even though I personally begged President Walker to consider Vanderbilt's offer, I knew that he would not. He understood clearly that Vanderbilt was attempting to buy him, and that the honor of his closest friend was being sullied. Perhaps he was intemperate in dismissing de Goincoura from his government and challenging him to a duel—but is intemperateness in defense of honor a fault? I am convinced, as are many other Southern men such as I, that a war between the South and the North is inevitable. If it comes, will we be intemperate to defend our honor and interests with the forthright forcefulness William Walker has taught us?

I find dishonor only in de Goincoura's actions in publishing President Walker's letter to the British. It was a cowardly act, the act of a man who cannot defend himself by arms. He was fully aware that once the New York newspapers were in possession of that letter, they would not rest until they had painted President Walker as a double-dealer and traitor to his native land. But if President Walker called Americans an "unworthy, psalm-singing lot," had we not proved ourselves to be just that?

It may well be remembered by history that the collapse of support for the Walker regime in the North, because of the publication of that letter, was the most fortuitous event of his career; for did it not drive him back into the arms of his native South, where there were many willing to come to the aid of a man who repudiated any ties with a government such as disgraced Washington at that time?

How quickly does the idealism of youth learn who its true friends are when faced with the perfidy of the self-serving world! It is my personal feeling, though I had made many friends among the better class of Nicaraguans, that President Walker's next actions were absolutely correct, given his circumstances. Cut off from the support he merited, his one hope was to increase the American—and particularly Southern— influence in Nicaragua as quickly and thoroughly as possible. His decree that all legal documents would be equally valid in either English or Spanish was the first step to this goal; the second was his decree that all titles to land had to be recorded properly. The unfamiliarity of the native populace with either English or the recording of titles meant, of course, that the American element suddenly experienced an enormous advantage in the acquisition of land and property, in a wholly legal manner. President Walker's sound schooling in American law served him well, my friends, and I recommend such a background to any young man who would seek his fortune in this world.

That he further alienated the property-owning class of the native populace by those decrees was unavoidable. Yet the Indians and the poor of Nicaragua were bound ever more fastly to him. It was not they who owned estates and property. To them he remained a true revolutionary and liberator. Well did they realize that their lot would be improved immeasurably under American masters, with the American sense of decency and fair play to protect them. And there William Walker remains fixed in my own mind, a true revolutionary and liberator—in spite of the distortions that have since been spread about his further decrees—but of those I cannot speak, since I was not a part of them. My recall to Washington a short time after the incident of my extending recognition to his government prevented me from playing any further role in Nicaraguan history.

Yet let me share a dream with you that William Walker shared with me after his assumption of the presidency of Nicaragua. Imagine a great American-led, Anglo-Saxon empire, my friends, extending from South America through the entire isthmus of Central America, reaching into the Caribbean to embrace Cuba, and eventually moving north through all of Mexico to the border of the United States itself. Is it not a grand and noble dream? Do not we in America, who have been so smiled upon by the Creator, deserve the right to dream it?

It was William Walker's dream. It remains my dream still. If the government I represented has not the capacity to dream it with us, then I say let war come between the South and the North. Let us create a government which knows its own interests, which dares to dream with us. Let us unfetter our William Walkers, that they may lead us into the future!

IT WAS REALITY, I believe, that came between William Walker and myself at last. Now that's an easy word to use, and you may think I mean that Walker was mad if I say he and I didn't live in the same world, but he wasn't. In some ways, he was the sanest man I had ever known, because he had a vision of the way things ought to be that he held on to through everything. No, it was not that vision which was at fault; it was all the steps he took on his way to it that got him lost in the darkest part of the woods.

I don't know just when I began to pull away from him, but I'll tell you a day and a time when I first realized for a fact that a great gulf had become fixed between us.

It was after that second battle of Rivas, when the Costa Ricans had left the city to the rats and the cholera. It had been a terrible time for me. All during that battle I had run from wounded man to wounded man, often having to use my revolver to kill one man in order to get to another, and I had to save men according not to their wounds, but to the color of their skin. When we came back to Granada, I sat alone for a full day before I even began to be able to think of sleep.

And as we watched and waited for the cholera to do its work, my imagination would not leave me in peace. Each night I could see in my mind the nearly abandoned city, the rats gnawing at the Costa Ricans before they were fully dead, the convulsions and vomiting of men dying alone in doorways like dogs. When I spoke to the general about it and begged him to let me go into the city and show the Costa Ricans those few simple things they ought to do to lessen the death, he told me that the dying was God's will at work,

143

and that he too had taken his turn once at suffering because of God's will and the cholera. He took it as a sign, he said, that what had once been his enemy was now his friend. And he was a surgeon, a man of science!

I was with the first to go into the city after the Costa Ricans abandoned it, and I did what I could to ease those who had been left behind. But there was no hospital and no medicine save opium, and the flies hung like smoke over them and crawled so thickly into their noses and mouths that they choked before we could drive them away. Dante could have devised no worse hell than the town of Rivas during those days.

One day I rode out along the transit road from Rivas to San Juan del Sur, which was the route the Costa Ricans had taken when they fled. The bodies lay where they had fallen in the road; there had not been strength nor will enough left in the Costa Ricans to shove their comrades into the drainage ditches when they died. They were bloated and black by then, black bodies on the smooth white surface of Commodore Vanderbilt's road. The stench seemed to wilt the very leaves on the trees. They had been peasants, farmers on other men's lands, who found no better deaths than they had lives. If Americans brought them this road, the marvel of Central America, had not we also created these bodies to lie on it? Was that our mission, then? Was that our progress?

That was the first time I knew how wide the gulf was. Those bones and those bodies, the things my nose and eyes told me, were my reality. And I realized that General Walker hardly saw them, that the things his nose and his eyes and his heart told him were no more than shadows in a cave to him.

No, he hadn't caused the cholera: I suppose God might have been responsible for that after all. But what General Walker refused to see—and I tried to say it to him—was that all those men would have been at home with their families instead of swelling by the roadside if we hadn't been in Nicaragua. Before, I had been able to let myself be convinced that we had come to stop the killing. Now I couldn't—but General Walker wouldn't even *see* the killing.

Things had not gone well for us, in spite of the inauguration. We were living off the foraging parties of Rangers that went out into the countryside to round up what beeves and vegetables they could for us. Some may have told you that the inauguration of William Walker was a very great moment in his life. It was; but he was also becoming desperate. I was a watcher of things, remember, and there was nothing I watched more closely than William Walker. As he formed his Cuban bodyguard that surrounded him everywhere he went, as he got freer and freer with the executions of those who opposed him, as he resorted to lawyers' tricks to get the land away from the people who owned it (but didn't give it to the poor, mind you), and as he courted the slavers who came down from New Orleans and Savannah to look the country over, I recognized him less and less.

A little over a month after his inauguration, he sent one of his Cuban bodyguards to ask me if I would go for a walk along the beach of the lake with him. We walked along the gray sands just at evening, with his bodyguards a dozen paces behind us, when the lake was turning from its afternoon blue to its nighttime black. He began by talking of the usual things—the treatment of a tropical disease we had not encountered before, the state of our medical supplies—and then he began to talk about things he seldom brought up with me. It was almost as if he were making an argument for himself and not for me at all. He told me how disappointed he was that the rest of the world had not recognized his achievement, and how frustrated he was in his plans to get the natives in Nicaragua to increase their production on the land as they ought to. It was in the race, he said, the fault of mixing the Spanish and the Indian races so that the best parts of both were lost. Then he switched subjects, and talked of a woman he had known in New Orleans and had been engaged to. To this day I don't understand fully why he brought her into the talk, although by then I had come to be used to his talking not to me, but right through me.

"I have always detested slavery," he said suddenly.

"I know that, sir," I answered, and I waited for him to go on, but he didn't.

We walked awhile longer, the lake turning blacker and blacker beside us. Coconut husks and watermelon rinds washed up in the gray froth the waves threw onto the beach. "All things evolve," he said finally. "Are we agreed on that?"

"We are."

"Civilizations do not spring forth full grown."

"No," I said.

"You should be proud of your race, Guy. I see nothing mixed in you."

"Not that I know of, sir."

"It's just that, just the mixing that cannot be gotten around."

"So I've heard," I said.

"We have a bargain between us, do we not—your race and mine?"

"What might that be, Mr. President?"

"What your race has given mine is the means to pursue liberty and order. What mine has given yours is comfort, civilization, Christianity. I think that is a fair bargain."

"If that's the bargain, sir, it could be considered fair."

He stopped and stared away at some girls who were coming up from the lake waters with bundles of laundry on their heads. "There is a war building in the United States," he said after a time. "The South has no place to expand. There may be only one man on earth who can avert the horror of

146

that war. Only one man who can give the South a place to grow toward. Is there a nobler aim, Guy?"

"If that's the aim, sir, it is a noble one."

"The world will evolve beyond slavery someday, I'm convinced of it. But it hasn't yet. I must have a dependable labor force, Guy. I must have investment from the United States. I have no place to turn but to the South. Do you understand me?"

"I do, General."

"There is no place to begin but at the beginning. It is the primary form of the crystal we must change, not just the secondary. A civilization can't evolve beyond slavery until it first has slavery—that's the paradox."

"It is a paradox. Nonetheless, I'm pleased there's no slavery in Nicaragua."

"You will always be a free man, Guy. I want you to know that."

"I don't imagine you heard me, sir."

His eyes were huge in the dimness. "There has been no slavery in Nicaragua," he said.

"I beg you, General, don't do it."

He walked away from me toward the shadows of the forest alongside the beach, and in his black suit I lost him for a moment. "The decree is drawn. I intend to issue it tomorrow. I wanted you to know first."

And yet even after that, I stayed. I had gotten into the habit of hope. Do not blame me. Perhaps I did think of myself a little as a white man then, as the natives did, and since Walker had no time to actually bring in slaves before the end, I allowed myself to believe he truly might not. Would he have? I cannot say. I would have to understand William Walker to tell you that, and after that evening on the beach, I realized how impossible that would ever be. I think he was becoming who he was every minute I knew him, much more so than most men, and who he was at the very end, I have no way of knowing. But I can tell you this much: by the time we came back into Granada that night before he legalized slavery in Nicaragua, I was beginning to understand that what mattered far more than who he was was what he stood for. That's what fixed the gulf, though I was not man enough to act yet.

But I wanted to hold on to the hope so hard, so hard. I had found it no place else. Do not blame me.

WILLIAM WALKER

THAT POET Whitman I worked with on the newspaper in New Orleans was wrong, Guy; he perceived the perfect beauty of Democracy, but he confused it with the perishable flesh of man. Democracy is beautiful because it is a system. It transcends. It does not depend upon one mortal creature, or even upon many. Whole populations may perish, and the system will remain. This is the true paradox: only out of ugliness may beauty arise. The Greeks stood on the shoulders of slaves as they reached toward the firmament of perfect truth and beauty. From the corruption and death of war arose the American state. That loveliest of poems, the "Marseillaise," demands our acceptance that even the most tranquil fields must run red with blood before the beauty of the Rights of Man may bloom.

It is a further paradox, I recognize, that in order to save the people of Central America from their own base and imperfectly developed natures, it was necessary that Walker allow many of them to perish. We must believe that God forgave and understood, for we never lost sight of our ends.

Walker knew that only through passionate adherence to his eventual goal could his destiny be realized, that solely with a vision of ultimate perfection can man ever hope to approach the condition of God. Surely God understood.

The enemy was mortality: Guy Sartain, you of all men, a surgeon, should know mortality! Walker had to hurry. He was thirty-two years old. Alexander of Greece was dead by Walker's age. Keats was dead long before he was as old as Walker. Shelley was dead. Christ our Lord was in the fullness of his mission. There was no choice. Walker knew that in time, progress in the sciences would make slavery a thing of the past everywhere. He prayed so, for he loathed it. But not yet, not yet . . .

Walker never loved power, Guy; they lie who say he did. He understood simply that without power there can be no change, that we will be forever trapped by who we are.

TALMEDGE WARNER

AFTER THEM Costa Ricans turned and run back home, things was all right for a while. We still had hold of the best pieces of the country, but there wasn't a day gone by we didn't realize we wasn't cocks of the walk no more. Every time a company of Rangers would go out on foraging duty, they'd come back with the news that they'd run into a greaser patrol and like as not had lost a man or two. We didn't eat as good as we had, and whatever we got was grudged us. I don't doubt you've heard them stories the natives put out about us setting around in swallowtail coats and drinking champagne and eating quail ever night (let alone the stories that had us eating babies!). Beans and beef, it was, and fresh vegetables only if we was lucky. Better than some of us was used to, I grant you, but it was a poor man's war, ever step.

Most of us had it in mind that after Uncle Billy changed the laws for people to bring their niggers in, we'd see some things start happening. Not that me and the boys figured niggers would do none of us much good, since we didn't have the money to buy any. We figured the best we could do was marry native women with lots of brothers and hire on some *peones*—which wasn't as good as niggers but would do—if we ever got our land. But we expected things would get rolling in general.

You know what, though? I reckon we was just like field niggers to a lot of them rich people: if once we got the weeds cleared and all the snakes drove out, then they'd come down and plant their grass.

Anyway, come September, we organized us an expedition. See, there was this one hacienda called San Jacinto, up in the hills past a town called Tipitapa, where the greasers had done something we just couldn't let go by. A company of Rangers had been out foraging some cows there and these enemy greasers was holed up in the hacienda house and seen them at it. There was more than a patrol of them that time, we knew for a fact, because they tore into the Rangers so hard our boys had to run.

When we heard about it back in Granada, we was right upset. We wasn't used to running. Too, it was near about the end of the rainy season and we was tired of setting around, so a bunch of us went and asked Uncle Billy if we could go to San Jacinto and run them greasers off. Uncle Billy said yes, and that we could take sixty volunteers, since there couldn't be more than two or three hundred greasers to deal with. Word got out what we was up to, and half the Phalanx volunteered, seemed, so we had our pick. We decided we'd make a regular holiday out of it, and let some of the civilians come along who'd been pestering us to see some fighting. We thought so little of it, in fact, that we passed over Captain Holdich and Captain Henry and elected this man named Byron Cole to head us up. He hadn't seen much action, since he was a real easygoing sort who was better at telling stories and running off to San Francisco to get contracts signed than he was at soldiering. Uncle Billy had made him a major. But he was really a civilian and everybody liked him so we figured we'd let him have a shot at it.

I recollect it was still raining when we started up into the hills out of Tipitapa, the rain a-hissing and a-dripping in the trees around us, and a-running in a steady stream from my hat brim down onto the pommel of the flat Nicaraguan saddle we used. Behind us, the land was all in woods, and we could see it through the rain rising dense as the dark up to this volcano, that set and sent steam up into the clouds. The early morning air felt cool and good to me, even though my britches was wet and sticking to my legs. The road was climbing up from this low swampy place between the two big lakes, where there was ceiba trees arising up out of the swamps so tall and so covered with Spanish moss that I thought they looked like old-time prophets out of the Bible, reaching up to touch that red sunrise.

There in the hills was where it reminded me of Kentucky or Tennessee, and ever now and again we even came across a wood farmhouse with a great broad porch across the front of it like back home. But mostly there was nothing but these little mud huts alongside the road where the *peones* lived, with breakfast smoke already blowing out from the kitchen lean-tos they'd tacked onto the sides of the huts. The wood-smoke, and the warm smell that tortillas has, made me right easy.

"You boys still sure you want a civilian to lead this fandango?" Byron Cole hollered out along the line of march once, when we was a good ways up into the mountains.

"If it amounted to a hill of beans, we wouldn't!" Captain

Henry answered him. He'd done fought two duels that week, and his mood was good. Me and him got along most of the time, except when the mean was on him.

"Where you from, Tom?" Byron Cole, who was riding a mule, asked him.

"Texas, by God," Captain Henry yelled at him.

"How about you, Brian? Georgia, ain't it?"

"Alabama," Captain Holdich said.

"And that Ranger major, the one you boys claim run from here the first time, where's he call home?"

"Kentuck," I said. "Same as me."

"Why, then, there's your problem. Nothing but Southern boys in this damn army. No wonder you need a fat Yankee civilian like me to run a few greasers out of a farmhouse. Give me a pair of Green Mountain boys and I'd have had 'em out a week ago!" He whooped and kicked his mule into a gallop through a watermelon patch beside the road. Captain Henry tore out after him and the two of them run head on in the middle of the melon patch. They went down into the melons together, a-hooting and a-laughing and a-rolling over and over until they both come up wet and pink with rain and melon juice. Two sad natives I reckon the patch belonged to squatted over at its edge and watched with their mouths shut.

"Hell of a way to run an army," I heard a voice behind me say. "Ain't it fine?" I looked around and seen this reporter from the New Orleans *Picayune* that had got bored and come along—Callahan, his name was—a-grinning at me like a jackass eating cockleburrs.

"Ain't it?" I said, and grinned back. I felt better than I had in weeks. We was ourselves again.

We come up to the San Jacinto hacienda before midday. It set back off the main road at the end of a pair of wheel ruts, on top of this little rise. A empty corral spread out behind it where the rise dropped off into a little hollow, then the land rose up so steep and so thick with woods it might as

152

well have been a wall. Only way out was the way we'd come in. From the road, I could look way off in the distance and see Lake Managua, gray still under the clouds, though most of the rain had burned off, and a little mist still hung down in the hollows.

A couple of pickets without no shoes fired warning shots and run when we turned off the main road. "See!" Byron Cole yelled at us. "One look at this fierce passel and they're done, boys." All our spirits was high; Cole couldn't hardly get us to shut up long enough to make a plan. The civilians was worse than schoolboys, giggling and poking at each other, trying to pretend they wasn't worried.

We tied the mules and the horses near the main road and went crouching through the grass, which was high as your waist, until we could get a good look at the house. It wasn't much, this long white adobe building with a thatched roof and a porch that run along all four sides. But them walls would be a good two-foot thick, I knowed, and where the grass stopped there was a open space of maybe a hundred yards we'd have to get past; I picked out what was left of at least a couple of dozen campfires in the open space.

Well, Byron Cole and Captain Henry and Captain Holdich argued out what we ought to do for a while, and the more they argued, it seemed to me, the more nervous Byron Cole got. We'd done wrong, I thought. We shouldn't have never made him leader—we shouldn't have even let him come. He wasn't in no shape for this. Captain Holdich tried to calm him down, but Captain Henry kept trying to show him up and just making him more nervous.

"Like you say, Mr. Green Mountain," he'd tell Cole when he'd suggest a plan. "Ain't nothing but some greasers in a farmhouse. Don't matter."

Finally we decided there wasn't no way to do it but honest John: divide up and charge the place. Come on a-running and a-hollering from all sides with revolvers, which was kind of our trademark by then, and try to scare the greasers so much they'd just set down and die before we had to shoot them.

"Five U.S. dollars, gold, says no man gets to the porch afore me," Captain Henry said, grinning.

"Done," Byron Cole said, a-sweating.

"Done," Captain Holdich said. Him and Captain Henry didn't get on atall, so he couldn't let Captain Henry get up on him.

Captain Henry looked at me. I grinned. He knowed I hadn't seen five gold dollars to bet with since we'd left California.

We spread back through the grass, picking our men. There was to be three bunches of us, and me and the reporter from the *Picayune* wound up with Captain Holdich. Byron Cole started moving his bunch first, since he was going to charge from the empty corral behind the house, and it was furtherest away. He shook Captain Henry's and Captain Holdich's hands, sweating even more, and said "God bless you" to each one of them, and even to me.

After he was out of sight, we commenced to move. We kept wide of the house, to stay as far out of range as we could. Everywhere crickets come a-popping up out of the wet grass and gnats hung onto the little cuts the grass made on our hands and faces. Behind me, the *Picayune* man kept up this low, steady whistling as we went. Captain Holdich pulled us up facing a corner of the house. No use in coming head on into the windows he said. Make the bastards fire on a angle, a-getting in each other's way.

Except for them gun barrels poking out of the windows of the house, it could have been deserted. It was as peaceful a place as I'd been in Nicaragua, and I wondered if I might not talk Uncle Billy into giving it to me once we'd run them off. There wasn't nare sound but the crickets and the flies, and the breeze in the grass and in the magnolias that hung over that old whitewashed house, which set there like it was as much part of the hills and the woods as the limestone croppings on the mountain behind it.

Byron Cole's signal shot from the other side of the rise wasn't no louder than a firecracker. Almost before the echo died away in the little hollow, Captain Henry's shot answered him. I taken me a deep breath. Captain Holdich fired once into the air, and we was running. Twenty yards on each side of me the grass busted open and the boys come spilling out. I give a last glance behind me and seen the *Picayune* man cross hisself and come a-stumbling up to his feet.

As I run across the open space, a-kicking campfire ashes and cow patties, I kept my eyes steady on them gun barrels in the windows. They stayed still as stone. What in hell was they doing, I wondered as I run. Usually they was firing at us before we was within fifty yard of range. Could the sons of bitches have some officers that knowed what they was doing? I seen one muzzle that I was sure was pointed directly at me, and zigzagged. That quiet had done turned into the awfulest thing on earth. I knowed for sure we was in range, even if they had muskets. I run faster.

And then them windows exploded, all at once. One solid volley, and just as soon as that volley was over, the gun barrels jerked back inside the windows and another set taken their place in the blue smoke. Then another volley come— that round, heavy sound muskets makes. Somebody hollered out behind me. I looked down the line of the boys in my bunch; only two others besides me was still a-running. Captain Holdich was on his belly and flagging me down to the dirt with him like I was a steam engine. At least half a dozen of us was hit and a-bleeding. I looked off to my left and seen only Captain Henry still on his feet and a-moving.

Another set of barrels slid out into the windows. The two boys of my bunch who had still been a-running with me seen them and dove for the ground, but one of them was too late. A ball flipped him over on his side in midair.

And over to my right by the corral, I seen Byron Cole go sinking down to his knees, slow as a barge on a reef.

"Take the wounded," Captain Holdich yelled between volleys. I scuttled around on my belly and seen the *Picayune* man a-setting spraddle-legged on a cow pattie. He was holding his gut, and his hands was bloody.

"Git down," I hollered and made for him on all fours. The man looked at me like I'd no more than asked him for a light. He wasn't hardly no older than I was, with this scraggly goatee and mustache and thin hair that he wore long and pulled back like a Frenchman. When I got to within a yard of him, he looked back down at his gut.

"Confound," he said.

In the next volley, I seen pieces of his ear fly off toward the grass, and he toppled backwards. I stopped a few seconds by him, then crawled on ahead. When I got to the grass, I turned around to look at the house again. Captain Henry was leaping up onto the porch, all by hisself. He slapped it, like he was a-touching base in hide and seek, then crouched and run back toward his boys.

We got to the mules and horses a-dragging the wounded like sacks of flour. There wasn't no order to nothing. Them what got to the horses first taken them, and the wounded was slung over whichever ones was left. Wore out and out of breath, some of the boys passed me running for the woods. God knows if they ever come out.

At the swampy place just before Tipitapa, we stopped long enough to rip down a little wooden bridge behind us in a pure panic. In Tipitapa, the garrison caught that panic like the flu, and thrown up barricades, a-waiting for all them enemy greasers to come down outen the mountains after them.

Nobody come. In the night, we tended the wounded and got drunk.

Sometime way past midnight, I reckon, Captain Henry

come into the hut me and Captain Holdich was sharing. He had a demijohn of *aguardiente* that was already half empty, but he seemed steady enough on his feet. Captain Holdich and me had been drinking rum—he was good to his boys that way—and he didn't bother to get up from his hammock.

"You owe me five dollars. Gold," Captain Henry said.

"Did you collect from Cole?" Captain Holdich said.

"I'll take a I.O.U. Cole didn't know his ass from a hole in the ground."

"That why you came in here?"

"No. You a college man, right?"

"What's on your mind, Tom?" Captain Holdich was a-slurring his words right heavy. I prayed Captain Henry and him wasn't about to get mad and have no duel.

"I read. I read lots of books on military tactics. I was in that Mexican War."

"You got a drink to spare?"

Captain Henry passed him the demijohn. "I reckon you think you understand these people, don't you?"

"I don't understand anybody." He weren't making no bones that he weren't in no mood to talk.

"If they're like Mexes, then something happened today." Captain Henry said. "They whupped us. No excuses—just whupped us. That ever happen before?"

"Not without excuses." Captain Holdich handed him the demijohn back.

"There you are. That's bad."

"We went off half-cocked."

"That ain't the point. They got three armies a-setting up there a-waiting for something to get their courage up with. They see we can be whupped without excuses—not like down in Rivas—and they smell blood. Mark me."

"Uncle Billy can fix it," Captain Holdich said, and turned his face to the wall.

"You better hope to God he can, son." Captain Henry

glanced over at me like I was his witness. "We started something up yonder in them mountains we going to have to finish. And they's a wad of greasers between here and Texas."

He went out, and Captain Holdich commenced to snoring. The only light in the world, it seemed to me, was the candle stub in a little clay saucer that set in front of me on the table. Up above me, this lizard as long as my forearms was a-crawling along the ceiling and turning his head this way and that to try to see the candle and me. What happens when they stop believing we demons? some new boys had asked me once. Well, I thought, now I reckon we might be fixing to find out. I taken another drink.

RACHAEL BINGHAM

October 9th, '56 Home. I want to write the word, to look at it. If I could smell it and taste it, I would do that, too. I'm going home. In only five days Arthur and I will get on a lake steamer and cross to the Atlantic and go home to New York. As simple as that!

I won't have to think about William Walker in New York if I don't want to—I won't even have to read a newspaper. I'll be free of this nightmare he's convinced us we all have to live in—because it's the only dream *he* ever has.

It's Arthur's decision. (It would have been mine months ago.) His strength is fading, and we're losing the country, and everybody can see it but Walker and his men. Ever since they got themselves shot to pieces at that hacienda, they've tried to ignore the native armies moving down toward us

158

from the north. And now the natives are barricaded in the very next town over, Masaya, which is so close you can see it on a clear day. It's an awful town to take, Brian says, because there's a lake on the far side of it, and the land on this side is so steep it's almost cliffs. But that's just what they're going to try to do—tomorrow or the day after.

Taking towns, losing towns, taking towns back—oh, I'm so thoroughly sick of it! What does it matter who squats in the plaza of some town no one has ever heard of! Why can't they let these poor people go about their business of growing food and raising children and trying to get by?

We're going home. There's nothing left here for us; even Arthur sees that now. I think the natives have actually developed a sense, some special organ, to detect horrible things coming, the way you can sense a storm before it breaks. Our school closed last week. Granada is becoming a ghost town, except for Walker's Phalanx. The natives are slipping away in the night, even though Walker has ordered them not to. Not even his own men are obeying him. Desertions are commonplace, and I think there must pass whole days in which Walker can't find a single man sober enough to give an order to. And who can blame them? He's a president, but where is his country? In these past two weeks, he's given nearly all of it up but Granada and the Transit Route—which is all he claims to need.

We'll go to my sister's farm in Utica for a while, then we'll come back to New York when Arthur's stronger. He wants to be an impresario, he says, and I'll go back on the stage. We haven't talked beyond that—about living arrangements. I don't want to think about that part of it now. I'm going home: that's what matters.

Brian is fit to be tied. He says he's going to do all sorts of things that I know would be wrong for him—and for me. He says he's coming to New York and live, but I know he couldn't do that. We won't even know each other there. In

159

our real lives, we won't be who we are here. At least I pray to God we won't be.

I don't think he ever truly understood how much I hated this place and this war. In spite of everything, I don't think he hates it. I've always told myself that his loving me was all right, because I wouldn't hurt him. That's stopped now. I'm leaving him and I'm going to hurt him. But what would he want me to do? Stay? I know he still thinks that Walker will win somehow. It's possible he will. But dear God, might that not be even worse than his losing? What might we turn into in the world Walker wants to make?

It's Guy Sartain that I truly pity, not myself or Brian or Arthur. Arthur and I are leaving, and Brian could leave if he wanted. But where could Guy go? Walker's decree about slavery broke him, but what can he do about it?

—I know what I would be going back to, if I went home to Philadelphia, he said to me a week ago. —But I don't know what I'm going to find if I stay. I came down here because what I was leaving behind wasn't tolerable to me. It would be even less so now.

As each hour brings me nearer to leaving, I'm drawing farther and farther away from him, at least in my mind. Our conditions seemed so nearly alike here. That's what bonded us together, this place and what William Walker made of us.

I don't deny that I will miss Guy. I've always thought that when a prisoner leaves a prison, he must regret leaving some things, and feel nostalgia for certain people and certain moments.

Yes, I do feel bad for being able to leave when Guy can't, and for simply walking out on Brian. But I'm going. I'm going home.

Tuesday, October 11th, '56 I spent all yesterday packing, and part of this morning. People are still leaving the city in droves. I hear the sounds, and I think of Paris during the Terror. They're taking their cats with them, and rats are moving into the vacant houses. Leaving is in the air like the smell of the jasmine that's blossoming all over the city. Two more days and we'll be on a ship again, pointing north, with the sound of English around us.

The Phalanx left today, pointing north, too. Walker took almost the entire Phalanx with him, nearly eight hundred men, and left only two hundred—mostly civilians—here in Granada. It's as if he were Richard the Lion Hearted going off on a crusade—he's called all his garrisons in from every part of the country he still controls. I don't think there have ever been so many of his men together at one time before. He made a speech before they left and told them that, man for man, they were the finest fighting force on earth. I pray that he's right. They say that there are at least two thousand natives waiting for them behind barricades in Masaya.

Two days. Please, God, let them hold them off only two days.

Tuesday afternoon I put aside the packing long enough this morning to go and watch the Phalanx march out of the city. Brian was with them, and Guy. It might be my last chance to see them.

In the Jalteva section of the city, where the Indians live, there's a ruined church, and I climbed the church tower to watch from. The morning was fine, with the lake white-capping behind me and the green fields and groves and forests sending up a light, cool mist over the land. (I'll miss that, too, truly.) The head of the column, with all its drummers, was already past by the time I reached the top of the tower,

161

but I could see the new flag that Walker has designed flapping alongside his horse. He was almost hidden by it. It's a red star with five points, and each point is supposed to be one of the countries of Central America—for his "confederation." I believe that somewhere in that labyrinth of a mind he actually believes he's off to fight a battle today that will give him control over all of Central America!

As the column passed along the muddy road through the Indians' huts, I listened to the sounds and smelled the odors that have become my life here. Are there other smells, other sounds in the world? I no longer remember.

I heard the drums, and the squealing flutes, the mules braying, the supply carts rattling, couriers galloping, the heavy rumbling of the artillery carriages, the shouts of the officers (I tried to pick out Brian's voice, but they all sound alike giving orders) as their men changed from their high-stepping city march to a route march for the road. I thought I could smell the leather and the gun oil and the gunpowder and the sweat and the mule droppings. I wanted to imagine I could smell the jasmine, too, but I couldn't.

Walker's mounted Rangers pranced by, singing, then his First Rifles, his veterans, and I recognized the faces of only a few of his original "Immortals" among them. Then came Walker's Cuban bodyguard as bright as macaws in the most bizarre collection of uniforms. Then the Second Rifles (see, I know them all—how many parades have I watched here?) with Tom Henry leading them, his head in a bloody bandage from another duel. He was carrying a flag that looked as if he'd cut it out himself: Five or None, it said. Then Hornsby —General Hornsby now—grim as ever, at the head of two infantry battalions or companies or whatever they are— mostly new men, shuffling and afraid. And like street sweepers, a dozen Rangers came along at the rear to lash stragglers back into line. I could see the tops of their heads as they passed, their hats all stained with sweat and grease.

I watched Brian, riding up beside Walker, until he was out

of sight among the trees. Brian's shirt was as blood red as Walker's new flag, but Walker was no more than a black dot.

Tuesday evening We've waited all day for the sound of the artillery, but it hasn't begun yet. Arthur is convinced something has gone wrong. The artillery should be the first thing we hear, since it's Walker's pride now. I don't really care about Walker's pride; what this evening means to me is that we're a day closer to leaving. If I keep writing, can I write the cold knot out of my stomach? Can I make this last night—this final waiting—end more quickly?

The artillery and "the illustrious Henningsen." How might I speed the night with him? I suppose he'll do as well as anything might. His coming is the only good thing anyone has been able to find to say about these past weeks. He showed up on a chartered steamer the very day of the idiocy at the hacienda at San Jacinto, and he had with him—according to the *El Nicaraguense* I have here—"several thousand Minié rifles, mortars, mountain howitzers, powder, exploding shells, copies of his two latest books, a black servant, a hunting dog, and a pet honey bear named King Carlos," who rides his shoulder. He says he was sent down by his wife, who is the neice of a senator from Georgia, and by a man named George Law, who runs the steamship and railroad route through Panama. Law apparently would like to get around both Cornelius Vanderbilt, and Morgan and Garrison, and wind up with the Transit Route himself. As best I've been able to make out, Henningsen's wife doesn't care who winds up with what, as long as her husband does something glorious again.

Henningsen is a handsome, round-faced man in his early forties, at least six feet tall. His best recommendation seems to be that he loves both war and Lord Byron as much as Walker does. Arthur has read one of his books, about an uprising he was in against the Czar, and I think he stands a little in awe of him. Even Hornsby, who brags that the only book he's ever read is the Bible, has heard of him. The women here have been fighting to be invited to dinner when it's known he's going to be there. And yes, I'll admit, he *is* an impressive man, for his type.

Even the men have warmed to him. He tells stories in that British English of his about how he was in the Carlist revolution in Spain when he was nineteen, or about fighting Cossacks, or how he was with Kossuth when Kossuth fled Hungary, and they listen like children. Almost as soon as he stepped off his ship, Walker made him a general, and he set out to train the men with the new rifles and cannons that he brought. I heard Tom Henry admit at dinner after Henningsen had been here only a week that he knew more about war than any man in Nicaragua. I can't imagine Tom Henry giving anyone a higher compliment—for what that's worth.

The black mood Walker had been in lightened slightly with Henningsen's arrival. I've seen him at all hours with Henningsen in the fields at the edge of town practicing with their new toys, firing off the mortars so the horses will get used to them, showing the men how to set fuses, blowing up abandoned Indian huts as if they were doing something grand. When we are home again, I think I will refuse to take a part in any play that has the sound of a cannon in it.

Tuesday midnight Arthur has been drinking less since he made the decision to go home. I try to imagine what it will be like with him in New York, as changed as he is. If he gets his strength back in some decent place our life may at least approximate what it was before. In the world where we both belong, I've never known a man I would rather be with than Arthur. We could talk: we used to watch those married couples in restaurants who sit across from one another and

164

say less than half a dozen words during their whole meal, and we would tell each how lucky we were not to be them.

Will we be able to talk again? Whatever our "living arrangements," I think our life will be tolerable as long as only we can talk.

It is dawn now. The streets are filling with people, because from very far away we can hear the sound of artillery. One more day now. As long as they are fighting there in Masaya, surely Granada will be safe for this last day. I can sleep.

October 14th, '56   Arthur is dead. My husband is dead. My husband is dead.

October 16th, '56   Brian has been more understanding than I thought he would be. Whatever his motives, I don't care. I need what he is offering me. But Guy Sartain has been my salvation. He's been with me almost every moment he can take away from tending the wounded from the horrors here and at Masaya. Walker came by once to "offer his sympathies," and Guy wanted to leave, but I begged him to stay. I don't know what I would have said or done to Walker if Guy hadn't been there. Walker talked of "a loss of his own once," though, thank God, Guy's presence kept him from going into detail. I was particularly glad for Guy then, when Walker was obviously trying to say there was something in common between us, some human bond I should be able to understand.

It has been four days since Arthur's death. Tonight I want to try to write about it; I tried to write two days ago, but I couldn't. If I can write about it, perhaps it will be over, final.

It was sometime during mid-morning on the 12th, the day I first heard Walker's artillery—I was still asleep—when the alarm sounded. Church bells, bugles, rifles, shouting—I ran out into the street with my hair still down to see, and the street was in a terror. A man I knew from the customs office stopped long enough to tell me I should get Arthur and my servants and come to the church on the plaza. We were under attack, he said. The best he or anybody could tell, one of the enemy armies—the Guatemalans, he thought—had seen Walker and the Phalanx heading toward Masaya and decided to do just what Walker did last year: take Granada by a sneak attack while it was undefended.

I rushed back to tell Arthur what was happening, then went to call the girl and the *mozo* to come help me get him out of the house. But when I came back into the parlor, he'd wheeled himself over to one of our steamer trunks and was rummaging through it. He'd found that Navy revolver of his that I'd never seen him shoot, and had it lying on the settee beside him. I asked him what he was doing, and all he could talk about was a *flag!*

—Where is it, where's that British flag? he said. Is it in this trunk—where did you pack it?

I had no idea what he was talking about at first. Then I recalled that old Union Jack we'd been carting around for years. He'd gotten it from the set of some play or another before we were married, and wouldn't let go of it. For the life of me, I didn't even remember packing it.

At last he found it and ripped it out of the trunk.

—I knew there'd come a use for it, he said. Have the *mozo* put it over the door. They wouldn't dare touch a British flag.

—For the love of God, Arthur, I said to him.

—Get to the church, he said. They won't touch me.

He thrust the flag at me, then took a drink from his brandy flask. He wasn't drunk yet, but he was on his way. Then he picked up the revolver and checked to see that it was loaded.

—Do you think I want to bring you home with only the

clothes on your back? he said. Great God, a farm near Utica is bad enough. Do you think I'll let them plunder everything we've got, too?

I told the *mozo* to pick him up and carry him. Arthur pointed the revolver at him and told him to hang the flag over the door or he would shoot him. I gave the *mozo* the flag.

When the *mozo* came back, he and the girl took me away. I could have fought them and stayed, but I didn't. They kept telling me that the Guatemalans wouldn't touch a house with a British flag in front of it. I think I believed them—I don't know.

They put us in the church basement and told us that the last messenger who had gotten through from Walker said his enemies had already retreated to the plaza of Masaya. He was winning; I hated that, but I knew I had to pray that he did win.

We huddled together and listened to the howling and shouts and rifle fire all afternoon and through the night. No one could tell me about Arthur: our people had thrown up barricades around the plaza and were holding off the Guatemalans, or whoever they were, until Walker came, if he ever did, and that's all anyone knew.

At midnight, someone reminded us that the new day was the first anniversary of Walker's taking the city. The others sang a hymn. I didn't.

It was around nine the next morning when they let us out, right after the first of Walker's Rangers rode into town. They'd been within sight of the plaza of Masaya, the Ranger said, but had broken off to come back here when they got word we were under attack. He was exhausted. They'd fought for two days straight, he said, and now they were no better off than when they had started.

Guy was with the first troops after the Rangers to come into the city. Brian was with the rear guard. I was relieved. I wanted Guy to go with me back to the school, not Brian.

I waited for him to see to the wounded, and I forbade anyone to go ahead of us to the school, though several of the men offered.

When I saw the British flag gone from the front of the house, I knew what we would find. They'd taken everything they could carry, and ripped apart what they couldn't. Arthur was out of his wheelchair, on the floor. They had used bayonets on him. The Navy revolver was underneath him. They hadn't gotten to it.

When Guy picked it up, he looked at it and said to me, "It wasn't fired."

But I already knew it wouldn't have been.

I have no costumes now, no money to buy new ones, no family in Manhattan. Arthur arranged our bookings always, and I'm not foolish enough to believe it was my name that made them possible. Shall I go home to that, to charity or Utica?

For the moment this place is calm. I have a house here, and a few friends. I need time to gather myself, to let memories leak out, to think. But I will not let William Walker defeat me; I will not be like the rest of them and have no place else to go but here, no other world to wake up to but William Walker's nightmare.

BRIAN HOLDICH

WHEN GENERAL WALKER decided to destroy Granada, yes, I was there with him. At the time, I accepted the decision just as I accepted nearly everything else he did. I had nothing to compare him with, you see. When you're young, and in a war, very little you've been taught holds, because you have nothing in life to compare to what you're doing.

Here's how the decision came about. Every day then was confusion, and brought us a new rumor and a new panic. Granada became a pest house. Cholera, malaria, breakbone fever, and diseases even the surgeon hadn't heard of moved in. The hospital turned into a rat hole, in spite of everything Guy Sartain did to keep it together. He told the general that in another six weeks every American in Granada would be dead. The Rangers were raiding the countryside for any food they could get hold of. But the peasants shot at them, or joined the Allies and took their food with them.

It seemed to me that the better part of the people I had known were gone away or dead. And to make it worse, the damned Costa Ricans settled their rebellion in the south and got into the fight again. They came up and took the town of Rivas back, which left us totally surrounded.

So the general decided to take a few of us up to Masaya again. And if the first time we tried to take it was bad, the second time was hell. We kept at it for two days, with General Henningsen's shells exploding in the empty air because their fuses were too short, and when we left we knew we wouldn't be back. Half of us were dead or wounded. But even at that, some of the men had to beg the general on their knees to let us quit. I don't think he slept the whole two days.

We retreated at night, and near dawn drew up to rest on the last high spot before the road started to drop down through the woods into Granada. The general stayed on his horse by himself at the head of the column, staring down at the lights of Granada glowing against the sky. He must have sat there like a statue for nearly half an hour, listening to the moaning of the wounded, and the stamping and snorting of the horses and the mules, and the insects that were always with us in Nicaragua. As dawn started to break, I remounted and rode up along the column toward him. General Henningsen, who had been at the rear with the artillery, drew up alongside me. General Walker didn't seem to notice when we reined in beside him.

"Mr. President?" General Henningsen said.

"Yes."

"Is there anything wrong, sir?"

"No, General, nothing."

"It's coming on dawn, sir. I don't think I could hold off a daylight attack in the rear."

General Walker nodded. When he spoke, his voice sounded very weak and tired. "Granada is lovely from here, isn't it?" he said.

"It is, sir," General Henningsen said.

"If I recall, Cortéz first saw the city of the Aztecs from heights like this. When he entered it, his men thought it was a city from the romances they had read as children. One of them wrote that years afterward."

"Yes, I've read it."

"It must have grieved Cortéz beyond words to destroy that city."

"Cortéz was a sensitive man, yes," General Henningsen said.

"But it was a symbol more than it was a city, General. Cortéz had a new order to build, and he had a lesson to teach the old order. If the savages could have taken their capital back, they could have claimed a great victory."

Down along the column a mule brayed, and I lost what General Henningsen said, but it seemed to have pleased General Walker, because he said, "Thank you, General."

"My pleasure, sir."

"Captain Holdich," General Walker said to me. "I'll want you near me today. We'll be preparing evacuation orders for Granada."

"Yes sir," I said. I remember thinking that the dawn coming up over Granada was the color of dingy linen.

170

"You understand, don't you, Captain? You understand why this is necessary."

I was too tired, I believe, to think. I was out of the habit of thinking in those days. "Yes, sir," I said.

He turned back toward General Henningsen. "How soon can you commence?"

General Henningsen thought awhile. "With a decent city plan, I should say in three to four days, sir."

"The city will be ready in two," General Walker said. "Prepare to march."

WILLIAM WALKER

WALKER DID NOT love to destroy. If he had, he could truly have been called a monster. Those who say that destruction is this age's art are wrong. Walker knew that. But if the old, the decadent, cannot be regenerated, it must be destroyed. That is the primary law of nature. That is the great discovery and truth of our age. Those who love this miserable world into which they are born are the true monsters. Walker was blessed with an unlovely body, and learned to detest the things of the flesh. What does it matter if the physical is destroyed—a body, or a city? Symbols, visions, orders of things are the only important reality.

In New Orleans, Ellen and I communicated without even the carnality of speech to come between us. She would have understood what I had to do in Granada. This world was always a shadow play to her, of necessity. At times, I almost envied her her affliction; she lived in a much purer place than even Walker could reach in this life.

171

BRIAN HOLDICH

THE PLAN was this, gentlemen. General Walker would take the government and stores down to Virgin Bay on one lake steamer, and the women and children and invalids would go out onto the lake in the other, to the island volcano they called Omotepe. General Henningsen would be in charge of the destruction, since explosives were his specialty. Most of the men would stay with him, and when the thing was completed, everybody would join up in Rivas, where it was healthy and we could protect the Transit Route. While we'd been at Masaya, the rest of the army had taken Rivas back for what seemed like the hundredth time, so it was once again ready for us. When we were settled there, we'd get all the new recruits we needed, General Walker said, and General Henningsen could send for better ammunition. The allied countries would squabble amongst themselves and fall apart, given the nature of their race. All we had to do was wait it out. It sounded fine to most of us. Anything was better than Granada by then.

At the beginning, we told the men only that there was going to be an evacuation of the Phalanx. So for the first and second days—a Tuesday and a Wednesday in late November of '56, it was—they mostly stayed busy trying to bribe somebody to take their goods and their native women—if they had them— on the boat to Omotepe. But when General Walker got on his steamer and left, we sent the word out: give the natives a day to get what they had together, drive them out into the countryside, then start burning. Commence in the Indian section of the Jalteva, because the cane huts should catch quickly and be done with. Then build barricades around the city in

172

case anybody tries to stop us. Use fire on wood and thatch, powder charges on stone and adobe. Let the priests carry away what they can, then strip the churches. Search the houses of the rich for arms we can use.

And don't leave anything standing, anything at all.

From where I was in General Henningsen's office in the Government Palace, it sounded to me as if one long cry went out from the entire city when the news was spread. We had divided Granada into sections and sent squads out; in the center of town they usually found somebody on the block who spoke a little English. Out in the Jalteva, they fired their rifles and gestured. I think nobody misunderstood.

By noon of the third day, when I went out to make a progress report for General Henningsen—he had specifically asked General Walker to leave me behind, because of my Spanish—the streets were like the New Orleans docks after a steamer puts in. Carters were asking fifty dollars a load, and piling their carts far above their side panels with anything that would move—armoires, portraits, children, mirrors, crystal that made them rattle like milk wagons, and that more often than not broke. Men had to ride beside the carts with whips to keep away the thieves that dashed out at them. All the dogs in town seemed to have gone mad.

The people without carts carried chests, or old women in mantillas and combs, on their backs. Nuns tried to keep whole coveys of children together as they shoved them toward the roads out of the city, where I supposed they would head toward country houses or the allied armies in Masaya. I felt the noise would come near to suffocating me—doors slamming, weeping and shouting, things breaking, mules, jackasses, carts clattering, and now and again the rifle of one of our men to remind them to keep moving, keep moving.

In the Jalteva, the huts were nearly empty by mid-afternoon. The poor and the Indians had nothing to carry away but their old and sick and children, their hammocks and a few clay pots. I reported to General Henningsen that the burning could begin there within the day.

RACHAEL BINGHAM ▏▏▏

November 22nd, '56   I went to his room last night. Brian told me I shouldn't, but Guy, who had already tried to talk to him, said perhaps I would have better luck, since I'm a woman and might say more without risk of getting shot. His Cubans didn't want to let me in, but I made such a racket, he looked out himself to see what the matter was.

I was furious, near hysteria, I suppose, but I didn't care.

—My God, I told him, nobody has done anything like this since Attila.

—You'll be provided for, he said to me, as if I were a wardheeler begging a favor. You'll go to Omotepe with the other women.

—Has anyone asked the Indians there? I said. They hate outsiders. They'll slaughter us.

—You'll be provided for, he said again. He just stood and looked at me with those awful gray eyes, so far away from me I couldn't have gotten through to him with a cannon.

—I'm not going, I said.

—You have no choice, madam, he said.

—I do have a choice, I told him. I have a choice not to let you control my life anymore. You'll need nurses here. My friends are here. I'm free to go or stay where I want to. I'm not in your miserable army.

174

I thought he was going to have me tossed out, but if he had spit at me, I don't think I could have been more surprised by what he actually did.

He tried to touch me. He reached out as if he wanted to take my hands. I was dumbfounded—so dumbfounded I think I would actually have let him take them if he hadn't stopped himself. For a terrible moment I thought, This man is a human being, he can touch people, he could touch *me*; and I had no notion under heaven what I would do if he did.

But as I looked down, my eyes rested for a moment on the cross around his neck, and I think he saw me and dropped his hands.

—Of course you're free to stay where you please, he said.

—But you won't stop this? You're actually going to try to destroy this city.

—Yes, he said.

—Dear God, why?

He looked at me as if he were deciding whether to answer me or not, then he turned back to packing all those endless papers of his.

—I am an instrument, he said.

He left this morning, and Henningsen took command of the city. Guy came by just after to see that I was all right, then went to see to the wounded and sick that they're loading on boats to send to Omotepe. I didn't see Brian all during the day; I assume he's out doing his part in this, like the others. I don't blame him because I don't blame anyone—except Walker. They simply can't see past him. Or they're terrified of him. When they're wounded they call out first for their mothers, then for Uncle Billy. Do they worship him because he's so cold? Is that the kind of god they need?

Now that Walker has gone there's no control left at all. Henningsen simply isn't listened to. Some of the men have started to fire the huts out in the Jalteva before they're sure they're empty. From my patio, I can already see the sky to the south and west beginning to glow.

Worse, near dusk, as they were searching houses for arms, they discovered the wine cellars of the *grandes*. It's not midnight yet, and I don't think there are ten sober men in Granada. They're reeling down the streets carrying great casks of brandy and wine, even using them to light fires with. Henningsen came out with that ridiculous honey bear on his shoulder and his black valet beside him and tried to order some of them to the guardhouse, but they ignored him.

Brian came by at last after dark to check and see if Arthur's pistol was still loaded, and to make sure I knew how to use it. He said he had been wandering the streets looking for sober officers, with barely any luck. Looting had begun. He asked me if I wanted him to come back and stay the night. I told him yes.

Just after he left, my serving girl came to me in tears because she didn't know if her family had gotten out of the city safely. Since I had Arthur's pistol, I felt brave enough to tell her I would go see with her.

The first smoke from the fires in the Jalteva was drifting through the streets and rifle fire was echoing down them from all directions—that and sounds such as you'd expect to be coming from a madhouse. The emptiness was horrible. I felt as if we were walking in Pompeii, where everyone was dead.

Off the San Francisco plaza, by Minister Wheeler's old consulate, we ran across Tom Henry. I thought I might ask him for help until I saw he was staggering drunk. He was standing with a jug of American whiskey in his hand and staring down at a dead peasant.

When he saw me, he gestured toward the peasant and said, genuinely puzzled, "He run, damn him. What you reckon he was up to?"

My serving girl knelt and picked up a silver spoon beside

the peasant's hand, and gave it to me. I showed it to Tom Henry. "Same thing as you are, I imagine, Captain," I said to him.

He scowled and squatted to see the man better in the faint light. "Old 'un," he said. "Past breeding age, anyways. Don't matter."

Farther on, we passed shuttered houses I've visited and gone to fandangos in, empty shops I've bought things in, broken open and looted now. We passed the Walker House Hotel, where all the important people stayed when they came down to look the country over, and where all of Walker's official dinners and balls were held. It was dark, except for a candle in one room, where I could hear the sound of crockery smashing and men singing.

I believe I know why they're drinking. Not because it's so hard to murder a city. After all, they've come close to doing that before. But they aren't just murdering this one. They're raping it.

BRIAN HOLDICH

I KNOW that sometime I found men still on their feet for General Henningsen to begin the work of firing the town proper. The work was miserable: over and over again we had to send details back to refire houses that had only half burned. The men stopped in the streets to build bonfires for roasting the meat they found in larders, or fell asleep in doorways with their torches in their hands. Their faces were so black with soot they looked like minstrel singers; they ate what they could get their hands on and drank water from any well. By the evening of most days, two or three who had passed out drunk at noon were dead of the cholera.

I can't call to mind whole days anymore. But I still see the churches slowly going; first the great cracks in the thick adobe walls, then the roofs collapsing like umbrellas closing and dragging the walls inward with a great *whoomp*. But I didn't have the time to oversee as I needed to—I was too busy pulling drunken men out of the way of the falling adobe. I cursed adobe as we torched and retorched the houses.

I left Tom Henry to burn Mr. and Mrs. Bingham's academy, after we had moved Mrs. Bingham to La Niña Irena's house. That house stood on the street to the wharf, our only escape route if we were attacked, and would be torched among the last. The academy caught more easily than other buildings, because of the books there, and Henry's men cheered it. Mrs. Bingham, who had been widowed in the attack on Granada the month before, wept, I recall. She was exhausted from working in the hospital, and was inconsolable. I'd like to say that no woman bore more than she did, or bore it better, in our entire time in Nicaragua. During those last days in Granada, she was mother and sister to all of us. I don't know how many men died with their hand in hers, or with her voice the last they heard on earth. God knows she deserved a better reward than she got.

And I can still see General Henningsen, his honey bear clutching his shoulder, pacing in his braided uniform under the arches of the Government Palace, bellowing at everyone in sight. "Goddamn it," he'd say. "We should have been done with this nonsense two days ago." Or three, or four days ago, as the work limped along. It wasn't that he was an impatient man, you understand. All of us who were sober enough to think knew that the allied armies up in Masaya had been watching the smoke since the day we began burning. How long they could bear it, we didn't know.

And how long any of us could keep bearing that burning swirl of mornings and evenings, only God knew.

IRENA O'HORAN

I DIDN'T CARE. If Walker caught me and shot me, I didn't care. Some of my friends came to my hacienda the day after he drove them out of the city and they said to me, "Irena, we wanted to bring you some things out of your house, but we didn't even have time to bring our own. The world is ending."

"What's happened to my house?" I asked them. "Why do I need my things?"

"Because he's gone crazy," they told me. "He says he's going to destroy the whole city."

"Nobody goes that crazy," I told them. "*Qué mierda*. Nobody destroys cities now. Not even gringos. Not even that gringo."

"Before we were out of the city," they said to me, "we saw the smoke already. Go see."

That's why I didn't care. All the pictures of my mother and my father, of my grandparents, all the knitting and crocheting my mother and I had done, the bedspreads we had made and the letters I had saved, the dresses I had brought back from England the time I went—everything that made me who I was, *comprendes*? . . . and they were going to burn it up like kindling wood. How would *you* feel, if they came into your house like that, with torches? They might as well

179

set *me* on fire, I thought, so I took two *mozos* and went on a burro home to Granada to save what I could if there was still time.

When I got to the city it was night, and the night was yellow. Already the city was on fire almost to the plaza. I left my *mozos* and my burro and came up along the beach and through some of the streets that weren't all the way on fire yet. Nobody was there who cared to stop me. In those streets I thought I had walked into what hell will be when the gringos get there. Men were leaping in and out of the flames of burning buildings, yowling like monkeys, some of them singing, shoving each other, throwing wine on each other. Everything smelled like smoke, like things charred; it sounded only of the roar of fire and the falling of walls and timbers. From some of the houses I heard mules and cats and dogs braying and howling and barking, but I was choking on the smoke and afraid I would get sucked into the fire by the great wind it made, so I didn't stop. Anyhow, there were too many. I thought of the dog of my friend, Luz Cuadra, who Luz had written me had just had puppies, but I didn't go see, because her house was already almost a heap of ashes.

At the plaza, the fire made huge shadows that lashed over the ground and the cathedral and the Government Palace like the fronds of palm trees in a storm. Past there, toward my house, the gutters were full of sleeping gringos—or dead ones—half vanished under ashes the color of lead, like heaps of old rags. I could almost recognize my city there: I saw the Esquipulas church with fire coming out of its doors but the outline of it still the same against the yellow sky. And beyond it, the big square towers of the Guadalupe, that my grandfather had said reminded him of old castles in Down; then, even further, the trees and the blackness that is always the lake at night. You know what it was like? *Sabes*, it was like you came home one day and there were new people living

180

in your house, and they had pulled out everything you cared about and piled it on the floor and shit on it.

I didn't notice the light in the parlor of my house until I already had opened the door and was standing in the entry hall. So I walked on my toes to the parlor and pushed open the door just a crack. I think I expected to see a dozen of Walker's gringos waiting for me with a cannon. But there was nobody in the room but a woman—a woman I knew. Her name was Bingham, and she had almost been a friend of mine once. She was sitting on my couch, and she had a big pistol pointed at me.

I pushed open the door all the way, and said to her, "I've come to get some of my things."

"They'll shoot you if they find you," she said. "They say you're a spy."

I laughed at her a little bit. "*Sí*," I said. "I am."

"I'm sorry. They put me in here. It's your house."

"*Sí*," I said again. "It used to be."

She put the pistol down on a table and looked at me awhile with her face almost as if she wanted to cry. She was wearing one of my dresses, and there was blood on it. Her hair was dirty, and from the way she stood, I knew she was very tired. I think I would have felt sorry for her if she weren't in my house wearing one of my dresses.

"Do you want some tea?" she asked me.

I walked to my sideboard. "No," I said. "I want some wine."

I poured a glass of *tinto*, and she said, "May I have one too?"

I shrugged and gave her one, then I went and sat down on my couch where she had been sitting. I said, "I'll go soon."

"You shouldn't be here when comes daylight. I'll help you carry some things."

"If you want to," I said. "Are you by yourself?"

"Now I am. Brian will come later."

181

"Holdich?" I raised my eyebrows at her.

She sat down in a rocking chair. "He stays with me at night." She seemed glad to be able to say it to somebody.

"Your husband is dead, no?"

"It's been going on longer than that," she said to me. "There wasn't anybody to tell."

I shrugged again. "I don't care."

"I didn't mean for you to," she said. "I just wanted you to know somebody will be coming later."

I felt a little bad; this one wasn't burning my city. I thought to myself, this one probably has as little to do with it as I do, even though she's a gringa. So I said to her, "He never said anything about you to me."

Now she laughed a little. "No. I think after I'm long in my grave, he'll pretend he doesn't know me. He probably thinks he's protecting my honor, whatever he sees that as. They're all like that. It's an emblem for what they've done here, isn't it? They say everything is anything but what it is, and that makes them heros. It's the way they live with themselves—they keep believing their own lies. Did you see them in the streets tonight?"

I looked at her pistol on the table beside me. "Where is Walker?" I asked her. For a few seconds I thought I might try to kill him while I was there, but I wasn't a fool like Ponciano.

"He's not here. He went away on a lake steamer." She didn't meet my eyes.

All right, I thought, I'm a spy then, and you're still a gringa: don't tell me. I said, "He's too much a coward to watch it. Eh?"

"No," she said. "I think he'd like to."

That surprised me. I said, "I want to know something."

"About what?"

"Walker," I said. "Does he like women? You know."

"If he doesn't have to touch them, I suppose."

"So it's not just me—because I'm Nicaraguan."

"I don't think so," she said.

"Have you tried?" I asked her.

"No." She was not comfortable, I could see.

"But you've thought about it."

She waited before she answered me. "Yes."

"Does he like men then?"

She blushed a little. "I don't know that."

"I do," I said. "I don't think he likes to touch men, either. I think he's afraid to touch anybody, like a priest. All he likes to do is send people to hell. But if he wasn't afraid, and had his choice of men or women—*quién sabe*, who knows?"

"Then perhaps he ought to be felt sorry for."

"Him?" I spat on my rug, which they would burn up anyway. "Do you know why he's doing this?"

"Do you?"

"Yes," I told her. "You know what spite is?"

"Oh, yes," she said. "Oh, yes."

"He's doing it for spite, just that. He knows we love this city. He's killed our husbands and our brothers. And now he's killing our city. We won't love him, so he kills what we do love."

"Some of you love him."

"Who?" I said. "The *indios*? Or my servants? Oh, no. Not even them now. They understand very little sometimes, but one thing they understand very well. They understand Satan, señora."

She shook her head, like she didn't want to talk about that. "Then, why haven't your people tried to stop him?"

"Who knows?" If she thought I was a spy, then why shouldn't she be one, too? What I knew, I kept. I finished my wine and stood up.

She looked disappointed. "Brian won't be here for a good while yet."

"I want to go," I said. "I don't want to watch. What will you help me carry?"

"Whatever you want me to."

"Better a burro. You don't have any strength now." She tried to smile at me, and I knew I had been hard on her. I felt sorry for her then. I think she must have been truly glad to see me; I wondered how long it had been since she had had a woman to talk to, and I said to her, "You can come with me. You can stay with me at my hacienda."

She thought for a whole minute, it seemed to me. Then she said, "No, I have to stay. But thank you."

"Do you like this?" I said. "Do you like these people?"

"I think I'm more terrified of my own people than I've ever been of anything in my life, but I would be lost with your people. And if I ran, I'd be doing it because of him— I'd be running from him. I can't do that."

"Because of Walker? I said, amazed. "Who does it matter to?"

"To me."

Pues bien, I had offered. What more could I have done? No more than I could have for Luz Cuadra's dog and her puppies, *verdad*? I had no time, and everything was almost a heap of ashes already. So I said, "All right. I'll get my things. You can keep the dress."

She helped me carry my pictures and letters and some clothes to the beach. I left her there and she walked back to her gringos and my burning city. When I started out into the countryside, I didn't look back at any of it. God would see the gringos and my city; God would see it all.

TALMEDGE WARNER   ‖‖‖

WHAT WAS we to do? There wasn't nothing to stop us, nothing to stop nothing. Most of us wasn't hardly but children still, and Uncle Billy weren't there to tell us what to do. It was like all that burning and blowing up we done got inside of us, like we was on fire too and we had to keep building the fire bigger and bigger with all that liquor.

But when them enemy greasers finally got their peckers up and come at us, it all stopped. What I recollect is greasers, greasers, greasers, a-coming at us from every direction. Before General Henningsen could send a single man down for reinforcements, they had took this one particular church they called the Guadalupe, on the street to the wharf, and there we was, that city a-burning all around us and not no way out of it but through piles of greasers on every side. I don't know how—everything's all mixed up for me about all that now—but we managed to fight them off until the boys that wasn't fit seen that the party was over. We made charges at them through burning buildings, hit them with grape shot, stood and hacked at them with bayonets and swords, and when we had to, picked up rocks and chunked them. I thought we was gone for sure once when they come rushing in a great mob into what was left of the plaza. But General Henningsen was smarter than they was: he had two hundred pound of powder in the tower of the cathedral, and when he set a light to it, it blowed like ever Fourth of July I had ever seen in the world. Squashed near a company of them like bugs when it come tumbling down.

"No way out, gentlemen," I recollect him saying one evening when we was a-standing and looking down the street toward the wharf, where the greasers had barricaded their-selves in that Guadalupe church. It was drizzling rain, and they had skewered one of our boys on a lance and hung him from the bell tower. We stood there and watched him drip, and heard their officers a-shouting orders, and people singing, and this one guitar all by itself playing some sad greaser song. "No way out," General Henningsen said, "but straight."

"Straight which way, General?" Captain Holdich asked him.

"Yonder." He pointed down the street toward the wharf. "Foot by damn foot if we have to."

"There must be near three thousand of them, sir," Captain Holdich said.

General Henningsen's face was peaceful as a Sunday morning. "Foot by damn foot. The president will see to us when we take the wharf."

When he was gone, Captain Henry said to somebody, "That man's crazier than a goddamn bessie bug."

A-burning and dying and blowing up, a-burning and dying and blowing up—God A'mighty in heaven, wasn't there nothing else in the world?

FROM
THE SUPREME EXECUTIVE POWER
TO
THE GARRISON AT GRANADA

A
MESSAGE

SOLDIERS! Again and again we have been shown the nature
of the enemy with which we have to contend. Nothing but
the love of blood and the cowardly instincts of the savage
can be urged for his repeated acts of treachery and wanton
murder against you. Let then a sense of the justice and
grandeur of the cause in which we are engaged nerve us
for the fulfillment of our present task. Remember that you
suffer and struggle to redeem one of the loveliest of lands
from barbarian rule and savage despotism. In such a case
as this, who would not gladly endure a few days of priva-
tion and fatigue? Who would not undergo some little
sufferings and danger for the sake of having his name
enrolled among the benefactors of the race? Fulfill your
task with honor!

WM. WALKER
General-Commanding-in-Chief, N.A.
President of the Republic of Nicaragua

TO :—HIS EXCELLENCY, WILLIAM WALKER,
General-Commanding-in-Chief, N.A.
President of the Republic of Nicaragua

SIR :

I received today a communication, delivered by a deserter
named Price and an officer of the Guatemalan forces and
backed by a crowd of local civilians, from the allied armies
of Central America. In it, expressed in the smoothest words,
I and my force were offered complete liberty if we would but
hand ourselves and our arms to the enemy within two hours.
The alternative presented was complete annihilation, since
the letter contained the lying intelligence that you and your
entire force had been destroyed at Virgin Bay and Rivas.

I immediately intimated that I would open fire if this crowd
advanced any further, and penned the following answer :—

> TO : GENERALS ZAVALA, BELLOSO, AND THE OTHER REBELS
> AND PRIVATE LEADERS WHOSE NAMES I CANNOT WASTE THE
> TIME TO DECIPHER :—
> SIRS :—I have no parley to hold with men whom I know lie.
> I regret, for the good of the cause, to be obliged to offer
> you that if you lay down your arms in two hours your lives
> will be spared; if not, within six months I will, in the name
> of the government I represent, hang you all as high as
> Haman. Price, as a traitor, I intend to detain and shoot,
> but I return one of your prisoners captured yesterday.

> C. F. HENNINGSEN
> *Acting in the name of the Commander-in-Chief and*
> *President of the Republic of Nicaragua*

I then told the Guatemalan aide not to venture to address
me; that his advancing without being blindfolded into our
lines constituted an act of espionage; that if he had been a
Nicaraguan I would have shot him, as a Guatemalan I would

have detained him, but that my contempt for his chief was so great that I would, if he chose, show him through my lines personally and then dismiss him—an offer which he declined with great pallor and politeness. Having at their request allowed my principal officers to append their signatures to my answer, and read it by the sound of the bugle to the men, I dismissed back the aide and prisoner, and regret the error of having wasted two rounds of valuable ammunition to emphasize my reply, backed by three times three cheers for General William Walker, which the soldiers translated Uncle Billy.

C.F. HENNINGSEN, Major-General, N.A.

RACHAEL BINGHAM ||||||||||||||||||||||||||||||||||||||||||||||||||||||||||||||||

December 1st   Today we evacuated all the sick and wounded from La Niña Irena's house, where they were moved only a few days ago, and they burnt it. I took a few things she had left behind. If I see her ever again, I will give them to her. Tomorrow will be the twelfth day since this horror began. Last night I took what may be my last bath. I locked all the doors into La Niña's courtyard and had Brian pour water from the well over me. In the moon, the courtyard looked as if it were covered with a spring snow: the ashes clung to the roses, the jasmine, the bougainvillaea, the orange trees; they lay as smoothly as a bedspread on the garden seats, the tables, the well. I stood and let him scrub me with La Niña's French soap until I was sure he had rubbed my skin to the quick. The water made gray ink of the ashes at my feet.

Afterwards, we found bread and the last of the cheese in La Niña's larder. I put on one of La Niña's silken nightgowns and we ate in the bedroom where only the finest powder of ashes could come in. I have been hard on Brian. These last days since Walker's nightmare have swallowed us all beyond redemption; he has been good to me. I think he truly does love me.

We moved the sick and wounded a few paces down the street toward the wharf, to the Guadalupe church when we took it back. The men are digging trenches everywhere, all along the street. They're constantly under attack. It seems we are going to literally *dig* our way to the wharf, and pray that we can get word to Walker somehow when we reach it. That's what we've been reduced to—weasels tunneling our way to salvation.

When I went to the Guadalupe church before we started moving the invalids, Brian went with me. Even before we opened the door, we smelled the stench. Inside the scene was like a set for some insane *Faust*. The altar was still alive with all those saints and vines and fruits I've always loved, but it was ripped from the wall and lay in pieces across the front of the church. In the long streaks of sunlight from the empty windows, the floor of the nave was only rubble. Arms, legs, heads of plaster saints, jagged hunks of adobe, pieces of tables, broken chairs—and oh, dear Jesus, the bodies. The unburied bodies of our own men who had died drunk there at the first attack, bloated now twice their size and turning black, scattered along the walls; the fresher bodies of the natives, who had died during our artillery barrage, half dug up by the dogs from their shallow graves in the dirt floor. There must have been sixty or seventy of them sprawled among the limbs of the saints. Over in the corner, a private stood awkwardly watching us, a cloud of adobe dust rising around the body he had just thrown in the heap he had been making.

I put my kerchief around my face and said to Brian, —
Bury them.

—We can't, he said. All the picks and shovels are being used for the barricades.

—If we bring the sick in here, they'll all be dead in two days, I said.

—They'll be dead by tonight if we don't, he told me.

We have sunk into something subhuman by now. I have no more unmixed feelings about William Walker. I don't need to believe he is supernatural, or a priest of the devil, to take in what I saw today, and what I'm likely to see. There is no horror I can imagine in any supernatural world that we're not capable of creating in this one.

December 2nd I couldn't find this diary all morning, and I was desperate. Who else is there for me now? I tried to sleep some last night, but I woke up and found that the two men on either side of me had died. I don't want to sleep again.

Please let the firing stop. Please.

What is Henningsen feeding his honey bear? I couldn't get that out of my head until dawn.

Afternoon— Has Walker defeated me? How little that matters to me anymore! I want it to be over—however it has to be, just over.

December 3rd I can't find Brian. Guy says he's sick, but I can't let go long enough to find him among all the others.

If we co

GUY SARTAIN

I HAD NOT lived with myself well since William Walker's announcement to me during the summer, as you no doubt can imagine. I knew I was a coward. So I had worked as I had never worked before in my life, to conceal myself from myself. And when those weeks in Granada came—weeks that should have existed only in the Book of Revelation and not on this earth—I took them to signify I was being told to work even harder.

I slept an hour or so at a time, most often in corners on piles of dirty linen. All my fingernails were split and filthy; I had not had a bath since the burning began; and every hairy place on my body was infested with ticks and chiggers. I trained a freedman to be my helper, and Mrs. Bingham was my nurse. But no matter how much I worked, the death that infected that city stayed ahead of me. Imagine, if you can, the Guadalupe church that we moved into: imagine a huge room filled with putrefaction and dying, the sick and the well all living together, nothing to eat but our horses and mules and an occasional dog or cat. Imagine the vomiting and the cries of the shot and the dying, the rats, the smell of sulphur that was with us constantly, and no tools to bury the dead with. I was never surprised when someone come down with the cholera or a fever. I was only surprised to find that anyone hadn't.

I think it is the death of Mrs. Bingham that marks the time for me when I can begin to distingush separate events. She came down with the cholera in the morning. She survived nearly a day, longer than I would have thought. There was nothing unusual I can tell you about her dying. She vomited as everyone else did, lost control of her bowels, then of her mind, then passed from convulsions into a coma. Men and women die the same, sir.

General Henningsen ordered that a pick and shovel be spared and that she be buried at midnight in the cemetery behind the church, wrapped in Walker's new Nicaraguan flag. He had a bugler play taps, and an eleven-gun salute given to her. She would not have cared for that. She kept a diary too, which I tried to hide, but Henningsen found it and sealed it for Walker's records. I regret that greatly.

Why have I not mentioned Mrs. Bingham more? And why is it only her death that begins to bring that time in Granada together for me? Because it was William Walker who obsessed me almost always up until then, William Walker and myself. She had been my friend, yes. But I don't think it was until that confusion of days and weeks in Granada that enough was stripped away from me to let me realize I was in love with her. Since living and dying came to mean so little, how could White and Black matter? She was with me always, shooing rats, helping the freedman and myself bind wounds, giving opium when I thought it might do some good, sitting beside the ones I was losing until they died. She was wife to me in the best sense.

And yet in that, too, I had to be only a watcher.

I couldn't tell her how I felt, as I saw her work herself into the exhaustion that killed her. I was afraid to: no matter how little White and Black came to mean to me, how could I know what it would mean to her? She had a lover already. I knew that, even if no one else did. He was Captain Holdich, one of those who had treated me decently, so that I might have hated him less than I would have so many of the others. And yet I did come to hate him.

Just after she fell ill, she asked me to put her cot near Captain Holdich's: he had been taken with the breakbone fever and was in a state of delirium. I don't think he ever realized she was next to him. And by the time he came out of his fever, she was already buried. When he found out she was dead, he gave no sign that he was more than commonly grieved, as the rest of the men were. I expected that he might come to me, at least, about it, but he didn't. I only noticed one gesture: in the cemetery, General Henningsen had ordered the tombstones to be torn up and made part of the barricades, so none of the graves was marked. The natives had buried some of their men when they had occupied the church, and we had managed to steal away a pick and shovel now and again to bury the longest-dead of our own. There were more than a few fresh graves, then, in among the old. One day at dusk, I saw Captain Holdich wandering among the fresh graves, trying, I imagine, to find which one was hers. I don't know how he settled on any one of them as hers, but by and by he stopped at one grave and stood a long while beside it, with his head lowered. It could have been her grave, or the grave of a native he had shot himself.

I never heard him speak her name after that. It was so little he did, so little! And these were men whose world I had so desperately wanted to share, as if we were somehow of the same species!

I knew which grave was hers, but I didn't tell him. I had marked it with a little pattern of stones, so nobody could find it but myself.

I don't know precisely how many of us there were when we finally dug our way to the beach, but we were far fewer than half the number we had been when we started the burning. And when we got to the beach, we still had no letup. Behind us were the breakers of the lake, and nothing but dirt barricades between us and all the allied armies. We ate the last

194

dog, a brigade mascot whose name I remember, of all things to stay in my mind: Warrior. We ate General Henningsen's horse. One day the general's honey bear disappeared too. Before it was over we got down to one mule, and Walker's own horse. We planned to eat her last.

I had little to do during those days: they stretch out in my memory like that gray beach. The men had gotten into my opium supply and three of them died from swilling it, so General Henningsen ordered it thrown into the lake. It had been my only medicine. So I sat and let the rains bathe me when they came, and took a rifle and killed when we were attacked, and watched the lake like the others for a sign of the lake steamer, my hope growing fainter every day that Walker—and not reinforcements for the allied armies— would actually be on it. Foot by foot we had dug our way out, as General Henningsen said we would, and our way back into the ruins of Granada looked like a maze of muddy canals, or graves. We would not go that way again.

One of those gray days, I recall, General Henningsen, his braided tunic ragged and a rough beard growing on him, called us all together and made us a speech. He talked about Thermopylae and Masada, and told us that in the whole history of irregular warfare, no one had ever done quite what we had. Then he told us we were not fighting for ourselves alone: we were fighting for the honor of the white race. It had come to that, he said, a final contest between mongrels and white men. I was not moved or heartened, as he had no doubt intended.

And when at last we saw the steamer moving toward us beneath the great mounded clouds that floated above the lake, and saw that it still had Walker's red-starred flag flying from it, I did not shout and weep for Uncle Billy, as the others did along the barricades. Nor, when the next morning we heard the first sharp sounds of Mississippi rifles on the beach to the north, did I leap over the barricades as the others did to meet the sound. I knew we were rescued, that I had done what was required of me, and that I had justified my place. I had no more killing in mind.

The guns were first to go on board Walker's steamer (which I might add was named the *Virgin*, if you are a lover of ironies, sir) : General Henningsen saw to that. Then, while he sat on the broken wharf in lantern light on a bale of hemp and dictated his report to Walker, we ate; I saw to the sick; and Walker sent a detail of men to fire the Guadalupe church. We heard how the women and sick had put out in an iron launch, half-naked at midnight, to escape an Indian attack on their camp on Omotepe—and I wished Mrs. Bingham were with me to know her choice to stay with us was not such a bad one after all. We heard how our navy, which was one sloop, had sunk the whole Costa Rican navy, which was one brig. Mrs. Bingham would have appreciated that, too.

I hung back, watching the pieces of men being loaded onto the steamer and making a gesture occasionally to help, so no one would wonder that I was not boarding with the others. At last, with only one longboat left behind to take on the men who were burning the Guadalupe church, General Henningsen got up from his bale of hemp and walked a little way toward town. He stood at the edge of the road and looked across at the flames from the Guadalupe, which sent a weak yellow light over the ruins around it, and cast shadows with no shape over the beach.

After a time, General Henningsen bent down and picked up a lance from the sand, and a piece of charred rawhide. He wrote something on the rawhide with a burnt stick, then twisted the lance through the rawhide as if it had been a pennant, and drove it hard into the ground.

He passed me without speaking on the way to the longboat. I had to get close enough to the lance and rawhide to touch it in order to read it in the yellow light. And though his grammar was bad, Henningsen's meaning was clear: *Aquí fue Granada.* Here stood Granada.

I looked up and down the shoreline. As far as I could see in either direction, there was no other light save the burning church.

I recalled that I had once hoped that who William Walker was might somehow change what with each week, each day, each new horror, he was coming to stand for. But now I knew, irrevocably, there could never be a difference between those two things.

Tom Henry was the one who saw me from the longboat. I heard him splashing through the waves and shouting, "Get back here, nigger," just as I reached the trenches we had dug. By the time he got close enough to fire at me, I was already in the first of the trenches and running. Once I reached the charred city, he would never find me. I was as black as the ruins they'd left.

THE DESTRUCTION
OF GRANADA

GEN. HENNINGSEN'S REPORT OF OPERATIONS TO HIS EXCEL-
LENCY GEN. WILLIAM WALKER, COMMANDER-IN-CHIEF OF THE
ARMY OF NICARAGUA, AND PRESIDENT OF THE REPUBLIC

SIR—On the evening of the 22nd of last month I took
command of the city and force in Granada. Your orders
were to destroy Granada, and to evacuate the place, with
all the ordnance stores, artillery, sick, soldiers, and American and native families. Your order has been obeyed.
Granada has ceased to exist.

By the 11th ultimo all stores, artillery, ammunition,
citizens, troops, sick, and wounded were embarked, and a
placard on the high road opposite to the ruins of the last
house of the city, notified that "Here stood Granada."

I regret that this was not accomplished without a delay,
which requires particular explanation in reporting to a
commander so distinguished as yourself for a celerity in
operations which I was anxious but unable to imitate
through unavoidable obstacles.

These obstacles consisted, in the first place, in the confusion and demoralization which arose through the discovery of arms and ammunition in certain native and
foreign houses which gave our men a pretext for breaking
into large stores of wines and brandies, of which the
existence was not suspected, an abuse which I venture to
signalize for your especial reprobation.

In the second place, in the breaking out of cholera and
fever, caused partly by the above-mentioned intemperance,
and partly by the necessity of crowding sick and healthy

together for the purpose of an organization, without which an evacuation under such circumstances becomes on a small scale a Moscow retreat.

There is a third cause, which may or may not have increased the loss of time and men, though on the whole I am inclined to think it did not, but which I have to report as a military incident. I mean the fact that on the third day we were surprised, attacked, and surrounded by the so-called allied forces of Guatemala, Honduras, Salvador, and the Nicaraguan rebels, with whom we fought for seventeen consecutive days. This force has been variously estimated at from 2,000 to 2,800 men. The latter is the enemy's estimate, and I presume it to be substantially correct.

Our loss amounted to 110 officers and men killed and wounded, 40 deserters, 2 prisoners, 120 officers, soldiers, citizens, women, and children swept off by the pestilence; but of those I think that two-thirds would at all events have died if they had remained in Granada. I began the operation with a force of 419. The loss of the enemy cannot be less than 800 killed and wounded. We were informed by prisoners that they suffered from cholera, and pestilence and desertion, and all the natives in our camp were taken sooner, and more rapidly prostrated and carried off than the Americans.

In conclusion, I must state that after the first surprise we neither lost a single prisoner, gun, or arm of any description, except a lance, to which I appended a placard.

WILLIAM WALKER ⁜

HENNINGSEN UNDERSTOOD as best he was able. It was not the plan's fault. The plan was well made. It was only the weakness of the stuff with which he and Walker had to work that caused the suffering—the weakness of those who caused their own deaths. Who can feel with Walker's acuteness the pain of building visions upon the mire of flesh? What more sharply honed, profound suffering can there be than was his when he was told the story of Granada? He had failed. I learned early that it is easy to suffer as does an animal; the spirit alone suffers perfectly. If the swamp of the flesh sucked under the brave so readily, Walker knew that the greatest gift he could give the weak was his presence and example. Even Henningsen, as fine a figure as he thought himself, could not give them that so well. So if Granada was the great triumph of Walker's will, it was his failure, also. The strength of his presence could not reach out across the waters to Granada as it should have. He suffered because of that, and the imprecision of the destruction disgusted him. In his imagination, it had been otherwise.

Guy Sartain hurt him most of all. He had elevated Sartain far above the station he could have achieved had he not joined Walker; whatever he had said about the Negro race in general, he was careful to exclude Sartain from those generalities. He had shown friendship for Sartain, and had protected him. He had expected gratitude.

Walker tried to persuade the Bingham woman to leave the city. He will not accept responsibility for her. Even when she came to him in a rage, he did not turn her away without counseling her. At one point he was moved to take her hands and give her the example of Ellen, how he had begged her to leave New Orleans when the cholera was making a pest house of it. But Ellen had stayed, had made signs to him that he was a doctor and could save her, and had laughed at his fear for her. How could he have then entreated this woman, whom he did not love? He could not bear to involve himself again: he had breathed death so long that it was little more than air to him. To admit that a particular death, a city's or a woman's, still mattered to him would have been fatal. It would have poisoned the air upon which he had to subsist until his cause should be realized. That, too, is suffering.

And how can it be that a man is what he stands for, Guy, and that be taken as an absolute, a simplification of him? Over here a man stands for one thing; there another. What he stands for is as complex as who he is. Walker was his cause, his destiny, yes. But how can he be blamed for the partial glimpses of his destiny, the unfinished arches? Trees must be felled before houses can be built. Shall a man interrupted by treachery in the felling of trees for houses be accused of destroying only? Walker has a right to demand that he be judged not for what he did, but what he might have done, what he would have done. He demands the right!

PART
FIVE

CHÉLON

THEY TOOK me down to what had been Granada with them, *muchachos*, and if they could have put me in a cage to carry me, the *pendejos* would have done it. All the time El Gaulquer was fighting in Masaya, all the time he was burning up Granada, all those other times that I knew my volunteer *indios* could have made the difference for him, they kept me at my hacienda like a goose with his feet nailed down. And then when it was all over, they put me on my horse and dragged me along with them so they could watch me. If it hadn't been for *mi general* Maximo Jerez, they would have shot me and had done with it, I think.

The one who was general of the Guatemalans, whose name was Zavala, was the worst of them. He looked like a rat without any teeth. He wore a cocked hat and had a little beard and enough gold braid to buy a province with, but he couldn't keep his pants from being too short.

"They tell me you know Walker better than any of the others," he said to me once, as we were riding down to look at Granada, and his voice sounded like a rat's too.

"Whatever you want, my general," I said.

"Tell me then, does General Walker smoke?"

"No."

"Ah. Does he gamble?"

"No."

"Does he drink liquor?"

"Not much."

"Well, then. Does he have women?"

"I don't know," I said to him.

"Does he?"

"No."

"Then he loves only one thing, Colonel," he said to me. "The sensuality of power. How can you abide such a man?"

He said that to me because he was afraid of El Gualquer. They all were, every one of them, and I think they squabbled like hens among themselves so they would have an excuse to go home. Upside Down Rivas had to lick their boots to keep them from sending their armies against each other, instead of El Gualquer. If they beat the gringos, it would be because there were so many of them, or because of luck, or if God came down and got on a horse and told them what to do.

I wish I could have hated my general Jerez, but he was decent to me. Even though he knew I had told my *indios* to fire their guns up into the air and not at the gringos if the conscription got them, he was decent to me. That made me feel worse than thinking about coming down to Granada in a cage. But I'm going to tell you something. Only my *indios* truly understood about the gringos. They understood that no matter how many times you beat the gringos, you never beat the gringos. They understood that you couldn't kill El Gualquer, because if you killed him you didn't kill him. No? That's why they deserted and hid from the conscription and fired their guns into the air, not because I told them to. My general Jerez didn't understand that; for all his books, he didn't know anything about gringos.

I'll tell you some things, *compañeros*, so you can know what I mean.

When we rode toward Granada after the gringos left, I remember I could smell the ashes a league away, and when I first saw the city from the hill, it was a black stain. Then, as we came into town, the shoewearer officers who had lived there rode faster and faster. But still, I recognized places:

the walls of the Jalteva church, the street corner where a whore named Inocéncia had lived, a piece of the wall of a *pulpería* that Don Anselmo something had owned. Ay, *Dios*, I thought. Even in this the gringos were thorough.

The further we rode, the more excited the shoewearers from Granada got. They pointed at things and shouted at each other, and some of them turned away from the column toward what I think had been their houses, bawling like women and beating their saddles or their legs.

I had hated that town. I almost choked from happiness that it was gone.

When we came into what had been the plaza, our horses and ourselves were covered with gray ashes like winding sheets, and I said to my general Jerez, "It's beautiful, no?"

"It's still your country," he said to me.

"Not this place, *mi general*," I said.

I kept going through the town, and as I rode I began to understand the first thing that I want you to know about the gringos. My horse had to pick his way around the hunks of adobe and broken stone from the cathedral tower, around the broken muskets, around the black skeletons of dogs. I passed the walls of the Guadalupe church, and rode down the empty trenches the gringos had dug, where grass was already sprouting. At the beach, the sand was full of charred pieces of wood, of horse and mule bones, of scraps of leather and cloth and boot soles. Nothing of the warehouses at the wharf was standing but the stones of their foundations, nothing. *Nada*.

I spurred my horse in a big circle past the wharf and back toward the city, looking for a good clear space to see it from all at one time, and to finish understanding it. I found the place I wanted up by the road to Tipitapa, beside a lance somebody had stuck into the sand with a piece of leather on it. I looked at the ruins of the city, and here's what came to me.

Not just in capturing cities will the revolution come,

compañeros. And not in steamboats that some fat Indian can ride to San Francisco. When God in his justice comes, he doesn't carry treaties with him, he carries torches. Will there be lawyers in black coats at the apocalypse? Or ballot boxes? Had I been expecting all along that the one from the Stories would bring the new day without fire? Did I think that he could make us a new world while the old one still stood? The circle has to come around and close; my mother said it.

I looked at the place where Granada had been, and I knew that everything was as it should be, that this, this was the true morning of the new day.

Here is the second thing I learned, *compañeros*, and this is how I learned it.

The shoewearers and my own Democrats who were traitors kept me with them in the ruins of Granada, with ashes in our food, through Christmas, through the New Year, through Three Kings Day. It was the saddest Christmas I ever spent —without my daughters and my wife, no posadas, no piñatas, no cakes on Three Kings. They kept getting new men, but the old ones deserted as fast as the new ones came. Nobody could make up his mind what to do.

Every week we got news that El Gualquer was getting stronger and stronger down in Rivas. All the ships on the Transit brought him fresh men and new guns. The generals in Granada pissed in their pants, they were so frustrated, and my heart stayed warm. Every time I saw Mendez the Cock beating his horse, I knew El Gaulquer was winning. Every time I heard one of the generals from El Salvador yell at a general from Guatemala, or heard a general from Honduras mumble about asking permission from the Butcher to come home, or a general from Costa Rica wondering why the rest of the Costa Rican army hadn't been heard from, I knew El Gualquer was winning.

And when my general Jerez came to tell me that I should get ready to see my wife and daughters, because we were going back to León, I knew El Gualquer had won. The *cabrones'* great alliance was over. As long as El Gualquer still had the Transit Route, all he had to do was to wait, and grow stronger. And the next time, when El Gualquer burnt San Jose or Tegucigalpa or Havana, I would be with him.

That night that my general Jerez told me we were going home, I went down to the beach with my guitar to wait for the morning. I wanted to tell God how pleased I was that He was the old God still, and hadn't forgotten how to smite His enemies with the sound of thunder and trumpets. I stayed all night, and in the morning I saw what I thought was a vision on the lake. It was a steamboat, and I was sure at first El Gualquer was coming back to finish what he had started. But I looked closer as it came toward the wharf with its flower of smoke blooming up against that pink morning, and no—no, it was flying a Costa Rican flag! *Santos*, I thought, *madre puta*, and I got up on my poor stiff leg to go see.

The bunch of generals and aides and shoewearer *grandes* was so thick at the wharf that nobody thought to make me go away. But I stayed at the edge of the crowd near my general Jerez, just in case. The boat was the *San Carlos*, one of the Transit Company's lake boats with a wheel on the side. The whistles were hooting and everybody was yelling and the Costa Rican soldiers on the boat were hanging over the railing grinning like cats.

Then a Costa Rican shaped like an avocado with a little round beard and dressed in a fancy red and blue uniform climbed off the boat and up onto a piling to make a speech, and all the generals hugged each other like washwomen; and I thought if impossible things were truly starting to happen

209

again, like Costa Ricans coming in El Gualquer's steamboat, like boys turning into rabbits happened, then God and I had misunderstood each other. God woke up with a bad stomach, and everything you thought you had figured out, you didn't have figured out.

Or was it Science? Had the Costa Ricans discovered Science, too?

I tried to make my poor ears, which are cracked from so many cannons, hear what the avocado was saying. He was slicing the air with his hands like he was splitting coconuts, and I missed most of it at first—all the esteemeds and honoreds. But I got closer to him in time to hear him say that he was General of the Armies José something Mora, brother of the Most Excellent President of Costa Rica, Juan Rafael Mora. Well, *muchachos*, that by itself was enough to make me want to spit. Last year the people here were firing off rockets because we'd struck a paralyzing blow against the *cabrones* at Rivas, and this year they were all listening to this one and not a man among them had guts enough to shoot him.

And then he went on about the heroic soldiers of Costa Rica living off monkey shit in the jungles and facing wild beasts and disease, so they could surprise the maniac gringos' garrisons on the river that runs from the lake to the Atlantic Ocean. And how their great warriors, the ones who were grinning like cats behind him, had seized not only this steamboat, but every steamboat the Transit Company had, just by waiting for them to come into the river, so that the glorious allied armies of Central America were masters of their azure lake and thundering river again, and God be praised. And I thought, *hombre*, if they put a plug in your mouth so you couldn't talk, you'd fart yourself to death. But I felt my heart turning cold as a trout's.

And then he brought out his gringo.

The gringo stepped up to the railing of the steamboat, and he wasn't a gringo I had ever seen before. And he wasn't a gringo like El Gualquer's were. This one wore a coat with a collar made out of velvet, and side-whiskers, and he had on a silk bow tie that hung down over his lapels. And he wasn't a prisoner, not with the little smile he kept on his face while the avocado was yelling at us. And when the avocado told us who this gringo was, I thought he would topple off his piling he bowed so low to him.

This gringo, he said, was el señor Sylvanus Spencer, of the great city of New York, sent down especially to help out their holy shitty cause with guns and money and the idea to cut through the terrible jungle and surprise El Gualquer's men and take the Transit Route away from them, which his grinning cats had done so wonderfully. And everything—the guns and the money and the idea, everything—had been furnished by that great friend of Central America, el señor Cornelius Vanderbilt.

I pushed my way back through the hugging shoewearers. I stood and I looked at the water on the other side of the wharf, where somebody's skull was washing in among the watermelon rinds, and I thought, all right, God, you make sense again. And while I was telling God that, my general Jerez pushed through the people and bumped into me as he was doing it. I shoved a couple of shoewearers out of the way and went after him. He was going so furiously I almost had to hop on my bad leg to keep up.

"You should be pleased, Excellency. No?" I said to him.

When we were away from the mob of shoewearers, he said to me, "Pleased? Damn it, there's a gringo behind it again. Can't we do anything but die for one gringo or the other, no matter which way we go?"

"*Cómo*, Excellency?"

"*Mira, mi* Chélon. This Vanderbilt is more dangerous than Walker. Don't you see that? Once they find out it's easier to pay us to kill each other than to come do it themselves, what then?"

"What then, my general?"

"I don't know what then. But I know that I'd rather have Walker here to look in the eye and shoot at than somebody without a face three thousand miles away. That's honest, at least."

He started walking fast again. His face was red. I tried to keep up for a little while, but then I let him go, his coattails flapping after him like a mule's tail. I yelled after him, "We were killing ourselves anyway, Excellency."

He was already climbing up the hill to the gringos' ditches, but he stopped and shouted back down to me, "Yes, but at least we could hope that half of us would kill off the other half and settle something. We'll never run out of gringos!" And he disappeared over the top of the hill, into all those ditches and trenches and holes the gringos had left behind.

I suppose I felt sorry for him, *compañeros*. He was the best man he knew how to be, but he still missed the point. He couldn't figure it out about gringos. El Gualquer might fight his way out of Rivas yet, but it didn't really make any difference. We'd never run out of gringos. If this El Gualquer wasn't the one to do the job, there'd be another one like the one on the boat. The factories would still come, and the steamboats and icehouses and Democracy and Progress and Science and Hygiene. The new day would keep coming, in fire and thunder, and God would still be smarter than one fat Indian. God was bountiful: we'd never run out of gringos.

And that was the second thing I learned. I could go home now and count my cows and listen to the rain on my porch and wait for the next gringos. I would miss El Gualquer, but not so much.

I hobbled my way up the hill, and followed my general Jerez into the gringos' ditches and trenches and holes.

CORNELIUS VANDERBILT

I NEVER MET the son-of-a-bitch. But if I had, you know what I would have said to him? The mills of the gods grind slowly, but they grind sure.

TALMEDGE WARNER

THERE'S THIS picture I can't get out of my head of them months in Rivas. It was sometime in March—the year was '57—and times was right hard. All them enemy greasers had set up shop in San Jorge, this little town on the lake nearly at hollering distance from us. Well, three times we went to run them off, and three times we come back and they was still a-setting there. And there wasn't much left of us in them days—we was wore out, cut up, and hungry, and so when we come back from attacking them that last time and found out we couldn't get back home to Rivas, we could have sat down and cried.

See, a bunch of them had managed to get into this adobe house right beside the road, and they wasn't fixing to let us past. It was the only road, too. Try as he might, Uncle Billy couldn't get none of us to risk passing that house: we just couldn't bear to get shot at no more that day. So what he done was what makes the picture I can't get rid of. He looked

213

us all over like we was the sorriest bunch of scum he'd ever seen, then wheeled his horse around and galloped it right flat up in front of that house and set there a minute like he was a-daring any of them to shoot. I reckon they was too surprised to do nothing, and Uncle Billy taken out his revolver, aimed it at the window, and fired off all six rounds. Then he stuck it back in its holster, slow as Christmas, and rode on off down the road to Rivas.

That's it. I don't never think of Nicaragua now without seeing that skinny little man in that old black coat a-setting there in front of that house and firing his revolver off like there wasn't nobody else around for a hundred miles.

What does it mean? I don't know. There wasn't much else left for him, I reckon.

There weren't much presidential about Rivas. Day and night, they kept a-firing their cannons at us; one of them big twenty-four pound balls would come a-crashing in through somebody's roof and we'd run pick it up and take it to be melted down for balls for our own cannons. Back and forth, back and forth, without no end in sight. We was on rations of mule mutton again, and I seen one man shoot another one through the head one afternoon for stealing his jar of pickled corn.

Everywhere you'd look, there was these leaflet things the natives kept sending to us, promising us a real good life if we'd just go over to them. Sometimes there was this one greaser I had knowed before named Mendez the Cock would stand just out of rifle range and hold a native woman in front of him and stick his finger up her hickey and holler at us to come on over and have some of that, and I know the boys was sorely tempted, because I was. Them natives didn't have no sense of decency at all when they knowed we was down. Not a night

I'd go out on sentry duty that I wouldn't hear something like this:

"Who goes," one of the boys would yell.

"Me," some voice would say in English off in the dark.

"Who you?"

"Charlie Tarbox," or something like that.

"Charlie? Hey, Charlie. This here's Frisco."

"Frisco? Goddamn, what you doing out there?"

"Just a-having me a little snort after dinner. Want one?"

"I'm a-going to have to shoot you, Frisco. You done gone over, ain't you?"

"What you have for supper tonight, Charlie—mule or horse?"

"None of your damn nevermind."

"You come down here to eat horse? Me, I had me a hunk of beef the size of my foot. These folks treat you right good, if you give them a chance."

"I'm a-going to have to shoot you, Frisco. I swear to God I am."

I'd move off down the line, and when I come back an hour later, there'd be not a soul watching that sentry post.

I don't recollect when that American warship come into port down at San Juan del Sur—sometime around late February or early March, seems. We had our own ship out there still, this old sloop we'd took and renamed the *Granada* and had made us a navy out of. Well, the commander of this American ship paid a call on ours and said he was just down there as a observer. His name was Commander Davis, and his ship was the *Saint Mary*, and the first time I seen him was when he come into Rivas to visit the general. I thought he was from the moon. He was this man pushing fifty, and in that white uniform and his hair trimmed up good and a-handing out cigars and bourbon to the officers and patting the rest of us on the backs, he was like something I had damn near forgot there still was on earth. You got to imagine, a-seeing something like that for the first time in near two years, and all it could put you in mind of about home. The rest of the boys talked about it a right smart, but I didn't. Where Uncle Billy was was home to me, so far as I could tell.

He come back right often to see how we was a-getting on, and to check and see if the women and children that was still with us was in need of anything. It got to where I looked forward to him coming, though there wasn't nothing in it for me. I don't reckon by then I was thinking no more about what was in what for me. That piece of land up in the mountains had got further and further away. To tell you the truth, I don't rightly know what it was that kept me going in them days, except thinking about a piece of pork or a fresh orange or a drink of whiskey. But I was a sergeant-major and I hadn't never been no sergeant-major before, and that was something. Weren't it?

There was a woman from Iowa that I taken up with for a spell, sister of one of the boys that had got killed at Granada, but nothing ever come of it. When she got her foot took off by one of them cannonballs, and died of it, I didn't particularly grieve. That business down there by then was a little like doctoring, you see: after a while the dead people got piled up so high around you that your grieving got too watered down to make much difference. There wasn't no joy to nothing no more, but there wasn't no grieving, neither. And I reckon that's where I'd come to. It could have been worse.

COMMANDER
CHARLES HENRY DAVIS ⅢⅢⅢⅢⅢⅢⅢⅢⅢⅢⅢⅢⅢⅢⅢⅢⅢⅢⅢⅢⅢⅢⅢⅢⅢ

I COULDN'T LIKE the man; I don't know that anyone ever claimed to actually consider him good company. He would sit and parley with me, surrounded by that grim crew of officers of his in that hellhole he called his capital, and I always had the impression I was talking to a book.

My orders were not to interfere militarily, but to protect American property and to get as many American citizens out of there alive as I could, if it came to that. In the beginning I confined myself to friendly visits, and to trying to keep communications open between Walker's camp and the natives'. Most of the Americans, Walker included, seemed to believe that I intended to intervene on their behalf, and were clearly disappointed when I did not. Walker disliked me from the moment we met, I am convinced, though on the first occasion I had to actively confront him, he gained better cause to. I brought him two letters that had come to me via Panama. One of them was from the Accessory Transit Company, the other from a man named Edmund Randolph. I opened them, of course, in case there was anything in them that might affect my command. I don't think either of us was not expecting the one from the Transit Company, although I knew it would be a blow to him to see it in black and white. The Transit Company informed him they were terminating their service until the situation stabilized. The second one, from Randolph, was full of a dozen excuses for the Transit Company, and promises that he would see to it that service was resumed as soon as possible. As much as I didn't like Walker, I felt a certain amount of commiseration with him.

217

He took the letters and made as if to put them away, but I begged him to read them on the spot. I say "begged" deliberately. He insisted that I address him as Mr. President, and those eyes of his fastened on me like Medusa's if he detected the slightest hint that I might be trying to order him to do a thing.

He read the letters, and his face remained blank as a slab of marble.

"I'm sorry, Mr. President," I said when he was done.

"The Transit Company is a commercial venture. When there's no profit, I don't expect them to continue service, Commander," he answered me.

"You don't seem upset," I said.

"I'm no stranger to betrayal."

"Damn it, sir," I said. "You've lost your last link to the United States. Whether you've been betrayed is the least of your problems. You can't stay on here now."

"I intend to, sir."

I think I was surprised, and when I am surprised, my temper is no friend to me. "Mr. President," I said to him, "you've been in this town for four months now. You've seen your force fall from a thousand men to less than, I would judge, five hundred. Every day it falls more—not only from slaughter, but from desertions and from diseases that would shame a Turk. Your men are full of lice and vermin to an extent that, frankly, disgusts me. Your hospital is a disgrace to the species. Each day—perhaps each hour— one of your men falls unknown in the mud of this place and is left to be carried off by the vultures. I've seen them! Your officers are thieves. Three times you've gone after your enemies in San Jorge—three times! And each time you've come away with your tails between your legs. Yesterday I understand that an attack on you reached the very plaza of this town. You've lost control of the lake, the river, and every source of decent provision in the country. What do your men—and the children—eat? The British have warships in your ports. It's all I can do to keep them from sinking that . . . *navy* of yours from day to day. And now you've lost all hope of replenishing your supplies of either men or munitions. Do you, sir, mean to sit there and tell me you have no more concern for the lives of your men—or your own honor—than to keep up this damned playacting?"

And how did he answer me? "Pray, sir," he said, his voice almost a whisper, "do you speak to the elected president of a sovereign state this way in the name of President Buchanan? Or do you speak in the name of the United States Navy?"

"By God, sir, I'm speaking to you man to man. Haven't you got the slightest bit of reason to you?"

"If I weren't conscious of your uniform, you realize I would have no other course than to demand satisfaction of my honor now," he said.

I will tell you truly, I believe the man would have declared war on the United States if he'd been in the mood for it. I had told him the truth about himself, and the only way he knew to respond was to challenge me to a duel. In his desperate situation, he challenged to a duel the only man on earth who could help him!

What I got out of that day, though, was at least a partial success. Henningsen came into the conversation, and between the two of us we convinced Walker to allow the women and children, at least, to come aboard my sloop until I could get them passage down to Panama. I had something in mind by that, of course. Without the women and children there, Walker's men would have less to fight for. I don't think Walker saw that; women and children made no difference to him by then. He was past those kinds of concerns.

Against all reason, he sat in that miserable town until the end of April. First he claimed he was waiting for four hundred recruits who were stranded over on the Atlantic side of the country. Then when he got word that they'd blown themselves up in a steamer trying to run the natives' river blockade, I don't know what in hell he was waiting for. He just waited, while everything that he had fell apart around him like a paper lantern in a rainstorm. I say against all reason he held on. I don't believe that applies; the man had no more touch with reason, that I could tell, than a dog does with religion.

It's possible he was waiting for another one of his miracles. He kept telling me about some native colonel in the north he expected to come down with a whole army of Indian volunteers. That was a fairy tale. The plain truth is that William Walker had had a run of luck, and now it was over, pure and simple; but he was like the fellow who sends his family to the poorhouse and borrows another dollar to keep playing. I have no respect for that kind of indecency, no toleration for it.

Right around the first of May, the information came to me that he had ordered his ship be prepared to sail, and told his officers to get the men he had left ready to march. When I sent to find out more, I learned he was planning to fight his way down to San Juan del Sur and sail off onto the seas, like some sort of Viking.

I had tolerated the man's whims since February, and I could stand no more. He was starving and he was running, and I knew that if I ever was going to stop him I had to do it then, whatever I would face when I got back home. So I sent him a message: in two weeks I would weigh anchor and sail for home. And when I left, I would take his ship with me— or sink her if she resisted. He would be as utterly stranded as the crew of the *Bounty*. He called it an act of piracy. I called it mercy. I was his last hope. I prayed he had any reason at all left.

The surrender terms I got for him were more generous than he had any right to expect: the native commanders were well ready to be shut of him. They told me they did not care how he went, as long as he went, for I believe that no matter how utterly I stranded him among them, they were convinced he would find a way to come at them again. I think they would have slept in absolute ease only if I had driven a stake through his heart.

And yet still he quibbled. I had got the natives to agree to let me take him and his staff—with their sidearms—on board the *Saint Mary* at once, and to arrange to send his men back home by the next ship passing. Scot free, every soul of them, and surrendering to me, not them. But he would not take even those terms, if I could not get the native commanders to agree to pardon all his native supporters as well—for what good that would do. As soon as I was out of the country they would bayonet them every one. He knew that, and I knew that, but still he insisted. You could call that decency. Or you could say it was a gesture as worthy of Don Quixote himself as any you've ever seen. Take your pick.

I know my pick. When I asked him later where he had planned to go with that ship of his, he told me north. To a port called Realejo, where he'd first landed in Nicaragua. Then he was going to gather his Indian colonel and march on the city of León. Going to start all over again, he was.

BRIAN HOLDICH

THERE WAS no sun. General Walker stood before us on the steps of the church in the plaza and held a sheet of soggy paper in his hand. I had copied it out for him the night before, just after we convinced him that his final scheme to cut our way through the jungles and retake the Transit Route by surprise was hopeless. He wouldn't have quit, gentlemen, not as long as there was a man among us able to stand on our feet and follow him, I'm convinced of that.

221

The paper he held contained the surrender terms, a short speech, and the last general order I would ever hear him give, though others would hear more. General Henningsen had managed to draw the hundred and fifty of us still fit for duty up into something like a formation in the mud of the plaza. The few remaining native volunteers hung about under the arches of the shops and *pulperías* out of the drizzling rain. As many of our sick and wounded who could be moved, we had propped or laid beside them. The general hadn't slept, and his hoarse voice barely carried to the center of the plaza. I recall one or two of the men were crying, nonetheless.

I remember little of his talk, even though I wrote it out for him. I don't think it matters greatly now. My attention wandered. Off in the distance, thunder was rolling, and the horses the native armies had lent us to ride away on whinnied and stamped. Such things as that I remember more; and such things as the drunken native who sat alone in the mud beside the church with a cloth over his face and held a conversation with himself while the general talked; and the rain that gathered into drops on my hat and fell to my collar and seeped beneath my shirt. I was shivering. I truly tried to concentrate on the general's words, on his thin, black figure against the unfinished church, empty and roofless, whose unpaved floor the natives had made into a graveyard, but I think I had no more room for those words.

We rode out of Rivas at dusk, all the staff officers in formation by twos, with General Walker and the Guatemalan commander, Zavala, at the head of us. The general had forbidden us to look back. None of us did. Peasants lined the road to San Juan del Sur. Most jeered, but a few took off their hats as our column passed, and stood in silence. Some of them held torches, and crossed themselves, as if we were a religious procession.

Zavala went on board ship with us, just to be sure, and the general gave him his personal copy of the *Aeneid*, with all his notes in it. I don't think Zavala understood the general's irony—or, if he did, he hid it well.

After supper, the clouds blew inland enough for a moon to show through. I stood at the rail of the *Saint Mary* awhile, tasting my tiredness and the first stew I'd had in months. The horseshoe of the beach shone pale as a lace collar in the moonlight, and the flame trees were dark, and I thought that from here you could hardly tell we'd ever fought our war. We left nothing useful behind. A few lights climbed up the hills around the town, and I knew the people there were thinking about us, those of them who were still alive. We had left that behind—a memory of us—at least. What that memory is I cannot speculate.

I wasn't far enough away from my life there to judge it, but I knew I would not grieve for Nicaragua soon. I hoped that in time parts of it might wash away in my memory, like stains on a white cloth: the muddy plaza in Rivas that last day, the howling drunkards and the flames of Granada, the stickiness of blood on my boots. Then I might remember the white ceiba trees against the sky, the blue lakes, the yellow and sweet jasmine, the scarlet bougainvillaea that spilled over courtyard walls, the girls bathing in the surf, the pulpy air, the cicadas at evening, the reflection of volcanoes in water. Or at least I might be able to believe those were the things I remembered.

I tried to imagine what Jason's captains might have thought as they watched the Black Sea coast fall away from them on their way home. We were no different, were we, if all Jason's story had been told, as I've told this one? It is the times, gentlemen, only the times that make it seem otherwise.

I want to tell you something now. I have left things out— others may have told you about them, I don't know. If they haven't, then it's meant to be that way. There are things that are mine alone to keep and bear, things I felt down there

that are too private for me to drag out onto a stage for you—
that are, frankly, none of your damned business. Believe
what you will, and blame me for what you want. I'm who I
am, who I got to be in Nicaragua.

I pushed away from the railing and walked along the deck.
I passed Tom Henry and General Hornsby grunting at each
other, then General Henningsen rolling a cigarette and arguing about some sort of statistics with his aide. I didn't stop;
I had nothing to say to them. It was my habit to see if
General Walker needed me for anything before I went to bed.
And I thought he might say something to me that night—I
don't know what, but something he hadn't said before. I
wanted him to—only him, no one else. I considered that it
was owed me.

I knocked at his cabin. A voice—Commander Davis's—said
something through the door that I couldn't make out. I was
disappointed, though not surprised, that they were together.
I waited, then, hearing nothing else, decided Davis must have
told me to come in. I opened the door.

The two of them sat facing one another in the yellow
lantern light across a table. Commander Davis was very
erect, and I thought the look on his face almost fatherly, but
uncomfortable. His arm was stretched across the table toward
the general, but not touching him. General Walker's head was
in his hands. I stood at the door until the reason that neither
of them had spoken, nor looked at me, came clear. General
Walker was weeping.

I shut the door.

In those days, when for a while everything seemed possible,
I thought William Walker was a hero. Now I have learned
to judge things more dispassionately. I no longer draw. I
have sold my father's land and bought a cotton gin. It is more
fitting to the age.

PART SIX

TALMEDGE WARNER ||||||||||||||||||||||||||||||||||||||||||||||||||||||||||||||||||||||||||||

September, 1860   In the beginning, I come to Uncle Billy. In the end, he come to me. It had been right at three year since I'd seen him. A considerable of the boys had took it hard that he'd run off and left us to walk across the country from Rivas like he done, with them greasers a-jeering at us all the way. But I knowed he had to get somewhere in a bigger hurry than we did, so I let it go.

I'd kept up with him, though, as best I could. I was working down on a place called Island Thirty-seven then, out in the Mississippi near Memphis. There was a man owned it had brought in a bunch of niggers to make it look like he was a-farming, but what we was really doing was making whiskey for Memphis. It wasn't bad work, as them things go—just me and the niggers out there, none of us doing much but keeping the fires hot and watching the corn grow. But I wasn't nobody, you know?

I'd heard about all them rallies and parades in New Orleans and New York and such places for the general when he got home, and all them squabbles he had with one senator or another, and about the time he went up to Washington and him and old President Buchanan had sit down and argued everything out. There was a man rowed out from Memphis ever now and again to pass the time and drink some whiskey brought me the newspapers and read out of them to me. Both times that Uncle Billy tried to get back down there to

227

Nicaragua and got stopped by the government, I knowed about them. It weren't right: the American government didn't have no business fooling with what Uncle Billy wanted to do, and I felt right sorry for him. Then when he wrote that book of his about the war, this man come a-rowing out to me with it like I was King Solomon hisself. He said everybody in the world was reading about us, and we set by the fire while he read to me out of it. And it was all there, all the people I had knowed, all the places I had been, all the battles I had fought, all the mouldering dead down yonder a-waiting not to be abandoned. Uncle Billy told all of it, straight as it could be, except that he kept a-calling hisself *he*, like there was two of him. And when that man got through reading to me, I was near to bawling. I was somebody I hadn't been in a long time.

When the man rowed back to Memphis, he was carrying on about me like I was a hero. And I reckon that's how Tom Henry found me.

You couldn't have surprised me more when I seen Tom Henry a-setting in that man's boat a few weeks later than if you had told me I was Saint Peter. Major Henry, he was by then, and he was just as mean and horsefaced as ever.

"Talmedge," he said to me. "Uncle Billy needs you."

"I didn't hardly reckon he remembered me," I told him.

"Talmedge," he said. "Uncle Billy's a-setting down yonder in New Orleans getting ready to go again and he sent me for you. There ain't many of us real Immortals left."

"He fixing to go back to Nicaragua?"

"Right near. This time we going through Honduras first. They's these English people out on some islands there that the British is giving back to the Hondurans. Well, they don't want to give back, and they told Uncle Billy they'll set him up fine if he comes down and leads them a revolution."

"We ain't got nothing to do with Honduras," I said.

"No, no. We ain't a-going to stay. Once we get set up there, we go south. We get aholt of old Chélon down in Nicaragua, and there we are!"

"Reckon old Chélon's still alive?"

"They's other Indians. Don't matter," he said.

Well, I pondered on it, and here's what made my mind up. Uncle Billy wanted to make me a lieutenant, Tom Henry said. Needed officers that knowed the country. Now, I ain't a utter fool, and I said, "How come he wants me? How come he don't want General Hornsby and Henningsen and Captain Holdich and them?"

"They studying this other war that's a coming if that Lincoln gets hisself elected," he said. "They getting fixed to be big shots. Hell, Uncle Billy's still a-trying to stop that war, and they getting ready to fight it. Now which one makes more sense?"

That satisfied me: Uncle Billy was hard up. He wouldn't have sent for somebody like me to be a officer if he wasn't—I knowed that. "All right," I told Tom Henry. "I'm for it."

Well, we got down here to Honduras in August, and the getting here turned out to be as big a mess as most things that happened to me. The British navy got wind of our coming and didn't leave them islands when they was supposed to, so we couldn't land there. Then they got ahold of our supply ship and taken all our guns and things. Then we put in on this other island where there wasn't even no people, to wait the British out, and damn neared starved. But I tell you, I reckon Uncle Billy knowed it was his last chance, and we all did too, so no matter how bad it all commenced, nare soul said to him, "General Walker, let's go home."

So what did we do? We decided we was a-going to attack Honduras anyway. There was less than a hundred of us, and we didn't have but forty rounds of ammunition apiece, but that didn't make Uncle Billy no nevermind. He'd whipped the bastard once that was running the country, that big mulatto they called the Butcher, and I reckon he thought he could do it again.

Here was what he said we was going to do. We was going to take this town on the coast called Trujillo, where there was a cold Spanish fort that Cortéz hisself had built. Then we was going to hook up with the Democrats in the country, that was supposed to be off somewhere in the woods somewhere under this man called Trinidad Cabañas. Then we was going to take over Honduras, then go back into Nicaragua, like we said we was going to. The only problem was that nobody had no notion where this Cabañas and his soldiers was, and on top of that, he couldn't stand the sight of Uncle Billy. But Uncle Billy never was one to let that kind of thing concern him overly.

Well, for a while it went all right. We taken the fort like we'd planned, and figured all we had to do was set tight for a few days while somebody found that Cabañas and his boys, and in a month or so we'd be eating supper in the Butcher's house. Uncle Billy was hisself then—arranging things, writing proclamations, giving orders, cleaning things up. He was like a president again for a spell.

He sent Tom Henry off to find this Cabañas. Well, we set and waited and set and waited, and for four days Major Henry stayed gone. We was getting a considerable upset, especially when we got the news that there was God knows how many of the Butcher's troops a-coming after us, and not a day away from town. We wasn't the Immortals, remember—this bunch was nothing but Southern country boys that hadn't never fought nothing but razorback hogs before.

I was in the powder magazine of the old fort squatted down measuring out charges when Major Henry got back, and I wish to God I hadn't been. I heard him a-singing and a-bellowing before he even got to the gates, and I knowed that whatever else he'd found out there, he'd found him a jug. Uncle Billy'd pitch a fit, I told myself, and went back to what I was doing. See, measuring out gunpowder goes a right good way toward making a man nervous, and if there was going to be any fits pitched, I didn't want nothing to do with them.

Next thing I knowed, Major Henry was a-standing in the door. "General in here?"

"Don't know where he is, Major," I said. Lord God almighty, I thought, the man's smoking a cigar.

"Hell you don't. He ain't nowhere else." He staggered a little bit and taken a step into the room.

"Can't come in here, Major."

"What?" he said, and his eyes got narrow.

"You smoking a cigar, sir."

"You telling me what to do, white trash?" He taken another step into the room and flicked his cigar ashes toward the powder kegs.

"Get the hell out of here, Major."

He grunted, and grabbed ahold of his bowie knife before I could even get unsquatted. I didn't have no choice. I throwed myself at him to knock him out the door of the powder magazine and done my best to get to my pistol. I was scared. Drunk or not, he was the quickest man with a knife I ever seen. I shot him before I even thought of it.

His head jerked up against the wall like I'd hit him with a brickbat. He blinked once or twice, then let his knife go. He looked like he couldn't figure nothing out, then reached up for his cigar. But he didn't have no jaw no more, and when he found that out, he tried to say something but couldn't. Then he taken a couple of steps down the hall, and toppled over his side like a axed tree.

Uncle Billy sat up with him all night long, giving him morphine and sick-nursing him. He taken it hard, though he didn't say nare a word to me. He knowed I'd done what I had to. He let me stay with him part of the time, and the once or twice when Tom Henry opened his eyes and stared up at these big lizards on the ceiling the general said to him, real quiet, "Did you find them, Tom? Where are they, Tom?" But Major Henry's eyes just kept a-staring at them lizards in the candlelight, and then they would close again.

In the early morning, the general and me went out onto the ramparts and watched the smoke rising from the campfires of all these Honduran soldiers that had come in during the night. There must have been a hundred fires spread out in a great ragged circle everwhere we looked.

And by the middle of that morning, there was more smoke. Two British man-o'-wars coming a-steaming into the harbor, moving slow as crocodiles. When they reversed their paddles and stopped they was so close to the fort I could hear their anchor chains rattle and their boatswain piping quarters. Uncle Billy watched them without no more sign on his face than if they had been clouds.

That's how we found out whose pond we was a-fishing in.

One of them British officers come ashore, gleaming like a bugle. There had been three thousand American dollars in the fort that the Butcher had borrowed from the Queen, he said, and he was there to pick it up. The Queen wanted it back and he give us twenty-four hours. If we come up with the money, he'd let us leave on one of the ships in the harbor. If not, he'd come get us. Uncle Billy treated him like he'd been a waiter.

That evening we set with Tom Henry again. I think Uncle Billy give him less morphine this time, because Major Henry commenced to write things on a slate, things he wanted—water, piss, morphine. He couldn't eat—he didn't have nothing but a hole in his face. I hadn't never seen nobody I'd shot dying like that before. I don't reckon I want to again.

232

Uncle Billy kept changing the wet cloth on his face, just watching him, reading them words on the slate like they was Scripture, like he was expecting them to tell him something. We burned gunpowder to get rid of the gangrene smell, and once I went to wipe away the maggots that was eating at Major Henry's face. No, Uncle Billy told me, leave them. They was eating the infection.

By and by, sometime after midnight, Major Henry wrote the general's name on his slate. His eyes was a little clearer than they had been, and Uncle Billy leaned over and met them. The two of them set that way in the light from that old smoky tallow candle so long I thought they was gone to sleep, but presently Uncle Billy said, "Where shall we go, Tom?"

Major Henry studied on that a long time, trying to keep focused on Uncle Billy. He might have understood what Uncle Billy was a-getting at, but I don't think so. At last he taken the slate and wrote a word on it. I seen it, and was able to spell it out. Cabañas, it said.

"But where is he, Tom?" the general asked him.

Major Henry rolled his head back and forth and thumped the name on the slate. Uncle Billy nodded and set still. "Thank you, Tom," he said after a while.

He got up and taken a half-empty glass of lemonade off this shelf above the bed, and then he pulled the cork out of the bottle of morphine he had. He set the two of them side by side on the table beside Major Henry. The major watched him, then his eyes caught Uncle Billy's again for a second, and closed.

"Stay with him," Uncle Billy said to me. "Then I want you to have everybody who can walk on the parade ground in forty-five minutes." He changed the cloth on Major Henry's face one last time, then left.

After a spell, Major Henry rolled over on his cot and picked up the bottle of morphine and the glass of lemonade.

He didn't act like I was in the room with him atall. He poured the whole bottle of morphine into that glass of lemonade, then stirred it up good.

After he'd poured it down his throat, he eased back down and pulled the blanket over his face. I tucked it in for him so it wouldn't slip off. The rest didn't take long.

When we come upon the trenches and barricades of Cabañas camp, we'd been in the jungle five days. We'd had a guide for a while, but he snuck off the first time the Hondurans caught up with us, just after we slipped out of Trujillo. We run and walked, and went down rivers, and cut through swamps, and fought off Hondurans until I knowed that if it hadn't been for Uncle Billy a-pushing and a-pushing, even though he come down with the coast fever like the rest of us, we'd have all set down and rotted like them bananas that was all we had to eat.

And then there we was, a-standing at the edge of all them swamps and mangrove trees, and them barricades and trenches setting there afore us empty as a nun's hope chest. Nothing on one side of us but the ocean, nothing behind us but Honduran soldiers, nothing but this great, slow river in front of us, and nothing on the other side but jungles and mountains, all the way to Nicaragua.

The enemy greasers found us that night and settled in. And for a week, I reckon it was, they come at us—ever hour, near about, while we laid there in the rain in the rifle pits, a-sleeping when we could with our faces turned down to keep from smothering from raindrops big as rifle balls. So when at last we seen these two longboats sailing up the river with a man in the lead one searching the shores, and Uncle Billy told us to get ready for a attack, I couldn't think nothing but that besides me and Uncle Billy there was only twelve men able to fight. I laid down my rifle and closed my eyes against the rain. I just can't no more, Uncle Billy, I thought. After all this time, I just can't no more.

But when I opened my eyes, the boys was a-cheering—and the men on the longboats was a-cheering back and running up the Union Jack, and I thought, praise the Lord, thank you, Jesus.

The English officer that hove hisself over the gunwales and come a-striding up the beach toward us was red-faced and stiff-backed and tall and thick and blond—everything he ought to be, I reckon. He looked at Uncle Billy, who was dirty and hadn't shaved in two weeks, and was frail as a old woman, like he was expecting him to ask for a handout.

"Sir," he boomed out at Uncle Billy, like Uncle Billy was a whole regiment. "I demand that you surrender yourself immediately."

Uncle Billy thrown his head back so he could look the man in the eye. "To whom do I surrender, sir?"

"To myself, Captain Norvell Salmon, damn it," the man said.

"So I am surrendering to Her Majesty's Government," Uncle Billy said.

"Yes, damn it. To me."

Uncle Billy taken off his sword. "Under those circumstances, I surrender to you, Captain." I know how it hurt him, but at least it wasn't to them greasers he was surrendering.

The Englishman looked over toward us. "Where are the rest?"

"Dead," Uncle Billy said to him.

The Englishman weren't pleased. "Why in God's name didn't you surrender to me in the fort, man, and save all this?"

Uncle Billy looked him in the eye and stuck his foot out in front of him. "Because in the fort, sir, I could have been accused of having a choice. Now, before the world, I do not," he said, and though I couldn't see no world around but monkeys and snakes, I was proud of him.

That evening, they was filling out their records on their ship, and they come to each of us and asked us things— what's your name, what's your job, what's your citizenship, that sort of thing. Well, we all answered the way I reckon they wanted us to, until they come to Uncle Billy, and he said to that Englishman, "I am William Walker, President of the Republic of Nicaragua."

The Englishman looked over at this other officer, like he wanted to make sure he was a-listening, and said, "Would you repeat that?"

Uncle Billy did. "You understand, sir," the Englishman said, "that if you're not an American citizen, I am not bound to offer you the protection of the British flag."

"I surrendered to you, Captain," Uncle Billy said. His face was hard as a hangman's. "That was made clear."

"I ask you again, sir, do you claim American citizenship or not."

"I have answered you, sir."

"You're a fool, sir." The Englishman turned toward this other officer. "Separate him from the others. He'll be handed over to the Honduran authorities immediately we arrive in Trujillo."

Well, I don't know. Sometimes I ain't good at thinking things out. But that was Uncle Billy Walker the son-of-a-bitch was a-doing that to, and I reckon it might have been that his uniform was so clean that got to me worse than anything else.

I taken a step forward. "I'm his aide," I said, which might have been true if it had come to it.

That Britisher looked me up and down like I was a nigger. "That one, too," he said to the other officer.

Uncle Billy whirled around and taken my hand, and I like to have shit. He glared at the other boys and said, "Remem-

236

ber the last order I ever gave you—or ever will give you. Keep your places."

I been hearing Uncle Billy and the priest talking in the room next to me a right smart these days. Since Uncle Billy become a Catholic a while back, he seems to have took it to heart right well. When they ain't talking, Uncle Billy's been a-writing things as best he can with all them chains they got on him—protests, letters to newspapers, legal things, the sorts of writing he's good at. Sometimes he talks to hisself, I think. He won't let them feed him nothing but some water and bread. They got him in the powder magazine where I shot Tom Henry, and me next door to him.

They sending me off to some mines somewhere for four year. Uncle Billy taken care of me to the last: him and the American consul got together and let Uncle Billy have all the blame for everything. It don't bother me so much. There's worse work than mines, I reckon.

Since tomorrow's the day, they let me see him for a spell this evening. I've been a-thinking all these days we been in here about the things I wanted to say to him, but when I got in there with him, nothing come out like I thought it would. He looked so little setting there, see, and so wore out. I ain't got the words that some others might—but there ain't nobody else to tell it, and he just looked so little. I wanted to set down beside him and hug him and tell him it was going to be all right, but I knowed that weren't really true. It was over, and for the life of me I couldn't tell him all what he'd wanted so bad to happen was ever going to come to be the way he'd said it would. So what I told him was that we wasn't done with these people yet, a-hoping that would cheer him, but it didn't. One way or another, I said to him, they wouldn't never be rid of us, and he nodded like he knowed it was true, but it just didn't make him no difference. It was like already he weren't Uncle Billy no more. Oh, and I couldn't hardly stand that.

So then I told him I knowed there was others than me that he'd rather be with tonight, and that I was sorry I wasn't them, but that I didn't reckon none of them had ever loved him better than me. I'd come all the way with him, I said, and I'd go with him in the morning if he wanted me to.

He told me no, that there wasn't nobody he'd rather be with tonight. I knowed it wasn't true, but I cried a little bit anyway. He taken my hand again, and held it a while.

Oh, Lord, help me. I don't know who I'm a-going to be without Uncle Billy!

WILLIAM WALKER ||||||||||||||||||||||||||||||||||||||||||||||||||||||||||||||||||||||||

WHY IS THERE only this wind from the sea, these little particles of sand in it, the sound of that dog from the beach? There should be more. He had imagined there would be more.

The quick of him is untouched; there where the arches are finished is not touched.

He had not thought there would be such terror.

DEATH OF
WILLIAM WALKER

FROM AN EYEWITNESS IN HONDURAS

At daylight, General Walker, surrounded by a guard of seventy unkempt ruffians, was marched past our camp across a small stream. His face was pale, as usual, and I noticed a scar on his cheek received in the fights around Trujillo. Being a Catholic, he carried a small gold crucifix in his hand, which he was normally accustomed to wear around his neck. He looked neither to the left nor right, intent only on the Psalms of David, as I was later told they were, which the priest who accompanied him never ceased to recite. When they halted, the officer commanding the guard read a paper in Spanish, his orders, I presume, and then General Walker spoke a few moments in Spanish. We could not hear what he said, and besides, I did not understand Spanish. We could see from where we stood a newly made grave in the sands, near the edge of which the general stood while speaking to the Spanish guards, and those collected round it. While he was speaking there was a tap on the drum, a volley of musketry followed, and General Walker was dead.

To be sure of this, the captain of the firing party advanced, and placing the muzzle of his piece against the general's forehead, blew out his brains.

The soldiers then threw down their guns, and with brutal ferocity tumbled his body into this hole in the sands without coffin or shroud. They robbed his body of its clothing, quarreling among themselves over its division, then covered him up. They picked up their guns and hurried away, apparently afraid to linger near the spot where they had killed and buried him, as if he might yet rise up against them.

AFTERWORD

For the most part, the events of this novel are based on historical records. The interpretation and dramatization of those records are the author's: this is a work of fiction. For those who would like to read more purely "factual" accounts, I suggest Walker's own book, *The War in Nicaragua* (Mobile, 1860) or A.Z. Carr's *The World and William Walker* (New York, 1962). Both the Library of Congress and the National Archives can furnish further source material.

The author would like to acknowledge the assistance of the Latin American Collection and the Manuscript Room of the Library of Congress, and to thank the many kind people in Nicaragua, *territorio libre*, who helped him come to know their country.

And, as always, he blesses the crazy faith of Tom Engelhardt of Pantheon Books, and is grateful for the patient reading of Esther Newberg of International Creative Management.

ABOUT THE AUTHOR

ROBERT HOUSTON is a native of Alabama and holds a doctorate from the University of Iowa, Writer's Workshop. He is currently teaching in the writing program at the University of Arizona in Tucson and has regularly been on the faculty of both the Breadloaf School of English and the Breadloaf Writer's Conference. He is the author of seven novels including *Bisbee '17*, *Cholo*, and *Ararat* and has edited a volume of Spanish poetry translations. In researching *The Nation Thief*, Houston traveled extensively through Sandinist Nicaragua.